THE CONFESSION OF BROTHER HALUIN

ELLIS PETERS

THE CONFESSION OF BROTHER HALUIN

THE CADFAEL CHRONICLES XV

sphere

SPHERE

First published in Great Britain in 1988 by
Headline Book Publishing plc
Published in 1989 by Futura
Reprinted 1991
This edition published by Warner Futura in 1992
Reprinted 1993, 1994, 1995, 1996, 1998, 1999, 2000
Reprinted by Sphere in 2007, 2009, 2011

A CIP catalogue record for this book
is available from the British Library.

ISBN 978-0-7515-1115-4

Printed and bound in Great Britain by
Clays Ltd, St Ives plc

Sphere
An imprint of
Little, Brown Book Group
100 Victoria Embankment
London EC4Y 0DY

An Hachette UK Company
www.hachette.co.uk

www.littlebrown.co.uk

THE
CONFESSION
OF BROTHER
HALUIN

The Journey of Broth

aluin and Brother Cadfael

R. Tame

ELFORD

VIVERS

FAREWELL

ENET

LICHFIELD

Woodland

0 Miles 4

DJC

Chapter One

HE WORST of the winter came early, that year of 1142. After the prolonged autumn of mild, moist, elegiac days, December came in with heavy skies and dark, brief days that sagged upon the rooftrees and lay like oppressive hands upon the heart. In the scriptorium there was barely light enough at noon to form the letters, and the colours could not be used with any certainty, since the unrelenting and untimely dusk sapped all their brightness.

The weather-wise had predicted heavy snows, and in mid-month they came, not with blizzard winds, but in a blinding, silent fall that continued for several days and nights, smoothing out every undulation, blanching all colour out of the world, burying the sheep in the hills and the hovels in the valleys, smothering all sound, climbing every wall, turning roofs into ranges of white, impassable mountains, and the very air between earth and sky into an opaque, drifting whirlpool of flakes large as lilies. When the fall finally ceased, and the heavy swags of cloud lifted, the Foregate lay half buried, so nearly smoothed out into one white level that there were scarcely any shadows except where the tall buildings of the abbey soared out of the pure pallor, and the eerie, reflected

7

light made day even of night, where only a week before the ominous gloom had made night of day.

These December snows, which covered most of the west, did more than disrupt the lives of country people, starve some isolated hamlets, bury not a few hill shepherds with their flocks, and freeze all travel into enforced stillness; they overturned the fortunes of war, made sport of the preoccupations of princes, and sent history spinning off-course into the new year of 1143.

They also brought about a strange cycle of events in the abbey of Saint Peter and Saint Paul, at Shrewsbury.

In the five years that King Stephen and his cousin, the Empress Maud, had fought for the throne of England, fortune had swung between them like a pendulum many times, presenting the cup of victory to each in erratic turn, only to snatch it away again untasted, and offer it tantalisingly to the other contender. Now, in the white disguise of winter, it chose to turn probability topsy-turvy once again, and deliver the empress out of the king's mailed hands as by a miracle, just as his fist seemed closing securely on his prisoner, and his warfare triumphantly ending. Back to the beginning of the five-year struggle, and all to do again. But that was in Oxford, far away beyond the impassable snows, and some time would elapse before the news reached Shrewsbury.

What was happening in the abbey of Saint Peter and Saint Paul was no more than a small annoyance by comparison, or seemed so at first. An envoy from the bishop, lodged in one of the upper chambers of the guest-hall, and already irritated and displeased at being halted here perforce until the roads were passable again, was unpleasantly awakened in the night by the sudden descent of a stream of icy water on to his head, and made very sure that everyone within range of his powerful voice should hear of it without delay. Brother Denis the hospitaller made haste

8

to placate him, and move him to a dry bed elsewhere, but within the hour it became clear that while the first drenching soon slackened, a steady drip continued, and was soon joined by half a dozen more, spanning a circle some yards across. The great weight of snow on the southern roof of the guest-hall had somehow worked a passage through the lead and filtered in between the slates, perhaps even caved in a number of them. Pockets of the driven snow had felt the comparative warmth within, and with the mute malice of inanimate things had chosen to baptise the bishop's emissary. And the leak was rapidly getting worse.

There was urgent conference at chapter that morning over what should and could be done. Perilous and unpleasant work on roofs was certainly to be avoided if possible during such weather, but on the other hand, if repairs were delayed until the thaw came they were in for a flood, and the damage, limited at this point, might be greatly aggravated.

There were several among the brothers who had worked on the building of additions to the enclave, barns and stabling and storehouses, and Brother Conradin, who was still in his fifties and robust as a bull, had been one of the first child oblates, and worked as a boy under the monks of Seez, brought over by the founding earl to supervise the building of his abbey. Where the fabric was concerned, Brother Conradin's advice carried the greatest weight, and having viewed the extent of the leak in the guest-hall, he stated firmly that they could not afford to wait, or they might have to replace half the southern slope of the roof. They had timber, they had slates, they had lead. That southern slope overhung the drainage channel drawn off from the mill leat, frozen hard at present, but there would be no great difficulty in raising a scaffolding. True, it would be bitterly cold work up there, shifting the mountain of snow first, to ease away the deforming weight, and then replacing broken or displaced slates and repairing the lead flashings.

9

But if they worked in short spells, and were allowed a fire in the warming room all day as long as the work lasted, the job could be done.

Abbot Radulfus listened, nodded his formidable head with his usual prompt comprehension and decision, and said: 'Very well, do it!'

As soon as the long snowfall ceased, and the skies lifted, the tough inhabitants of the Foregate sallied forth from their houses, well muffled and armed with shovels and brooms and long-handled rakes, and began to clear their way out to the highroad, and between them dig out a passage to the bridge and the town, where no doubt the stout burgesses within the walls were tackling the same seasonal enemy. The frost still held, and day by day fretted away mysteriously into the air the surface fringes of every drift, by infinitely slow degrees lessening the load. By the time a few of the main highways were again passable, and a few travellers, either foolhardy or having no choice, were laboriously riding them, Brother Conradin had his scaffolding up, his ladders securely braced up the slope of the roof, and all hands taking their turn aloft in the withering cold, cautiously shifting the great burden of snow, to get at the fractured lead and broken slates. A moraine of crumpled, untidy snow hills formed along the frozen drainage channel, and one unwary brother, who had failed to hear or heed the warning shout from above, was briefly buried by a minor avalanche, and had to be dug out hurriedly and despatched to the warming room to thaw out.

By then way was open between town and Foregate, and news, however hampered and slow its passage, could be carried from Winchester even to Shrewsbury in time to reach the castle garrison and the sheriff of the shire some days before Christmas.

Hugh Beringar came down from the town hotfoot to share it with Abbot Radulfus. In a country debilitated by five years

10

of desultory civil war it behoved state and church to work closely together, and where sheriff and abbot were of like mind they could secure for their people a comparatively calm and orderly existence, and fend off the worst excesses of the times. Hugh was King Stephen's man, and held the shire for him loyally enough, but with even greater goodwill he held it for the folk who lived in it. He would welcome, and this autumn and winter had certainly been expecting, the king's triumph at last, but his chief preoccupation was to hand over to his lord a county relatively prosperous, contented and intact when the last battle was over.

He came looking for Brother Cadfael as soon as he had left the abbot's lodging, and found his friend busy stirring a bubbling pot over his brazier, in his workshop in the herb-garden. The inevitable coughs and colds of winter, the chilblained hands and heels, kept him busy replenishing the medicine cupboard in the infirmary, and thanks to the necessary brazier his timber workshop was somewhat warmer to work in than the carrels of the scriptorium.

Hugh came bursting in upon him in a gust of cold air and a wave of what was for him perceptible excitement, though its outward signs would have escaped anyone who knew him less well than Cadfael did. Only the crisp exasperation of his movements and the abruptness of his greeting caused Cadfael to cease his stirring and fix attentively on the young sheriff's face, the pointed brilliance of his black eyes and the little pulse in his cheek.

'It's all overturned!' said Hugh. 'All to do again from the beginning!' And whatever that meant, and Cadfael did not trouble to ask, since he was certainly about to be told, there was no saying whether exasperation and frustration were not outmatched in Hugh's voice and face by amused relief. He flung himself down on the bench against the timber wall, and dangled his hands between his knees in a gesture of helpless resignation.

11

'A courier got through from the south this morning,' he said, raising his eyes to his friend's attentive face. 'She's gone! Out of the trap, and fled away to join her brother at Wallingford. The king's lost his prize. Even when he has her between his hands he lets her slip through his fingers. I wonder, I wonder,' said Hugh, opening his eyes wide at a new thought, 'whether he did not turn a blind eye and let her go, when it came to the point! It would be like him. God knows he wanted her badly enough, but he may have taken fright when it came to puzzling what he could do with her when he had her. It's one question I'd love to ask him – but never shall!' he concluded with an oblique grin.

'Are you telling me,' asked Cadfael cautiously, eyeing him across the brazier, 'that the empress is escaped out of Oxford, after all? With the king's army all round her, and stores down to starvation level in the castle, from what we last heard? And how did even she contrive it? Tell me next she's grown wings and flown over the king's lines to Wallingford! She could hardly walk through his siege vallations on foot, even if she managed to get out of the castle unseen.'

'Ah, but she did, Cadfael! She did both! She got out of the castle unseen, and passed through some part at least of Stephen's lines. To the best they can guess, she must have been let down by a rope from the rear of the tower towards the river, she and two or three of her men with her. There could not have been more. They muffled themselves all in white to be invisible against the snow. Indeed by all accounts it was snowing then, to hide them the better. They crossed the river on the ice, and walked the six miles or so to Abingdon, for it was there they got horses to take them on to Wallingford. Give her her due, Cadfael, this is a rare woman. From all accounts there's no living with her when she's in high feather, but by God I can see how a man could follow her when she's down.'

12

'So she's back with FitzCount, after all,' said Cadfael on a long, marvelling breath. Barely a month ago it had seemed certain that the empress and her most faithful and devoted ally were irrevocably cut off from each other, and might never meet again in this world.

Ever since September the lady had been under close siege in Oxford castle, the king's armies drawn tightly round her, the town in his hands, and he content to sit back and starve out her battered garrison. And now, all in one bold bid and one snowy night, she was out of her chains, free to re-muster her forces and take up the fight again on equal terms. Surely there never had been such a king as Stephen for conjuring defeat out of victory. But it was a quality they shared, perhaps native to their blood, for the empress too, when she was gloriously installed in Westminister, and her coronation but a few days away, had borne herself so arrogantly and harshly towards the obstinate burgesses of her capital that they had risen in fury and driven her out. It seemed that as often as either of them got within touch of the crown fortune took fright at the prospect of being in the service of either, and hurriedly snatched the prize away.

'So after all,' said Cadfael more placidly, as he lifted his bubbling pot to the grid at the side of the brazier, to simmer in peace, 'at least Stephen has got rid of his problem. He need worry no longer what to do with her.'

'True,' agreed Hugh wryly, 'he'd never have had the iron in him to put her in chains, as she did to him when she had him prisoner after Lincoln, and she's proved it would take more than stone walls to hold her. I fancy he's been blinking the issue all these months, looking no further than the moment when he would force her surrender. He's eased of all the troubles that would have been no more than beginning the day he made her prisoner. Better, perhaps, if he could winnow away her hopes so far that she'd be forced to go back to Normandy. But we've come to know the lady

13

better,' he acknowledged ruefully. 'She never gives up.'

'And how has King Stephen stomached his loss?' asked Cadfael curiously.

'As I've come to expect of him by this time,' said Hugh, with resigned affection. 'As soon as the lady was well out of it, Oxford Castle surrendered to him. Without her, he'd lost interest in the rest of the starved rats within. Most men would have taken out their rage on the garrison. Once, as you'll remember all too well, he let himself be persuaded to take such a revenge, here at Shrewsbury, God knows against his nature. Never again! As like as not it was the memory of Shrewsbury that kept Oxford safe. He let them march out untouched, on condition they dispersed to their homes. He's left the castle well garrisoned and supplied for his own cause, and made off to Winchester with his brother the bishop, to keep Christmas. And he's sent to call all his midland sheriffs there to keep it with him. It's long since he was in these parts, no doubt he's anxious to look us over afresh, and make sure that all his defences hold fast.'

'Now?' said Cadfael, surprised. 'To Winchester? You'll never make the journey in time.'

'Yes, we shall. We have four days, and according to the courier the thaw's well forward, further south, and the roads clear. I'll be away tomorrow.'

'And leave Aline and your boy to keep the feast without you! And Giles just past his third birthday, too!' Hugh's son was a Christmas babe, and had entered the world in the most extreme of winters, in frost and snow and bitter gales. Cadfael was his godfather and most devoted admirer.

'Ah, Stephen won't keep us long,' said Hugh confidently. 'He needs us where he placed us, to keep an eye on his shire revenues. I shall be home by the year's end, if all goes well. But Aline will be glad if you could pay her a visit or two while I'm gone. Father Abbot won't grudge you leave now and then, and that long lad of yours – Winfrid, is it? – he's getting handy enough with the salves and medicines to be left on his own for an hour or two.'

'Very gladly I'll mind your flock for you at home,' said Cadfael heartily, 'while you're strutting at court. But you'll be missed, all the same. What a turnabout this has been! Five years of it now, and nothing gained on either part. And with the new year, no doubt it must all begin again. All that effort and waste, and nothing is changed.'

'Oh, yes, there's something changed, for what it's worth!' Hugh uttered a brief bark of laughter. 'There's a new contender on the scene, Cadfael. Geoffrey could spare no more than a meagre handful of knights to his wife's aid, but he's sent her something it seems he can part with more willingly. Either that or, as may very well be true, he's taken Stephen's measure shrewdly enough to know past doubt what he dare wager in safety. He's sent over their son in his Uncle Robert's care, to see if the English will rally to him rather than to his mother. Henry Plantagenet, nine years old – or did they say ten? No more than that! Robert brought him to her at Wallingford. By this time I fancy the boy's been whisked away to Bristol or Gloucester, out of harm's way. But if Stephen laid hold of him, what could he do with him? As like as not put him on board ship at his own expense, and send him well guarded back to France.'

'Do you tell me so?' Cadfael's eyes had opened wide in astonishment and curiosity. 'So there's a new star on the horizon, is there? And starting young! It seems one soul at least has a blessed Christmas assured, with her liberty won, and her son in her arms again. His coming will give her heart, no question. But I doubt if he'll do much more for her cause.'

'Not yet!' said Hugh, with prophetic caution. 'We'll wait and see what his mettle is. With his mother's stomach and Geoffrey's wit he may give the king trouble enough in a few years' time. We'd best make better use of what time we have, and see to it the boy goes back to Anjou and stays there, and best of all, takes his mother with him. I wish,' said Hugh fervently, rising with a sigh, 'Stephen's own son promised better, we'd have no need to fear what the empress's sprig may have to show.' He shook off present doubts with an impatient twitch of his lean shoulders. 'Well, I'll be off and make ready for the road. We'll be away at first light.'

Cadfael lifted his cooling pot aside to the earth floor, and went out with his friend through the walled stillness of the herb-garden, where all his small, neat beds slept warmly through the frosts under deep snow. As soon as they let themselves out on to the path that skirted the frozen pools they could see distantly, beyond the glassy surface and the broad gardens on the northern side, the long slope of the guest-hall roof overhanging the drainage channel, the dark timber cage of scaffolding and ladders, and the two muffled figures working on the uncovered slates.

'I see you have your troubles, too,' said Hugh.

'Who escapes them, in winter? It's the weight of the snow that's shifted the slates, broken some of them, and found a way through to douse the bishop's chaplain in his bed. If we left it till the thaw we'd have a flood, and far worse damage to repair.'

'And your master-builder reckons he can make it good, frost or no frost.' Hugh had recognised the brawny figure halfway up the long ladder, hefting a hodful of slates surely few of his younger labourers could have lifted. 'Bitter work up there, though,' said Hugh, eyeing the highest platform of the scaffolding, stacked with a great pile of slates, and the two diminutive figures moving with painful caution on the exposed roof.

'We take it in short spells, and there's a fire in the warming-room when we come down. We elders are excused the service, but most of us take a turn, barring the sick and infirm. It's fair, but I doubt if it pleases Conradin. It irks him having foolhardy youngsters up there, and he'd just as soon work only the ones he's sure of, though I will say he keeps a close watch on them. If he sees any blanch at being up so high, he soon has them on solid earth again. We can't all have the head for it.'

'Have you been up there?' asked Hugh curiously.

'I did my stint yesterday, before the light began to fail. Short days are no help, but another week should see it finished.'

Hugh narrowed his eyes against a sudden brief lance of sunlight that reflected back dazzlingly from the crystalline whiteness. 'Who are those two up there now? Is that Brother Urien? The dark fellow? Who's the other one?'

'Brother Haluin.' The thin, alert figure was all but obscured by the jut of the scaffolding, but Cadfael had seen the pair climb the ladders barely an hour earlier.

'What, Anselm's best illuminator? How comes it you allow such abuse of an artist? He'll ruin his hands in this bitter cold. Small chance of him handling a fine brush for the next week or two, after grappling with slates.'

'Anselm would have begged him off,' Cadfael admitted, 'but Haluin would have none of it. No one would have grudged him the mercy, seeing how valuable his work is, but if there's a hair shirt anywhere within reach Haluin will claim it and wear it. A lifelong penitent, that lad, God knows for what imagined sins, for I never knew him so much as break a rule since he entered as a novice, and seeing he was no more than eighteen when he took his first vows, I doubt if he'd had time to do the world much harm up to then. But there are some born to do penance by nature. Maybe they lift the load for some of us who take it quite comfortably that we're humankind, and not angels. If the overflow from Haluin's penitence and piety washes off a few of my shortcomings, may it redound to him for credit in the accounting. And I shan't complain.'

It was too cold to linger very long in the deep snow, watching the cautious activities on the guest-hall roof. They resumed their passage through the gardens, skirting the frozen pools where Brother Simeon had chopped jagged holes to let in air to the fish below, and crossing the mill-leat that fed the ponds by the narrow plank bridge glazed over with a thin and treacherous crust of ice. Closer now, the piers of the scaffolding jutted from the south wall of the guest-hall across the drainage channel, and the workers on the roof were hidden from sight.

'I had him with me among the herbs as a novice, long ago,' said Cadfael as they threaded the snowy beds of the upper garden and emerged into the great court. 'Haluin, I mean. It was not long after I ended my own novitiate. I came in at past forty, and he barely turned eighteen. They sent him to me because he was lettered, and had the Latin at his finger-ends, and after three or four years I was still learning. He comes of a landed family, and would have inherited a good manor if he hadn't chosen the cloister. A cousin has it now. The boy had been put out to a noble household, as the custom is, and was clerk to his lord's estate, being uncommonly bright at learning and figuring. I often wondered why he changed course, but as every man within here knows, there's no questioning a vocation. It comes when it will, and there's no refusal.'

'It would have been simpler to plant the lad straight into the scriptorium, if he came in with so much learning,' said Hugh practically. 'I've seen some of his work, he'd be wasted on any other labour.'

'Ah, but his conscience would have him pass through every stage of the common apprenticeship before he came to rest. I had him for three years among the herbs, then he did two years more at the hospital of Saint Giles, among the sick and crippled, and two more labouring in the gardens at the Gaye, and helping with the sheep out at Rhydycroesau, before he'd settle to do what we found he could do best. Even now, as you saw, he'll have no privilege because he has a delicate hand with the brushes and pens. If others must slither perilously on a snowy roof, so will be. A good fault, mind you,' admitted Cadfael, 'but he takes it to extremes, and the Rule disapproves extremes.'

They crossed the great court towards the gatehouse, where Hugh's horse was tethered, the tall, raw-boned grey that was always his favourite mount, and could have carried twice or three times his master's light weight.

'There'll be no more snow tonight,' said Cadfael, eyeing the veiled sky and sniffing the light, languid wind, 'nor for a few days more, I fancy. Nor hard frost, either, we're on the edge of it. I pray you'll have a tolerable ride south.'

'We'll be away at dawn. And back, God willing, by the new year.' Hugh gathered his bridle and swung himself into the high saddle. 'May the thaw hold off until your roof's weatherproof again! And don't forget Aline will be expecting you.'

He was off out of the gate, with a sharp echo of hooves ringing from the cobbles, and a single brilliant spark that had come and gone almost before the iron shoe left the frozen ground. Cadfael turned back to the door of the infirmary, and went to check the stores in Brother Edmund's medicine cupboard. Another hour, and the light would be already dimming, in these shortest days of the year. Brother Urien and Brother Haluin would be the last pair up on the roof for this day.

Exactly how it happened no one ever clearly established. Brother Urien, who had obeyed Brother Conradin's order to come down as soon as the call came, pieced together what he thought the most probable account, but even he admitted there could be no certainty. Conradin, accustomed to being obeyed, and sensibly concluding that no one in his right senses would wish to linger a moment longer than he must in the bitter cold, had simply shouted his command, and turned away to clear the last of the day's broken slates out of the way of his descending workmen. Brother Urien let himself down thankfully to the boards of the scaffolding, and fumbled his way carefully down the long ladder to the ground, only too happy to leave the work. He was strong and willing, and had no special skills but a wealth of hard experience, and what he did would be well done, but he saw no need to do more than was asked of him. He drew off some yards to look up at what had been accomplished, and saw Brother Haluin, instead of descending the short ladder braced up the slope of the roof on his side, mount several rungs higher, and lean out sidelong to clear away a further sweep of snow and extend the range of the uncovered slates. It appeared that he had seen reason to suspect that the damage extended further on that side, and wished to sweep away the snow there to remove its weight and prevent worse harm.

The rounded bank of snow shifted, slid down in great folds upon itself, and fell, partly upon the end of the planks and the stack of slates waiting there, partly over the edge and sheer to the ground below. No such avalanche had been intended, but the frozen mass loosed its hold of the steep slates and dropped away in one solid block, to shatter as it struck the scaffolding. Haluin had leaned too far. The ladder slid with the snow that had helped to keep it stable, and he fell rather before than with it, struck the end of the planks a glancing blow, and crashed down without a cry to the frozen channel below. Ladder and snowfall dropped upon the planks and hurled them after him in a great downpour of heavy, sharp-edged slates, slashing into his flesh.

Brother Conradin, busy almost beneath his scaffolding, had leaped clear only just in time, spattered and stung and half-blinded for a moment by the blown drift of the fall.

Brother Urien, standing well back, and arrested in the very act of calling up to his companion to stop, for the light was too far gone, uttered instead a great cry of warning, too late to save, and sprang forward, to be half-buried by the edge of the fall. Shaking off snow, they reached Brother Haluin together.

It was Brother Urien who came in haste and grim silence looking for Cadfael, while Conradin ran out the other way into the great court, and sent the first brother he encountered to fetch Brother Edmund the infirmarer. Cadfael was in his workshop, just turfing over his brazier for the night, when Urien erupted into the doorway, a dark, dour man burning with ill news.

'Brother, come quickly! Brother Haluin has fallen from the roof!'

Cadfael, no less sparing of words, swung about, clouted down the last turf, and reached for a woollen blanket from the shelf.

'Dead?' The drop must be forty feet at least, timber by way of obstacles on the way down, and packed ice below, but if by chance he had fallen into deep snow made deeper still by the clearance of the roof, he might yet be lucky.

'There's breath in him. But for how long? Conradin's gone for more helpers, Edmund knows by now.'

'Come!' said Cadfael, and was out of the door and running for the little bridge over the leat, only to change his mind and dart along the narrow neck of causeway between the abbey pools, and leap the leat at the end of it, to come the more quickly to where Haluin lay. From the great court the gleam of two torches advanced to meet them, and Brother Edmund with a couple of helpers and a hand-litter, hard on Brother Conradin's heels.

Brother Haluin, buried to the knees under heavy slates, with blood staining the ice beneath his head, lay still in the middle of the turmoil he had caused.

21

Chapter Two

HATEVER the risks of moving him, to leave him where he was for a moment longer than was necessary would have been to consent to and abet the death that already had a fast hold on him. In mute and purposeful haste they lifted aside the fallen planks and dug out with their hands the knife-edged slates that crushed and lacerated his feet and ankles into a pulp of blood and bone. He was far gone from them, and felt nothing that was done to him as they eased him out of the icy bed of the drain enough to get slings under him, and hoisted him on to the litter. In mourne procession they bore him out through the darkened gardens to the infirmary, where Brother Edmund had prepared a bed for him in a small cell apart from the old and infirm who spent their last years there.

'He cannot live,' said Edmund, looking down at the remote and pallid face.

So Cadfael thought, too. So did they all. But still there was breath in him, even if it was a harsh, groaning breath that spoke of head injuries perhaps past mending; and they went to work on him as on one who could and must live, even against their own virtual certainty that he could not.

23

With infinite, wincing care they stripped him of his icy garments, and padded him round with blankets wrapped about heated stones, while Cadfael went over him gently for broken bones, and set and bound the left forearm that grated as he handled it, and still brought never a flicker to the motionless face. He felt carefully about Haluin's head before cleaning and dressing the bleeding wound, but could not determine whether the skull was fractured. The bitter, snoring breathing indicated that it was, but be could not be sure. As for the broken feet and ankles, Cadfael laboured over them for a long time after they had covered the rest of Brother Haluin with warmed brychans against simple death of cold, his body laid straight and shored securely every way to guard against the shock and pain of movement should he regain his senses. As no one believed he would, unless it was an obstinate, secret remnant of belief that caused them so to exert themselves to nourish even the failing spark.

'He will never walk again,' said Brother Edmund, shuddering at the shattered feet Cadfael was laboriously bathing.

'Never without aid,' Cadfael agreed sombrely. 'Never on these.' But for all that he went on patiently putting together again, as best he could, the mangled remains.

Long, narrow, elegant feet Brother Haluin had had, in keeping with his slender build. The deep and savage cuts the slates had made penetrated to the bone in places, here and there had splintered the bone. It took a long time to clean away the bloody fragments, and bind up each foot at least into its human shape, and encase it in a hastily improvised cradle of felt, well padded within, to hold it still and let it heal as near as possible to what it had once been. If, of course, there was to be healing.

And all the while Brother Haluin lay snoring painfully and oblivious of all that was done to him, very far sunk beneath the lights and shadows of the world, until even his breathing subsided gradually into a mere shallow whisper, no more than the stirring of a solitary leaf in a scarcely perceptible breeze, and they thought that he was gone. But the leaf continued to stir, however faintly.

'If he comes to himself, even for a moment, call me at once,' said Abbot Radulfus, and left them to their watch.

Brother Edmund was gone to get some sleep. Cadfael shared the night watch with Brother Rhun, newest and youngest among the choir monks. One on either side of the bed, they stared steadily upon the unbroken sleep beyond sleep of a body anointed and blessed and armed for death.

It was many years since Haluin had passed out of Cadfael's care to go to manual labour in the Gaye. Cadfael re-examined with deep attention lineaments he had almost forgotten in their early detail, and found now both changed and poignantly familiar. Not a big man, Brother Haluin, but somewhat taller than the middle height, with long, fine, shapely bones, and more sinew and less flesh on them now than when first he came into the cloister, a boy still short of his full growth, and just hardening into manhood. Thirty-five or thirty-six he must be now, barely eighteen then, with the softness and bloom still on him. His face was a long oval, the bones of cheek and jaw strong and clear, the thin, arched brows almost black, shades darker than the mane of crisp brown hair he had sacrificed to the tonsure. The face upturned now from the pillow was blanched to a clay-white pallor, the hollows of the cheeks and deep pits of the closed eyes blue as shadows in the snow, and round the drawn lips the same livid blueness was gathering even as they watched. In the small hours of the night, when the life sinks to its frailest, he would end or mend.

Across the bed Brother Rhun kneeled, attentive, unintimidated by another's death any more than he would be, some day, by his own. Even in the dimness of this small, stony room Rhun's radiant fairness, his face creamy with youth, his ring of flaxen hair and aquamarine eyes, diffused a lambent brightness. Only someone of Rhun's virgin certainty could sit serenely by a deathbed, with such ardent loving-kindness and yet no taint of pity. Cadfael had seen other young creatures come to the cloister with something of the same charmed faith, only to see it threatened, dulled and corroded gradually by the sheer burden of being human under the erosion of the years. That would never happen to Rhun. Saint Winifred, who had bestowed on him the physical perfection he had lacked, would not suffer the gift to be marred by any maiming of his spirit.

The night passed slowly, with no perceptible change in Brother Haluin's unrelenting stillness. It was towards dawn when at last Rhun said softly: 'Look, he is stirring!'

The faintest quiver had passed over the livid face, the dark brows drew together, the eyelids tightened with the first distant awareness of pain, the lips lengthened in a brief grimace of stress and alarm. They waited for what seemed a long while, unable to do more than wipe the moist forehead, and the trickle of spittle that oozed from the corner of the drawn mouth.

In the first dim, reflected snow-light before dawn Brother Haluin opened his eyes, onyx-black in their blue hollows, and moved his lips to emit a hair-fine thread of a voice that Rhun had to stoop his young, sharp ear to catch and interpret.

'Confession . . .' said the whisper from the threshold between life and death, and for a while that was all.

'Go and bring Father Abbot,' said Cadfael.

Rhun departed silently and swiftly. Haluin lay gathering his senses, and by the growing clarity and sharpening focus of his eyes he knew where he was and who sat beside him, and was mustering what life and wit remained to him for a purpose. Cadfael saw the quickening of pain in the strained whiteness of mouth and jaw, and made to trickle a little of

26

the draught of poppies between his patient's lips, but Haluin kept them tightly clenched and turned his head away. He wanted nothing to dull or hamper his senses, not yet, not until he had got out of him what he had to say.

'Father Abbot is coming,' said Cadfael, close to the pillow. 'Wait, and speak but once.'

Abbot Radulfus was at the door by then, stooping under the low lintel. He took the stool Rhun had vacated, and leaned down to the injured man. Rhun had remained without, ready to run errands if he should be needed, and had drawn the door closed between. Cadfael rose to withdraw likewise, and suddenly yellow sparks of anxiety flared in Haluin's hollow eyes, and a brief convulsion went through his body and fetched a moan of pain, as though he had willed to lift a hand to arrest Cadfael's going, but could not do it. The abbot leaned closer, to be seen as well as heard.

'I am here, my son. I am listening. What is it troubles you?'

Haluin drew in breath, hoarding it to have a voice to speak with. 'I have sins . . .' he said, '. . . never told.' The words came slowly and with much labour, but clearly. 'One against Cadfael . . . Long past . . . never confessed . . .'

The abbot looked up at Cadfael across the bed. 'Stay! He wishes it.' And to Haluin, touching the lax hand that was too weak to be lifted: 'Speak as you can, we shall be listening. Spare many words, we can read between.'

'My vows,' said the thread-fine voice remotely. 'Impure . . . not out of devotion . . . Despair!'

'Many have entered for wrong reasons,' said the abbot, 'and remained for the right ones. Certainly in the four years of my abbacy here I have found no fault in your true service. On this head have no fear. God may have brought you into the cloister roundabout for his own good reasons.'

'I served de Clary at Hales,' said the thin voice. 'Better,

27

his lady – he being in the Holy Land then. His daughter
. . .' A long silence while doggedly and patiently he
renewed his endurance to deliver more and worse. 'I loved
her . . . and was loved. But the mother . . . my suit was not
welcome. What was forbidden us we took . . .'

Another and longer silence. The blue, sunken lids were
lowered for a moment over the burning eyes. 'We lay
together,' he said clearly. 'That sin I did confess, but never
named her. The lady cast me out. Out of despair I came here
. . . at least to do no more harm. And the worst harm yet to
come!'

The abbot closed his hand firmly on the nerveless hand at
Haluin's side, to hold him fast by the grip, for the face on
the pillow had sunken into a mask of clay, and a long
shudder passed through the bruised and broken body, and
left it tensed and chill to the touch.

'Rest!' said Radulfus, close to the sufferer's ear. 'Take
ease! God hears even what is not said.'

It seemed to Cadfael, watching, that Haluin's hand
responded, however feeble its hold. He brought the drink of
wine and herbs with which he had been moistening the
patient's mouth while he lay senseless, and trickled a few
drops between the parted lips, and for the first time the
offering was accepted, and the strings of the lean throat
made the effort to swallow. His time was not yet. Whatever
more he might have to heave off his heart, there was yet
time for it. They fed him sips of wine, and watched the clay
of his features again cohere into flesh, however pale and
feeble. This time, when he came back to them, it was very
faintly and with eyes still closed.

'Father . . .?' questioned the remote voice fearfully.

'I am here. I will not leave you.'

'Her mother came . . . I did not know till then Bertrade
was with child! The lady was in terror of her lord's anger
when he came home. I served then with Brother Cadfael, I

28

had learned . . . I knew the herbs . . . I stole and gave her . . . hyssop, fleur-de-luce . . . Cadfael knows better uses for them!'

Yes, better by far! But what could help a badly congested chest and a killing cough, in small doses, or fight off the jaundice that turned a man yellow, could also put an end to the carrying of a child, in an obscene misuse abhorrent to the church and perilous even to the woman it was meant to deliver. From fear of an angry father, fear of shame before the world, fear of marriage prospects ruined and family feuds inflamed. Had the girl's mother entreated him, or had he persuaded her? Years of remorse and self-punishment had not exorcised the horror that still wrung his flesh and contorted his visage.

'They died,' he said, harsh and loud with pain. 'My love and the child, both. Her mother sent me word – dead and buried. A fever, they gave it out. Dead of a fever – nothing more to fear. My sin, my most grievous sin . . . God knows I am sorry!'

'Where true penitence is,' said Abbot Radulfus, 'God does surely know. Well, this grief is told. Have you done, or is there more yet to tell?'

'I have done,' said Brother Haluin. 'But to beg pardon. I ask it of God – and of Cadfael, that I abused his trust and his art. And of the lady of Hales, for the great grief I brought upon her.' Now that it was out he had better control of voice and words, the crippling tension was gone from his tongue, and weak though his utterance was, it was lucid and resigned. 'I would die cleansed and forgiven,' he said.

'Brother Cadfael will speak on his own behalf,' said the abbot. 'For God, I will speak as he gives me grace.'

'I forgive freely,' said Cadfael, choosing words with more than his accustomed care, 'whatever offence was done against my craft under great stress of mind. And that the means and the knowledge were there to tempt you, and I not

29

there to dissuade, this I take to myself as much as ever I can charge them to you. I wish you peace!'

What Abbot Radulfus had to say upon God's behalf took longer. There were some among the brothers, Cadfael thought, who would have been startled and incredulous if they could have heard, at finding their abbot's formidable austerity could also hold so much measured and authoritative tenderness. A lightened conscience and a clean death were what Haluin desired. It was too late to exact penance from a dying man, and deathbed comfort cannot be priced, only given freely.

'A broken and a contrite heart,' said Radulfus, 'is the only sacrifice required of you, and will not be despised.' And he gave absolution and the solemn blessing, and so left the sickroom, beckoning Cadfael with him. On Haluin's face the ease of gratitude had darkened again into the indifference of exhaustion, and the fires were dead in eyes dulled and half-closed between swoon and sleep.

In the outer room Rhun was waiting patiently, drawn somewhat aside to avoid hearing, even unwittingly, any word of that confession.

'Go in and sit with him,' said the abbot. 'He may sleep now, there will be no ill dreams. If there should be any change in him, fetch Brother Edmund. And if Brother Cadfael should be needed, send to my lodging for him.'

In the panelled parlour in the abbot's lodge they sat together, the only two people who would ever hear of the offence with which Haluin charged himself, or have the right in private to speak of his confession.

'I have been here only four years,' said Radulfus directly, 'and know nothing of the circumstances in which Haluin came here. It seems one of his earliest duties here was to help you among the herbs, and there he acquired this knowledge he put to such ill use. Is it certain this draught he concocted could kill? Or may this truly have been a death from fever?'

'If the girl's mother used it on her, she could hardly be mistaken,' said Cadfael ruefully. 'Yes, I've known hyssop to kill. I was foolish to keep it among my stores, there are other herbs that could take its place. But in small doses, both herb and root, dried and powdered, are excellent for the yellow distemper, and useful with horehound against chest troubles, though the blue-flowered kind is milder and better for that. I've known women use it to procure abortion, in great doses that purge to the extreme. Small wonder if sometimes the poor girl dies.'

'And this was surely during his novitiate, for he cannot have been here long if this child was his, as he supposes. He can have been only a boy.'

'Barely eighteen, and the girl surely no more, if as old. It is some extenuation,' said Cadfael firmly, 'if they were in the same household, seeing each other daily, of equal birth, for he comes of a good family, and as open to love as are most children. In fact,' said Cadfael, kindling, 'what I wonder at is that his suit should have been rejected out of hand. He was an only son, there was a good manor would have been his if he had not taken vows. And he was a very pleasing youth, as I recall, lettered and gifted. Many a knight would have welcomed him as a match for his daughter.'

'It may be her father already had other plans for her,' said Radulfus. 'He may have betrothed her to someone else in childhood. And her mother would hardly venture to countenance a match in her husband's absence, if she went in such awe of him.'

'She need not, however, have rejected the boy utterly. If she had let him hope he would have waited, surely, and not tried to force her hand by forestalling marriage. Though it may be I do him wrong there,' Cadfael relented. 'It was not calculation, I fancy, that brought him into the girl's bed, but

31

too rash affection. Haluin would never make a schemer.'

'Well, for better or worse,' said Radulfus with a weary sigh, 'it was done, and cannot be undone. He is not the first, and will not be the last young man to fall into that error, nor she the first nor the last poor child to suffer for it. At least she has kept her good name. Easy to see why he feared to confide, for her sake, even under the seal of confession. But it is all long ago, eighteen years, his age when it befell. Let us at least secure him a peaceful ending.'

It was the general view that a peaceful ending was the best that could be hoped for for Brother Haluin, and that prayers for him ought not to presume to look towards any other outcome, all the more as his brief return to his senses rapidly lapsed again into a deeper unconsciousness, and for seven days, while the festival of the Nativity came and passed, he lay oblivious of the comings and goings of his brethren round his bed, ate nothing, uttered no sound but the hardly perceptible flutter of his breath. Yet that breath, however faint, was steady and even, and as often as drops of honeyed wine were presented to his lips, they were accepted, and the cords of his throat moved of themselves, docilely swallowing, while the broad, chilly brow and closed eyes never by the least quiver or contraction revealed awareness of what his body did.

'As if only his body is here,' said Brother Edmund, soberly pondering, 'and his spirit gone elsewhere until the house is again furbished and clean and waiting to be lived in.'

A sound biblical analogy, Cadfael considered, for certainly Haluin had himself cast out the devils that inhabited him, and the dwelling they vacated might well lie empty for a while, all the more if there was to be that unlooked-for and improble act of healing, after all. For however this prolonged withdrawal might resemble dying, Brother

32

Haluin would not die. Then we had better keep a good watch, thought Cadfael, taking the parable to its fitting close, and make sure seven devils worse than the first never manage to get a foot in the door while he's absent. And prayers for Haluin continued with unremitting fervour throughout the festivities of Christmas and the solemn opening of the new year.

The thaw was beginning by that time, and even then it was a slow thaw, wearing away each day, by slow degrees, the heavy wastes of snow from the great fall. The work on the roof was finished without further mishap, the scaffolding taken down, and the guest-hall once again weatherproof. All that remained of the great upheaval was this still and silent witness in his isolated bed in the infirmary, declining either to live or die.

Then, in the night of the Epiphany, Brother Haluin opened his eyes and drew a long, slow breath like any other man awaking without alarm, and cast his wondering gaze round the narrow room until it rested upon Brother Cadfael, mute and attentive on the stool beside him.

'I am thirsty,' said Haluin trustingly, like a child, and lay passive on Cadfael's arm to drink.

They half expected him to sink again into his unconscious state, but he remained languid but aware all that day, and in the night his sleep was natural sleep, shallow but tranquil. After that he turned his face to life, and did not again look over his shoulder. Once risen from the semblance of death he came back to the territory of pain, and its signature was on his drawn brow and set lips, but he bore it without complaint. His broken arm had knitted while he lay ignorant of his injuries, and caused him only the irritating aches of healing wounds, and it seemed both to Cadfael and Edmund, after a day or two of keeping close watch on him, that whatever had been shaken out of place within his head had healed as the outer wound had healed, medicined by

33

stillness and repose. For his mind was clear. He remembered the icy roof, he remembered his fall, and once when he was alone with Cadfael he showed that he recalled very clearly his confession, for he said after a long while of silent thought:

'I did shamefully by you, long ago, now you tend and medicine me, and I have made no amends.'

'I've asked none,' said Cadfael equably, and began with patient care to unfold the wrappings from one maimed foot, to renew the dressings he had been replacing night and morning all this time.

'But I need to pay all that is due. How else can I be clean?'

'You have made full confession,' said Cadfael reasonably, 'you have received absolution from Father Abbot himself, beware of asking more.'

'But I have done no penance. Absolution so cheaply won leaves me still a debtor,' said Haluin heavily.

Cadfael had laid bare the left foot, the worse mangled of the pair. The surface cuts and wounds had healed over, but what had happened to the labyrinth of small bones within could never be put right, they had fused into a misshapen clot, twisted and scarred, discoloured in angry dark reds and purples. Yet the seamed skin had knitted and covered all.

'If you have debts,' said Cadfael bluntly, 'they bid fair to be paid in pain to the day you die. You see this? You will never set this firmly to ground again. I doubt if you will ever walk again.'

'Yes,' said Haluin, staring out through the narrow chink of the window at the darkening wintry sky, 'yes, I shall walk. I will walk. If God allows, I will go on my own feet again, though I must borrow crutches to help them bear me. And if Father Abbot gives me his countenance, when I have learned to use what props are left to me I will go myself to Hales, to beg forgiveness of Adelais de Clary, and keep a night's vigil at Bertrade's tomb.'

34

In his own mind Cadfael doubted if either the dead or the living would take any great comfort from Haluin's fondly resolved atonement, or still be nursing any profound recollection of him, after eighteen years. But if the pious intent gave the lad courage and determination to live and labour and be fruitful again, why discourage him? So all he said was:

'Well, let's first mend all that can be mended, and put back some of that lost blood into you, for you'll get no leave to go anywhere as you are now.' And contemplating the right foot, which at least still bore some resemblance to a human foot, and had a perceptible and undamaged anklebone, he went on thoughtfully: 'We might make some sort of thick felt boots for you, well padded within. You might get one foot to the ground yet, though you'll need the crutches. Not yet – not yet, nor for weeks yet, more likely months. But we'll take your measure, and see what we can fashion between us.'

On reflection, Cadfael felt that it might be wise to warn Abbot Radulfus of the expiation Brother Haluin had in mind, and did so after chapter, in the privacy of the abbot's parlour.

'Once he had heaved the load off his heart,' said Cadfael simply, 'he would have died content if it had been his fortune to die. But he is going to live. His mind is clear, his will is strong, and if his body is meagre it's wiry enough, and now that he sees a life ahead of him he'll not be content to creep out of his sins by way of absolution without penance. If he was of a lighter mind, and could be coaxed to forget this resolve as he gets well, for my part I would not blame him, I'd be glad of it. But penitence without penance will never be enough for Haluin. I'll hold him back as long as I can, but trust me, we shall hear of this again, as soon as he feels able to attempt it.'

'I can hardly frown upon so fitting a wish,' said the abbot reasonably, 'but I can forbid it until he is fit to undertake it. If it will give him peace of mind I have no right to stand in his way. It may also be of some belated comfort to this unhappy lady whose daughter died so wretchedly. I am not familiar,' said Radulfus, pondering the proposed pilgrimage warily, 'with this manor of Hales, though I have heard the name of de Clary. Do you know where it lies?'

'Towards the eastern edge of the shire, Father, it must be a matter of twenty-five miles or so from Shrewsbury.'

'And this lord who was absent in the Holy Land – he can have been told nothing of the true manner of his daughter's death, if his lady went in such awe of him. It is many years past, but if he is still living this visit must not take place. It would be a very ill thing for Brother Haluin to salve his own soul by bringing further trouble and danger upon the lady of Hales. Whatever her errors, she has suffered for them.'

'For all I know, Father,' Cadfael admitted, 'they may both be dead some years since. I saw the place once, on the way from Lichfield on an errand for Abbot Heribert, but I know nothing of the household of de Clary.'

'Hugh Beringar will know,' said the abbot confidently. 'He has all the nobility of the shire at his finger-ends. When he returns from Winchester we may ask him. There's no haste. Even if Haluin must have his penance, it cannot be yet. He is not yet out of his bed.'

Chapter Three

UGH AND his escort came home four days after Epiphany. Much of the snow was gone by then, the weather grey, the days short and sombre, the nights hovering on the edge of frost, so that the thaw continued its gradual way, and there was no flooding. After such a heavy fall a rapid thaw would have seen a great mass of water coming down the river and draining from every drift, and the Severn would have backed up the Meole Brook and flooded the lower part of the fields, even if the enclave itself escaped inundation. This year they were spared that trouble, and Hugh, kicking off his boots and shrugging off his cloak in his own house by Saint Mary's church, with his wife bringing him his furred shoes and his son clinging to his sword-belt and clamouring to have his new, painted wooden knight duly admired, was able to report an easy journey for the time of year, and a satisfactory reception at court for his stewardship.

'Though I doubt if this Christmas truce will last long,' he said to Cadfael later, after acquainting the abbot with all the news from Winchester. 'He's swallowed the failure at Oxford gallantly enough, but for all that he's on his mettle for vengeance, he'll not sit still for long, winter or no. He

37

wants Wareham back, but it's well stocked, and manned to the battlements, and Stephen never did have the patience for a siege. He'd like a fortress more to the west, to carry the war to Robert's country. There's no guessing what he'll try first. But he wants none of me or my men there in the south, he's far too wary of the earl of Chester to keep me long out of my shire. Thank God, for I'm of the same mind myself,' said Hugh blithely. 'And how have you been faring? Sorry I am to hear your best illuminator had a fall that all but ended him. Father Abbot told me of it. I can hardly have left you an hour, that day, when it happened. Is it true he's mending well?'

'Better than any of us ever expected,' said Cadfael, 'least of all the man himself, for he was certainly bent on clearing his soul for death. But he's out of the shadow, and in a day or two we'll have him out of his bed. But his feet are crippled for life, the slates chopped them piecemeal. Brother Luke is cutting some crutches to his measure. Hugh,' said Cadfael directly, ' what do you know of the de Clarys who hold the manor of Hales? There was one of them was a crusader nearly twenty years back. I never knew him, he was after my time in the east. Is he still living?'

'Bertrand de Clary,' said Hugh promptly, and looked up at his friend with quickening interest. 'What of him? He died years back, ten or more it must be. His son holds the honour now. I've had no dealings with them, Hales is the only manor they hold in this shire, the *caput* and most of their lands are in Staffordshire. Why, what's put de Clary in your mind?'

'Why, Haluin has. He was in their service before he took the cowl. It seems he feels he has left unpaid some debt he still owes in that direction. It came to mind when he made what he took to be his deathbed confession. In something he feels he offended, and has it on his conscience still.'

That was all that could be told, even to Hugh, the

confessional being sacred, and if nothing more was offered, Hugh would ask for nothing more, however he might speculate on what had not been said.

'He's set on making the journey to set the account straight, when he's fit to undertake it. I was wondering . . . If this Bertrand's widow is no longer in the land of the living, either, as well Haluin should know it at once, and put it out of his mind.'

Hugh was eyeing his friend with steady interest and a tolerant smile. 'And you want him to have nothing to trouble about, body or mind, but getting back into the way of living as soon as may be. I'm no help, Cadfael. The widow's living still. She's there at Hales, she paid her dues last Michaelmas. Her son's married to a Staffordshire wife, and has a young son to succeed him, and from all accounts his mother is not of a nature to share another woman's household without meddling. Hales is her favourite home, she keeps there from choice and leaves her son to rule his own roost, while she makes sure of ruling hers. No doubt it suits them both very well. I should not be even so well-informed,' he said by way of explanation, 'if we had not ridden some miles of the way from Winchester with a company of de Clary's men, dispersing from the siege of Oxford. The man himself I never saw, he was still delayed at court when we left. He'll be on his way home by now, unless Stephen keeps him for whatever move he has next in mind.'

Cadfael received this news philosophically but without pleasure. So she was still living, this woman who had sought to help her daughter to an abortion, and succeeded only in helping her to her death. Not the first nor the last to come by such a death. But what must the mother's despair and guilt have been then, and what bitter memories must remain even now, beneath the ashes of eighteen years? Better, surely, to let them lie buried still. But Haluin's self-torturing conscience and salvation-hungry soul had their

39

rights, too. And after all, he had been just eighteen years old! The woman who had forbidden him any aspiration to her daughter's affection must have been double his age. She might, thought Cadfael almost indignantly, have had the wisdom to see how things began to be between those two, and taken steps to separate them in time.

'Did you ever feel, Hugh, that it might be better to let even ill alone,' wondered Cadfael ruefully, 'rather than let loose worse? Ah, well! He has not even tried his crutches yet. Who knows what changes a few weeks may bring.'

They lifted Brother Haluin out of his bed in the middle of January, found him a corner near the infirmary fire, since he could not move about freely like the others to combat the cold, and treated his body, stiff from long lying, with oil and massage to get the sinews working again. To occupy his hands and mind they brought him his colours and a little desk to work on, and gave him a simpler page to adorn until his fingers should regain their deftness and steadiness. His mangled feet had healed and fused into misshapen forms, and there was no question as yet of letting him attempt to stand on them, but Cadfael allowed him to try the crutches Brother Luke had made for him, with support on either side, to get accustomed to the heft and balance of them, and the shaped and padded props under his armpits. If neither foot could ever be brought to support him again, even the crutches would not be of any use, but both Cadfael and Edmund agreed that there was every hope of the right foot being restored to use in time, and even the left might eventually provide a grain of assistance, with a little ingenuity in shoeing the invalid.

To that end Cadfael called in, at the end of the month, young Philip Corviser, the provost's son, and they put their heads together over the problem, and between them produced a pair of boots as ill-matched in appearance as were the feet for which they were intended, but adapted as best they could devise to give strong support. They were of thick felt with a leather sole, built up well above the ankles and laced close with leather thongs to support and protect the damaged flesh and make full use of the shin-bones, which were intact. Philip was pleased with his work, but wary of praise until the boots were tried on, and found to be wearable without pain, and blessedly warm in this wintry weather.

And all that was done for him Brother Haluin accepted gratefully and humbly, and went on doggedly refreshing eye and hand with his reds and blues and delicately laid gold. But as often as the hours of leisure came round he would be precariously hoisting himself out of his corner bench with shoulders braced upon his crutches, poised to reach for the support of wall or bench if his balance was shaken. It took some time for the sinews to recover their toughness in his wasted legs, but early in February he could set his right foot firmly to the ground, and even stand on it briefly without other support, and from that time on he began to use his crutches in earnest, and to master them. He was seen again, dutiful and punctual, in his stall at chapter, and in the choir at every office. By the end of February he could even set the blocked toe of his left boot to the ground, to help hold him steady and secure on his crutches, though never again would that foot be able to support his weight, light though he was.

In one thing he was fortunate, that the winter, once that first early snowfall had thawed and vanished, was not a hard one. There were occasional spells of frost, but none that lasted long, and after January such snow-showers as there were were fitful and slight, and did not lie long. When he had his balance and was used to his new gait he could exercise his skills outdoors as well as in, and grew expert, fearful only of the cobbles of the court when they were glazed with frost.

At the beginning of March, with the days lengthening, and the first cautious and reluctant signs of spring in the air,

Brother Haluin rose in chapter, when all the urgent business of the day was over, and meekly but resolutely made a plea which only Abbot Radulfus and Brother Cadfael could fully understand.

'Father,' he said, his dark eyes fixed unwaveringly on the abbot's face, 'you know that in my trouble I conceived a desire to make a certain pilgrimage, if I should by God's grace be restored. Great mercy has been shown to me, and if you will give me leave, I wish now to register my vow in heaven. I beg your sanction and the prayers of my brothers that I may fulfil what I promise, and return in peace.'

Radulfus regarded the petitioner in silence for a disturbingly long time, his face revealing neither approval nor disapproval, though the fixity of his gaze brought a surge of blood into Haluin's hollow cheeks.

'Come to me after chapter,' said the abbot then, 'and I will hear what you intend, and judge whether you are yet fit to undertake it.'

In the abbot's parlour Haluin repeated his request in open terms, as to men before whom his spirit was naked and known. Cadfael knew why he himself had been summoned to attend. Two reasons, indeed, stood clear: he was the only other witness of Haluin's confession, and might therefore be admitted into his counsels; and he could speak as to Haluin's fitness to set out on such a journey. He had not yet guessed at a third reason, but he was not quite easy in his mind as he listened.

'I must not and will not hold you back,' said the abbot, 'from what is needful for your soul's health. But I think you ask too soon. You cannot yet have regained your strength. And it is not yet spring, however well we happen to have fared these last weeks. There may still be bitter weather to come. Think how recently you have been close to death, and spare putting yourself in such hardship until you are fitter to bear it.'

'Father,' said Haluin ardently, 'it is because I have been close to death that I must not delay. How if death should reach for me again before I can expiate my sin? I have seen how it can lay its hand on a man in a moment, in the twinkling of an eye. I have had my warning. I must heed it. If I die in paying the penance due from me, that I will embrace as fitting. But to die and not have made any amend, that would be endless reproach to me. Father,' he said, burning up like a stirred fire, 'I truly loved her, I loved her according to the way of marriage, I would have loved her lifelong. And I destroyed her. I have hidden my sins too long, now that I have confessed them I long to complete the atonement.'

'And have you thought of the miles you must go and return? Are you in any case to ride?

Haluin shook his head vigorously at that. 'Father, I have vowed already in my heart and will repeat the vow on the altar, to go on foot to the place where she is buried, and on foot return – on these feet that brought me to the earth and made me to face the truth of my unshriven offences. I can go, I have learned how the innocent lame must go. Why should not I, who am guilty of so much, suffer the same labours? I can endure it. Brother Cadfael knows!'

Brother Cadfael was none too pleased at being called in witness, and none too happy about saying anything which could promote this obsessed enterprise, but neither could he see any genuine peace of mind for this tormented creature until the expiation was completed.

'I do know he has the will and the courage,' he said. 'Whether he has the strength is another matter. And whether he has the right to force his body to the death in order to cleanse his soul is something on which I will not judge.'

Radulfus pondered for some minutes in sombre silence, eyeing the petitioner with a fixity which should have caused him to stir uneasily and lower his gaze had there been anything false or pretentious in his purpose. But Haluin's wide, earnest eyes sustained the encounter ardently.

'Well, I acknowledge your desire to atone, late though it comes,' said the abbot at last, 'and I understand the better since the delay of years has not been for your own sake. Go, then, make the attempt. But I will not permit you to go alone. There must be someone with you in case you founder, and should that happen, you must allow him to make such dispositions for your safety as he sees fit. If you endure the journey well, he need not do anything to impair your sacrifice, but if you fall by the wayside, then he stands as my representative, and you must obey him as you obey me.'

'Father,' said Haluin in anxious protest, 'my sin is mine alone, my confession sealed and sacred. How can I let another man come so close, without myself breaking that seal? It would be a violation even to cause wonder and question concerning this penance of mine.'

'You shall have a companion who need neither wonder nor question,' said the abbot, 'since he already knows, at your own telling. Brother Cadfael shall come with you. His company and his prayers can only be of comfort and benefit to you. Your confidence and the lady's memory will be in no danger, and he is well qualified to care for you along the way.' And to Cadfael, turning, he said: 'Will you undertake this charge? I do not believe he is fit to go alone.'

Small choice, thought Cadfael, but not altogether displeased at the instruction, either. There was still, somewhere deep within him, a morsel of the *vagus* who had roamed the world from Wales to Jerusalem and back to Normandy for forty years before committing himself to stability within the cloister, and an expedition sanctioned, even ordered by authority could be welcomed as blessed, instead of evaded as a temptation.

'If you so wish, Father,' he said, 'I will.'

'This journey will take several days. I take it that Brother Winfrid will be competent to dispense whatever may be needed, with Edmund to guide him?'

'For a few days,' agreed Cadfael, 'they should manage well enough. I have stocked the infirmary cupboard only yesterday, and in the workshop there's a good supply of all the common remedies usually called for in the winter. Should something unforeseen be needed, Brother Oswin could come back from Saint Giles to help for a while.'

'Good! Then, son Haluin, you may prepare for this journey, and set out when you are ready, tomorrow if you will. But you will submit yourself to Brother Cadfael if your strength fails you, and do his bidding as faithfully as within these walls you have always done mine.'

'Father,' said Haluin fervently, 'I will.'

At the altar of Saint Winifred Brother Haluin recorded his solemn vow that same evening after Vespers, to leave himself no way out, with a white-faced vehemence which indicated to Cadfael, who witnessed it at Haluin's own wish, that this implacable penitent in his deepest heart knew and feared the labour and pain he was imposing on himself, and embraced it with a passion and resolution Cadfael would rather have seen devoted to a more practical and fruitful enterprise. For who would benefit by this journey, even though it passed successfully, except the penitent himself, at least partially restored to his self-respect? Certainly not the poor girl who had committed no worse sin than to venture too much for love, and who surely was long since in a state of grace. Nor the mother who must long ago have put this evil dream behind her, and must now be confronted by it once again after years. And Cadfael was not of the opinion that a man's main business in this world was to save his own soul. There are other ailing souls, as there are ailing bodies, in need of a hoist towards health.

But Haluin's needs were not his needs. Haluin's bitter years of silent self-blame certainly called for a remedy.

'On these most holy relics,' said Brother Haluin, with his palm pressed against the drapings that covered the reliquary, 'I record my penitential vow: that I will not rest until I have gone on foot to the tomb in which Bertrade de Clary lies, and there passed a night's vigil in prayer for her soul, and again on foot returned here to the place of my due service. And if I fail of this, may I live forsworn and die unforgiven.'

They set out after Prime, on the fourth morning of March, out at the gate and along the Foregate towards Saint Giles and the highroad due east. The day was cloudy and still, the air chill but not wintry cold. Cadfael viewed the way ahead in his mind, and found it not too intimidating. They would be leaving the western hills behind them, and with every mile eastward the country about them would subside peaceably into a green level. The road was dry, for there had been no recent rain, and the cloud cover above was high and pale, and threatened none, and there was a grassy verge such as could be found only on the king's highways, wide on either side the track, easy walking even for a crippled man. The first mile or two might pass without grief, but after that the constant labour would begin to tell. He would have to be the judge of when to call a halt, for Haluin was likely to grit his teeth and press on until he dropped. Somewhere under the Wrekin they would find a hospitable refuge for the night, for there were abbey tenants there among the cottagers, and any hut along the way would willingly give them a place by the fire for a midday rest. Food they had with them in the scrip Cadfael carried.

In the brisk hopefulness of morning, with Haluin's energy and eagerness at their best, they made good speed, and rested at noon very pleasurably with the parish priest at

Attingham. But in the afternoon the pace slowed somewhat, and the strain began to tell upon Haluin's hardworking shoulders, aching from the constant weight and endlessly repeated stress, and the cold as evening approached numbed his hands on the grips of his crutches, in spite of their mufflings of woollen cloth. Cadfael called a halt as soon as the light began to fade into the windless March dusk, grey and without distances, and turned aside into the village of Uppington, to beg a bed for the night at the manor.

Haluin had been understandably silent along the road, needing all his breath and all his resolution for the effort of walking. Fed and at ease in the evening, he sat watching Cadfael in accepting silence still for a while.

'Brother,' he said at last, 'I take it very kindly that you've come with me on this journey. With no other but you could I speak without conceal of that old grief, and before ever we see Shrewsbury again I may sorely need to speak of it. The worst of me you already know, and I will never say word in excuse. But in eighteen years I have never until now spoken her name aloud, and now to utter it is like food after starvation.'

'Speak or be silent as the need takes you,' said Cadfael, 'and I'll hear or be deaf according to your wish. But as for tonight you should take your rest, for you've come a good third part of the way, and tomorrow, I warn you, you'll find some aches and pains you knew nothing of, from labouring so hard and so long.'

'I am tired,' admitted Haluin, with a sudden and singularly touching smile, as brief as it was sweet. 'You think we cannot reach Hales tomorrow, then?'

'Don't think of it! No, we'll get as far as the Augustinian canons at Wombridge, and spend another night there. And you'll have done well to get so far in the time, so don't grudge the one day more.'

'As you think best,' said Haluin submissively, and lay

47

down to sleep with the confiding simplicity of a child charmed and protected by his prayers.

The next day was less kind, for there was a thin, spasmodic rain that stung at times with sleet, and a colder wind from the north-east, from which the long, green, craggy bulk of the Wrekin gave them no shelter as the road skirted it to the north. But they reached the priory before dusk, though Haluin's lips were fast clenched in determination by then, and the skin drawn tight and livid over his cheekbones with exhaustion, and Cadfael was glad to get him into the warmth, and go to work with oiled hands on the sinews of his arms and shoulders, and the thighs that had carried him so bravely all day long.

And the third day, early in the afternoon, they came to the manor of Hales.

The manor house lay a little aside from the village and the church, timber-built on a stone undercroft, in level, well-drained fields, with gentle wooded slopes beyond. Within its wooden fence stable and barn and bakehouse were ranged along the pale, well maintained and neat. Brother Haluin stood in the open gateway, and looked at the place of his old service with a face fixed and still, only his eyes alive and full of pain.

'Four years,' he said, 'I kept the manor roll here. Bertrand de Clary was my father's overlord, I was sent here before I was fourteen, to be page to his lady. Will you believe, the man himself I never saw, before I came here he was already in the Holy Land? This is but one of his manors, the only one in these parts, but his son was already installed in his place, and ruled the honour from Staffordshire. She always liked Hales best, she left her son to his lordship and settled here, and it was here I came. Better for her if I had never entered this house. Better far for Bertrade!'

'It's too late,' said Cadfael mildly, 'to do right whatever

48

was done amiss then. This day is for doing a right what you have pledged yourself to do now, and for that it is not too late. You'll be freer with her, maybe, if I wait for you without.'

'No,' said Haluin. 'Come with me! I need your witness, I know it will be just.'

A tow-haired youth came out of the stable with a pitchfork in his hands, steaming gently in the chill air. At sight of two black Benedictine habits in the gateway he turned and came towards them, leisurely and amiable.

'If you're wanting a bed and a meal, Brothers, come in, your cloth's always welcome here. There's good lying in the loft, and they'll feed you in the kitchen if you'll please to walk through.'

'I do remember,' said Haluin, his eyes still fixed upon a distant past, 'your lady kept always a hospitable house for travellers. But I shall need no bed this night. I have an errand to the lady Adelais de Clary herself, if she will give me audience. A few minutes of her time is all I ask.'

The boy shrugged, staring them over with grey, unreadable Saxon eyes, and waved them towards the stone steps that led up to the hall door.

'Go in and ask for her woman, Gerta, she'll see if the lady'll speak with you.' And he stood to watch them as they crossed the yard, before turning back to his labours among the horses.

A manservant was just coming up the steps from the kitchen into the passage as they entered the great doorway. He came to ask their business, and being told, sent off a kitchen boy to carry word to the lady's woman of the chamber, who presently came out from the hall to see who these monastic guests might be. A woman of about forty years, very brisk and neat, plain in her dress and plain in her face, for she was pock-marked. But of her confidence in office there was no question. She looked them over somewhat superciliously, and listened to Haluin's meekly uttered request without a responsive smile, in no hurry to open a door of which she clearly felt herself the privileged custodian.

'From the abbey at Shrewsbury, you come? And on the lord abbot's business, I suppose?'

'On an errand the lord abbot has sanctioned,' said Haluin.

'It is not the same,' said Gerta sharply. 'What other than abbey business can send a monk of Shrewsbury here? If this is some matter of your own, let my lady know with whom she is dealing.'

'Tell her,' said Haluin patiently, leaning heavily on his crutches, and with eyes lowered from the woman's unwelcoming face, 'that Brother Haluin, a Benedictine monk of Shrewsbury abbey, humbly begs her of her grace to receive him.'

The name meant nothing to her. Clearly she had not been in Adelais de Clary's service, or certainly not in her confidence or even close enough to guess at her preoccupations, eighteen years ago. Some other woman, perhaps nearer her mistress's years, had filled this intimate office then. Close body-servants, grown into their mistress's trust and into their own blood-loyalty, carry a great treasury of secrets, often to their deaths. There must somewhere, Cadfael thought, watching in silence, be a woman who would have stiffened and opened her eyes wide at that name, even if she had not instantly known the changed and time-worn face.

'I will ask,' said the tirewoman, with a touch of condescension still, and went away through the hall to a leather-curtained doorway at the far end. Some minutes passed before she appeared again, drawing back the hangings, and without troubling to approach them, called from the doorway: 'My lady says you may come.'

The solar they entered was small and dim, for the windward of the two windows was shuttered fast against the weather, and the tapestries that draped the walls were old, and in rich dark colours. There was no fireplace, but a stone hearth laid close to the most sheltered corner carried a charcoal brazier, and between that and the one window that gave light a woman was sitting at a little embroidery frame, on a cushioned stool. Against the light from the window she showed as a tall, erect shape, dark-clothed, while the glow of the brazier shone in copper highlights on her shadowed face. She had left her needle thrust into the stretched cloth. Her hands were clenched fast on the raised arms of the stool, and her eyes were on the doorway, into which Brother Haluin lurched painfully on his crutches, his one serviceable foot sore with use and bearing him wincingly at every step, the blocked toe of his left foot barely touching the floor as a meagre aid to balance. Constant leaning into the crutches had hunched his shoulders and bent his straight back. Having heard his name, she must surely have expected something nearer to the lively, comely young man she had cast out all those years ago. What could she make now of this mangled wreckage?

He was barely within the room when she rose abruptly to her feet, stiff as a lance. Over their heads she spoke first to the waiting-woman, who had made to follow them in.

'Leave us!' said Adelais de Clary. And to Haluin, as the leather curtain swung heavily into place between solar and hall: 'What is this? What have they done to you?'

Chapter Four

HE MUST, Cadfael reckoned, growing used to the play of light and shadow within the room, be within ten years of his own age, but she looked younger. The dark hair that was coiled in heavy braids on either side of her head was barely touched with grey, and the imperious, fine bones of her face had kept their imperishable elegance though the flesh that covered them was a little shrunken and sapless now, and her body had grown angular and lean as the juices of youth dried up. Her hands, though shapely still, betrayed her with swollen knuckles and seamed veins, there was a languor upon her pale skin at throat and wrist where once the rounded gloss of youth had been. But for all that, in the oval face, the long, resolute lips and large eyes in their deep settings Cadfael saw the ashes of great beauty. No, not ashes, embers, still alive and as hot at least as the coals burning in the heart of the brazier.

'Come nearer!' she said. And when Haluin stood before her with the light upon his face, pale and cold light from the window, flushed from the fire: 'It is you!' she said. 'I wondered. How have you come to this?'

Her voice was low-pitched, full and authoritative, but the

first implication of dismay and concern was gone. She looked at him neither compassionately nor coldly, but with a kind of detached indifference, a curiosity of no deep root.

'This is no man's blame but mine,' said Haluin, 'Don't regard it! I have what I earned. I came by a great fall, but by the grace of God I am alive, who by this time had thought to be dead. And as I have eased my soul to God and my confessor for old sins, so I come to beg forgiveness of you.'

'Was that needful?' she said, marvelling. 'After so many years, and all this way?'

'Yes, it was needful. I do greatly need to hear you say that you forgive me the wrong I did, and the grief I brought upon you. There can be no rest for me now until the leaf is washed clear of every last stain.'

'And you have told over all the old writing,' said Adelais with some bitterness, 'all that was secret and shameful, have you? To your confessor! And how many more? This good brother who bears you company? The whole household at chapter? Could you not bear to be still a sinner unshriven, rather than betray my daughter's name to the world, and she so long in her grave? I would have gone sinful into purgatory rather!'

'And so would I!' cried Haluin, wrung. 'But no, it is not so. Brother Cadfael bears me company because he is the only one who knows, excepting only Abbot Radulfus, who heard my confession. No other will ever know from us. Brother Cadfael was also grossly wronged in what I did, he had a right to give or withhold forgiveness. It was from his store and after his teaching that I stole those medicines I gave to you.'

She turned her gaze upon Cadfael in a long, steady stare, and her face, for once seen clearly, was intent and still. 'Well,' she said, again turning away into indifference, 'it was very long ago. Who would remember now? And I am not dying yet. What do I know! I shall need a priest myself

54

some day, I could better have answered you then. Well, to put an end to it . . . Have what you ask! I do forgive you. I would not add to what you suffer. Go back in peace to your cloister. I forgive you as I hope for forgiveness.'

It was said without passion; the brief spurt of anger was already gone. It cost her no effort to absolve him, she did it as neutrally, it seemed, and with as little feeling as she would have handed out food to a beggar. Of gentlewomen of her nobility alms could properly be asked, and granting was a form of largesse, the due fulfilment of a rite of lordship. But what she gave lightly came as relieving grace to Haluin. The braced tension went out of his leaning shoulders and stiffly clenched hands. He bent his head humbly before her, and uttered his thanks in a low and halting voice, like a man momentarily dazed.

'Madam, your mercy lifts a load from me, and from my heart I am grateful.'

'Go back to the life you have chosen and the duties you have undertaken,' she said, again seating herself, though she did not yet reach for her needle. 'Think no more of what happened long ago. You say you have a life spared. Use it as best you can, and so will I mine.'

It was dismissal, and as such Haluin accepted it. He made her a deep reverence, and turned carefully upon his crutches, and Cadfael reached a hand to steady him in the movement. She had not so much as bidden them be seated, perhaps too shaken by so sudden and startling a visit, but as they reached the doorway she called after them suddenly:

'Stay if you will, take rest and meat in my house. My servants will provide you everything you need.'

'I thank you,' said Haluin, 'but our leave of absence enjoins a return as soon as my pilgrimage here is done.'

'God hasten your way home, then,' said Adelais de Clary, and with a steady hand took up her needle again.

* * *

55

The church lay a short distance from the manor, where two tracks crossed, and the huddle of village house-plots gathered close about the churchyard wall.

'The tomb is within,' said Haluin, as they entered at the gate. 'It was never opened when I was here, but Bertrand's father is buried here, and surely it must have been opened for Bertrade. She died here. I am sorry, Cadfael, that I refused hospitality also for you, I had not thought in time. I shall need no bed tonight.'

'You said no word of that to the lady,' Cadfael observed.

'No. I hardly know why. When I saw her again my heart misgave me that I did ill to bring before her again that old pain, that the very sight of me was an offence to her. Yet she did forgive. I am the better for that, and she surely none the worse. But you could have slept easy tonight. No need for two to watch.'

'I'm better fitted for a night on my knees than you,' said Cadfael. 'And I am not sure the welcome there would have been very warm. She wished us gone. No, it's very well as it is. Mostly likely she thinks we're on the homeward way already, off her land and out of her life.'

Haluin halted for a second with his hand on the heavy iron ring latch of the church door, his face in shadow. The door swung open, creaking, and he gripped his crutches to ease himself down the two wide, shallow steps into the nave. It was dim and stonily chilly within. Cadfael waited a moment on the steps till his eyes grew accustomed to the changed light, but Haluin set off at once up the nave towards the altar. Nothing here was greatly changed in eighteen years, and nothing had been forgotten. Even the rough edges of the floor tiles were known to him. He turned aside towards the righthand wall, his crutches ringing hollowly, and Cadfael, following, found him standing beside a stone table-tomb fitted between the pillars. The carved image recumbent there was in crude chain-mail, and had

56

one leg crossed over the other, and a hand on his sword-hilt. Another crusader, surely the father of Bertrand, who in his turn had followed him to the Holy Land. This one, Cadfael calculated, might well have been with Robert of Normandy's army in my time, at the taking of Jerusalem. Clearly the de Clary men were proud of their warfare in the east.

A man came through from the sacristy, and seeing two unmistakable Benedictine habits, turned amicably to come towards them. A man of middle age, in a rusty black cassock, advancing upon them with a mildly enquiring expression and a welcoming smile. Haluin heard his steps, soft as they were, and swung about gladly to greet a remembered neighbour, only to recoil on the instant at seeing a stranger.

'Good day, Brothers! God be with you!' said the priest of Hales. 'To travellers of your cloth my house is always open, like this house of God. Have you come far?'

'From Shrewsbury,' said Haluin, strongly recovering himself. 'Forgive me, Father, if I was taken aback. I had expected to see Father Wulfnoth. Foolish of me, indeed, for I have not been here for many years, and he was growing grey when I knew him, but to me in youth it seemed he would be here for ever. Now I dare hardly ask!'

'Father Wulfnoth is gone to his rest,' said the priest, 'seven years ago now it must be. Ten years back I came here, after he was brought to his bed by a seizure, and three years I looked after him until he died. I was newly priest then, I learned much from Wulfnoth, his mind was clear and bright if the flesh had failed him.' His good-natured round face offered sympathetic curiosity. 'You know this church and this manor, then? Were you born in Hales?'

'No, not that. But for some years I served with the lady Adelais at the manor. Church and village I knew well, before I took the cowl at Shrewsbury. Now,' said Haluin earnestly, observing how brightly he was studied, and feeling the need to account for his return, 'I have good need to

57

give thanks for escaping alive from a mishap that might have caused my death, and I have taken thought to discharge, while I may, every debt I have on my conscience. Of which number, one brings me here to this tomb. There was a lady of the de Clary family whom I reverenced, and she died untimely. I should like to spend the night here at her burial place, in prayers for her. It was long before your time, eighteen years ago now. It will not disturb you if I spend the night here within?'

'Why, as to that, you'd be welcome,' said the priest heartily, 'and I could light a cresset for you, it gives some help against the cold. But surely, Brother, you're under some mistake. True, what you say puts this before my time, but Father Wulfnoth told me much concerning the church and the manor, he'd been in the service of the lords of Hales all his life. It was they helped him to his studies and set him up here as priest. There has been no burial here in this tomb since the old lord died, this one who's carved here on the stone. And that was more than thirty years back, it's his grandson rules now. A lady of the family, you say? And died young?'

'A kinswoman,' said Haluin, low-voiced and shaken, his eyes lowered to the stone which had not been raised for thirty years. 'She died here at Hales, I had thought she must be buried here.' He would not name her, or betray more than he must of himself and what moved him, even to this kindly man. And Cadfael stood back from them, watched, and held his peace.

'And only eighteen years ago? Then be certain, Brother, she is not here. If you knew Father Wulfnoth, you know you can rely upon what he told me. And I know his wits were sharp until the day he died.'

'I do believe it,' said Haluin, quivering with the chill of disappointment. 'He would not be mistaken. So – she is not here!'

'But this is not the chief seat of the de Clary honour,' the

58

priest pointed out gently, 'for that's Elford, in Staffordshire. The present lord Audemar took his father there for burial, the family has a great vault there. If there are any close kin dead these last years, that's where they'll be. No doubt the lady you speak of was also taken there to lie among her kinsfolk.'

Haluin seized upon the hope hungrily. 'Yes . . . yes, it could well be so, it must be so. There I shall find her.'

'I have no doubt of it,' said the priest. 'But it's a long way to go afoot.' He had sensed an urgency that was very unlikely to listen to reason, but he did his best to temper it. 'You'd be well advised to go mounted, if you must go now, or put it off for longer days and better weather. At least come within, to my house, and take meat with me, and rest overnight.'

But that Haluin would not do, so much was already clear to Brother Cadfael. Not while there was still an hour or more of daylight left at the windows, and he had still the strength to go a mile further. He excused himself with slightly guilty thanks, and took a restrained leave of the good man, who watched them in wondering speculation until they had climbed the steps to the porch, and closed the door after them.

'No!' said Cadfael firmly, as soon as they were clear of the churchyard, and passing along the track between the village houses to reach the highroad. 'That you cannot do!'

'I can, I must!' Brother Haluin responded with no less determination. 'Why should I not?'

'Because, in the first place, you do not know how far it is to Elford. As far again as we have come, and half as far after that. And you know very well how hard you have pushed yourself already. And in the second place, because you were given leave to attempt this journey in the belief that it would end here, and we two return from here. And so

59

we should. No, never shake your head at me, you know very well Father Abbot never envisaged more than that, and would never have given you leave for more. We should turn back here.'

'How can I?' Haluin's voice was implacably reasonable, even tranquil. His way was perfectly clear to him, and he was patient with dissent. 'If I turn back, I am forsworn. I have not yet done what I vowed to do, I should go back self-condemned and contemptible. Father Abbot would not wish that, however little either he or I expected so long a penance. He gave me leave until I had accomplished what I swore to do. If he were here to be asked, he would tell me to go on. I said I would not rest until I had gone on foot to the tomb where Bertrade lies buried, and there passed a night in prayer and vigil, and that I have not done.'

'Through no fault of yours,' said Cadfael strenuously.

'Does that excuse me? It is a just judgement on me that I must go double the way. If I fail of this, I said, may I live forsworn and die unforgiven. On the blessed relics of Saint Winifred, who has been so good to us all, I swore it. How can I turn back? I would rather die on the road, at least still faithfully trying to redeem my vow, than abandon my faith and honour, and go back shamed.'

And who was that speaking, Cadfael wondered, the dutiful monk, or the son of a good Norman house, from a line at least as old as King William's when he came reaching for the crown of England, and without the irregularity of bastardy, at that. No doubt but pride is a sin, and unbecoming a Benedictine brother, but not so easily shed with the spurs and title of nobility.

Haluin, too, had caught the fleeting implication of arrogance, and flushed at the recognition, but would not draw back from it. He halted abruptly, swaying on his crutches, and detached a hand in haste to take Cadfael by the wrist. 'Don't chide me! Well I know you could, and your face shows me I deserve it, but spare to condemn. I can do no other. Oh, Cadfael, I do know every argument you could justly use against me, I have thought of them, I think of them still, but still I am bound. Bound by vows I will not, dare not break. Though my abbot judge me rebellious and disobedient, though my abbey cast me out, that I must bear. But to take back what I have pledged to Bertrade, that I will not bear.'

The flush of blood mantling in his pale cheeks became him, warmed away the faded look of emaciation from illness, and even stripped some years from him. In stillness he stood upright, stretching his bent back upward between the braced crutches. No persuasion was going to move him. As well accept it.

'But you, Cadfael,' he said, gripping the wrist he held, 'you have made no such vow, you are not bound. No need for you to go further, you have done all that was expected of you. Go back now, and speak for me to the lord abbot.'

'Son,' said Cadfael, between sympathy and exasperation, 'I am fettered as fast as you, and you should know it. My orders are to go with you in case you founder, and to take care of you if you do. You are on your own business, I am on the abbot's. If I cannot take you back with me I cannot go back.'

'But your work,' protested Haluin, dismayed but unwavering. 'Mine can well wait, but you'll be missed. How will they manage without you for so long?'

'As best they can. There's no man living who cannot be done without,' said Cadfael sturdily, 'and just as well, since there's a term to life for every man. No, say no more. If your mind's made up, so is mine. Where you go, I go. And since we have barely an hour of daylight left to us, and I fancy you have no wish to seek a bed here in Hales, we had better move gently on, and look for a shelter along the way.'

* * *

61

Adelais de Clary rose in the morning and went to Mass, as was her regular habit. She was meticulous in her religious observances and in almsgiving, keeping up the old custom of her husband's household. And if her charity seemed sometimes a little cold and distant, at least it was constant and reliable. Whenever the parish priest had a special case in need of relief, he brought it to her for remedy.

He walked with her to the gate after the office, dutiful in attendance. 'I had two Benedictines come visiting yesterday,' he said as she was drawing her cloak about her against a freshening March wind. 'Two brothers from Shrewsbury.'

'Indeed!' said Adelais. 'What did they want with you?'

'The one of them was crippled, and went on crutches. He said he was once in your service, before he took the cowl. He remembered Father Wulfnoth. I thought they would have come to pay their respects to you. Did they not?'

She did not answer that, but only observed idly, gazing into distance as though only half her mind was on what was said: 'I remember, I did have a clerk once who entered the monastery at Shrewsbury. What was his business here at the church?'

'He said he had been spared by death, and was about making up all his accounts, to be better prepared. I found them beside the tomb of your lord's father. They were in some error that a woman of your house was buried there, eighteen years ago. The lame one had it in mind to spend a night's vigil there in prayers for her.'

'A strange mistake,' said Adelais with the same tolerant disinterest. 'No doubt you undeceived him?'

'I told him it was not so. I was not here then, of course, but I knew from Father Wulfnoth that the tomb had not been opened for many years, and what the young brother supposed could not be true. I told him that all of your house now are buried at Elford, where the head of the manor lies.'

'A long, hard journey that would be, for a lame man

afoot,' said Adelais with easy sympathy. 'I hope he did not intend to continue his travels so far?'

'I think, madam, he did. For they declined to rest and eat with me, and sleep the night over, but set off again at once. There I shall find her, the young one said. Yes, I am sure they will have turned eastward when they reached the high-road. A long, hard journey, indeed, but his will was good to perform it.'

His relationship with his patroness was a comfortable and easy one, he did not hesitate to ask directly: 'Will he indeed find the gentlewoman he's seeking at Elford?'

'He well may,' said Adelais, pacing evenly and serenely beside him. 'Eighteen years is a long time, and I cannot enter into his mind. I was younger then, I kept a bigger household. There were cousins, some left without fortune. My lord kept a father's hand on all of his blood. In his absence and as his regent, so did I.'

They had reached the churchyard gate, and halted there. The morning was soft and green, but very still, and the cloud-cover hung heavy and low.

'There will be more snow yet,' said the priest, 'if it does not turn to rain.' And he went on inconsequently: 'Eighteen years! It may be that this monk in his time with you was drawn to one of these young cousins, after the way of the young, and her early death was a greater grief to him than ever he ventured to let you know.'

'It may be so,' said Adelais distantly, and drew up the hood of her cloak against a few infinitely fine spears of sleet that drifted on the still air, and stung her cheek. 'Good day, Father!'

'I will pray,' said the priest after her, 'that his pilgrimage to her grave may bring comfort and benefit to him living, and to the lady dead.'

'Do so, Father,' said Adelais without turning her head. 'And do not fail to add a prayer for me and all the women of

63

my house, that time may lie lightly on us when our day comes.'

Caldfael lay awake in the hay-loft of a forester's holding in the royal forest of Chenet, listening to the measured breathing of his companion, too constant and too tense for sleep. it was the second night since they had left Hales. The first they had spent with a solitary cottar and his wife a mile or so beyond the hamlet of Weston, and the day between had been long, and this second shelter in the early reaches of the forest came very warmly and gratefully. They had gone early to their beds in the loft, for Haluin, at whose insistence they had continued so far into the evening, was close to exhaustion. Sleep, Cadfael noted, came to him readily and peacefully, a restoring mercy to a soul very troubled and wrung when awake. There are many ways by which God tempers the burden. Haluin rose every morning refreshed and resolute.

It was not yet light, there might still be an hour to dawn. There was no movement, no rustling of the dry hay from the corner where Haluin lay, but Cadfael knew he was awake now, and the stillness was good, for it meant that he lay in the languor of ease of body, wherever the wakeful mind within might have strayed.

'Cadfael?' said a still, remote voice out of the darkness, 'Are you awake?'

'I am,' he said as softly.

'You have never asked me anything. Of the thing I did. Of *her* . . .'

'There is no need,' said Cadfael. 'What you wish to tell will be told without asking.'

'I was never free to speak of her,' said Haluin, 'until now. And now only to you, who know.' There was a silence. He bled words slowly and arduously, as the shy and solitary do. After a while he resumed softly: 'She was not beautiful, as

64

her mother was. She had not that dark radiance, but something more kindly. There was nothing dark or secret in her, but everything open and sunlit, like a flower. She was not afraid of anything – not then. She trusted everyone. She had never been betrayed – not then. Only once, and she died of it.'

Another and longer silence, and this time the hay stirred briefly, like a sigh. Then he asked almost timidly: 'Cadfael, you were half your life in the world – did you ever love a woman?'

'Yes,' said Cadfael, 'I have loved.'

'Then you know how it was with us. For we did love, she and I. It hurts most of all,' said Brother Haluin, looking back in resigned and wondering pain, 'when you are young. There is nowhere to hide from it, no shield you can raise between. To see her every day . . . and to know that it was with her as it was with me . . .'

Even if he had put it from him all these years, and tried to turn hands and mind and spirit to the service he had undertaken, of his own will, in his extremity, he had forgotten nothing, it was there within him ready to quicken at a breath, like a sleeping fire when a door is opened. Now at least it could escape into air, into the world of other men, where it could touch other men's sufferings and receive and give compassion. From Cadfael there were no words needed, only the simple acknowledgement of companionship, the assurance of a listening ear.

Haluin fell asleep with a last lingering word on his lips, murmured almost inaudibly after lengthening silences. It might have been her name, Bertrade, or it might have been 'buried'. No matter! What mattered was that he had uttered it on the edge of sleep, and now would blessedly sleep again after all his harsh labour along the way, perhaps long past the coming of the light. So much the better! One day more spent on this pilgrimage might grieve his impatient spirit,

65

but it would certainly benefit his harshly driven body.

Cadfael arose very quietly, and left his companion deeply asleep and virtually a prisoner in the loft, since he would need help to get to his feet and descend the ladder. With the trapdoor left open, a listener below would hear when the sleeper stirred, but by the look of his relaxed body and the thin face smoothed of its tensions he would sleep for some time.

Cadfael went out into the clear, sharp morning, to snuff the still air, redolent of the lingering winter scents of forestland still half asleep. From the forester's small assart among the trees it was possible to see the cleared grey of the track in broken glimpses between the old trunks, for the growth was close enough to keep the ground almost clear of underbrush. A handcart trundled along the road, laden with kindling from the fallen deadwood of the autumn, and the chattering flight of disturbed birds accompanied it in a shimmer of fluttered branches and drifting leaves. The forester was already up and about his morning tasks, his cow lumbering in to be milked, his dog weaving busily about his heels. A dry day, the sky overcast but lofty, the light good. A fine day for the road. By night they could be in Chenet itself, and the manor, in the king's holding, would take them in. Tomorrow to Lichfield, and there Cadfael was determined they should halt for another long night's rest, however ardently Haluin might argue for pressing on the remaining few miles to Elford. After a proper sleep in Lichfield Haluin should be in better condition to endure the next night's vigil pledged in Bertrade's memory, and face the beginning of the return journey, during which, God be praised, there need be no haste at all, and no cause to drive himself to the limits of endurance.

Sounds came muffled and soft along the beaten earth of the track, but Cadfael caught rather the vibration of hooves than the impact. Horses coming briskly from the west, two

66

horses, for their gaits quivered in counterpoint, coming at a brisk trot, fresh from a night's rest and ready for the day. Travellers heading, perhaps, for Lichfield, after spending the night at the manor of Stretton, two miles back along the road. Cadfael stood to watch them pass.

Two men in dun-coloured gear, leather-coated, easy in the saddle, their seats and the handling of their mounts so strongly alike that either they had learned from childhood together, or the one had taught the other. And indeed, the one was double the bulk of the other and clearly a generation the elder, and though they were too distant and too briefly seen to have features, the whole shape of them indicated that they were kin. Two privileged grooms to some noble house, each with a woman pillion behind him. Women warmly cloaked for travelling look all much alike, and yet Cadfael stared after the first of these with roused attention, and kept his eyes on her until the horses and their riders had vanished along the road, and the soft drumming of hooves faded into distance.

She was still within his eyelids as he turned back into the hay-hut, pricking uneasily at his memory, urging, against all his dismissal of the possibility as folly, that he had seen her before, and further, that if he would but admit it he knew very well where.

But whether that was true or not, and whatever it augured if it was, there was nothing he could do about it. He shrugged it into the back of his mind, and went in, to listen for the moment when Haluin should awake and have need of him.

They came through groves of trees into an expanse of level meadows, a little bleached and grey as yet in the cold air, but fertile and well cultivated, a rich little island in a shire otherwise somewhat derelict still after the harsh pacification of fifty years back. There before them lay the sleek curves of the River Tame, the steep-pitched roof of a mill, and the close cluster of the houses of Elford, beyond the water.

In the warm and welcoming hospitality of the clerics of Lichfield they had spent a restful night, and received full directions as to the best road to Elford, and with the first light of dawn they had set off on the last four miles or so of this penitential journey. And here before them lay the goal of Haluin's pilgrimage, almost within reach, only an expanse of peaceful fields and a wooden footbridge between him and his absolution. A fortunate place, prosperous where much was impoverished, with not one mill by the waterside, but two, for they could see the second one upstream, with ample meadowland, and rich soil where the arable fields showed. A place that might well promise blessing and peace of mind after labour and pain.

The pale thread of the path led them forward, and the roofs of Elford rose before them, circled with trees and bushes still naked and dark at this distant view, not yet so far advanced in bud as to show the first faint, elusive smoke of green. They crossed the bridge, the uneven planks causing Haluin to watch carefully how he placed his crutches, and came into the track between the houses. A neat village, with housewives and husbandmen going cheerfully and confidently about their daily business, alert to strangers but civil and welcoming to the Benedictine habit. They exchanged greetings along the way, and Haluin, cheered and vindicated at the successful completion of his journey, began to flush and brighten with pleasure at being offered this spontaneous omen of acceptance and release.

No need to ask how to reach the church, they had seen its low tower before they crossed the bridge. It had been built since the Normans came, sturdy in grey stone, with a spacious churchyard very well stockaded for sanctuary at need, and full of old and handsome trees. They entered under the round-arched portico, and came into the familiar cool, echoing gloom of all stone-built churches, smelling faintly of dust, and wax candles, and strongly and reassuringly of home, the chosen abiding-place.

Haluin had halted in the tiled silence of the nave to get his bearings. Here there was no Lady Chapel to accommodate a patron's tomb between the altars, the lords of Elford must lie aside, built into the stones of the walls they had raised. The red eye of light from the altar lamp showed them where the tomb lay, a great table slab filling a niche in the right-hand wall. Some dead de Clary, perhaps the first who came over with King William, and got his reward later, showed as a sleeping figure in relief on the sealing stone. Haluin had started forward towards it, only to check and draw back after the first echoing step, for there was a woman on her knees beside the tomb.

They saw her only as a shadowy figure, for the cloak she wore was dark grey like the stone in this dim light, and they knew her for a woman and not a man because the hood of the cloak was thrown back from her head, uncovering a white linen coif and a gauze veil over it. They would have retired into the porch to let her complete her prayers in peace, but she had heard the impact of the crutches on the tiled floor, and turned her head sharply to look towards them. In a single graceful, abrupt movement she rose to her feet, and coming towards them, stepped into the light from a window, and showed them the proud, aging, beautiful face of Adelais de Clary.

Chapter Five

OU?' SHE said, staring, and turning her startled gaze from one face to the other, seeking, it seemed, some logic in this unexpected visitation. Her voice was neutral, neither welcoming nor repelling them. 'I had not thought to see you again so soon. Is there something more you have to ask of me, Haluin, that you have followed me here? You have only to ask. I have said I forgive.'

'Madam,' said Haluin, shaken and quivering from the apparition of his former mistress in this unexpected place, 'we have not followed you. Indeed I never thought to find you here. For your forbearance I'm grateful, and I would not for the world trouble you further. I have come here only in fulfilment of a vow I made. I had thought to spend a night in prayer at Hales, believing that my lady your daughter must be buried there. But we heard from the priest that it is not so. It's here at Elford she lies, in the tomb of her grandsires. So I have continued this far. And all I have to beg of you is your leave to keep my vigil here through this coming night, in deliverance of what I have sworn. Then we will depart, and trouble you no more.'

'I will not deny,' she said, but with a softening voice,

71

'that I shall be glad to have you gone. No ill-will! But this wound you have opened again for me I would willingly swathe away out of sight until it heals. Your face is a contagion that makes it open and bleed afresh. Do you think I should have taken horse and ridden here so fast if you had not put that old grief in my mind?'

'I trust,' said Haluin in a low and shaken voice, 'you may find, madam, as I hope to find, the wound cleansed of all its rancours by this atonement. It is my prayer that for you this time the healing may be sweet and wholesome.'

'And for you?' she said sharply, and turned a little away from him, with a motion of her hand that forbade any answer. 'Sweet and wholesome! You ask much of God, and more of me.' In the sidelong light from the window her face was fierce and sad. 'You have learned a monk's way with words,' she said. 'Well, it is a long time! Your voice was lighter once, so was your step. This at least I grant you, you are here at a very heavy cost. Do not deny me the grace of offering you rest and meat this time. I have a dwelling of my own here, within my son's manor pale. Come within and rest at least until Vespers, if you must punish your flesh on the stones here through the night.'

'Then I may have my night of prayer?' asked Haluin hungrily.

'Why not? Have you not just seen me entreating God in the same cause?' she said. 'I see you broken. I would not have you forsworn. Yes, have your penitential vigil, but take food in my house first. I'll send my grooms to fetch you,' she said, 'when you have made your devotions here.'

She was almost at the door, paying no attention to Haluin's hesitant thanks, and affording him no opportunity to refuse her hospitality, when she suddenly halted and swung round to them again.

'But say no word,' she said earnestly, 'to any other about your purpose here. My daughter's name and fame are safe enough under the stone, let them lie quiet there. I would not have any other reminded as I have been reminded. Let it be only between us two, and this good brother who bears you company.'

'Madam,' said Haluin devoutly, 'there shall be no word said to any other soul but between us three, neither now nor at any other time, neither here nor in any other place.'

'You ease my mind,' she said, and in a moment she was gone, and the door drawn quietly to after her.

Haluin could not kneel without something firm before him to which to cling, and Cadfael's arm about him to ease his weight down gently, sharing the burden with his companion's one serviceable foot. They offered their dutiful prayer at the altar side by side, and Cadfael, open-eyed as Haluin kneeled long, traced with measured concern the worn lines of the young man's face. He had survived the hard journey afoot, but not without a heavy cost. The night on the stones here would be cold, cramping and long, but Haluin would insist on the last extreme of self-punishment. And after that, the long road back. As well, indeed, if the lady could persuade him to remain for at least a second night, if only as a concession and grace to her now they had, in a fashion, come to terms with their shared and haunted past.

For it could certainly be true that Haluin's sudden visit had sent her on her own pilgrimage, hotfoot here to confront her own part in that old tragedy. Passing by at a smart trot the forester's assart near Chenet, with only a maid-servant and two grooms in her train, and striking an elusive spark in Cadfael's memory. It could well be true. Or would such a seed have borne fruit so fast? The implication of haste was there. Cadfael saw again the two double-laden horses passing in the early morning, going steadily and with purpose. In haste to pay a half-forgotten debt of affection and remorse? Or to arrive before someone else, and be ready and armed to receive him? She wanted them satisfied and gone, but that was natural enough. They had trespassed on her peace, and held up an old, flawed mirror before her beautiful face.

'Help me up!' said Haluin, and raised his arms like a child to be lifted to his feet; and that was the first time that he had asked for help, always before it had been proffered, and his acceptance humble and resigned rather than grateful.

'You did not speak one word throughout,' he said suddenly, marvelling, as they turned towards the church door. 'I had not one word to speak,' said Cadfael. 'But I heard many words. And even the silences between them were not altogether inarticulate.'

Adelais de Clary's groom was waiting for them in the porch, as she had promised, leaning indolently with one shoulder propped against the jamb of the door, as though he had been waiting for some time, but with immovable patience. His appearance confirmed everything Brother Cadfael had elaborated, in his own mind, from the few glimpses he had had of the riders between the trees. The younger of the pair, this, a brawny young man of perhaps thirty years, thickset, bull-necked, unmistakably in the Norman mould. Perhaps the third or fourth generation from a progenitor who had come over as a man-at-arms with the first de Clary. The strong original stock still prevailed, though intermarriage with English women had tempered the fairness of his hair into a straw-brown, and somewhat moderated the brutal bones of his face. He still wore his hair cropped into a close cap in the Norman manner, and his strong jaw clean-shaven, and he still had the bright, light, impenetrable eyes of the north. At their coming he sprang erect, more at ease in movement than in repose.

'My lady sends me to show you the way.'

His voice was flat and clipped, and he waited for no reply, but set off out of the churchyard before them, at a pace Haluin could not well maintain. The groom looked back at the gate and waited, and thereafter abated his speed, though it obviously chafed him to move slowly. He said nothing of his own volition, and replied to question or simple civility cordially enough, but briefly. Yes, Elford was a very fine property, good land and a good lord. Audemar's competent management of his honour was acknowledged indifferently; this young man's allegiance was to Adelais rather than to her son. Yes, his father was in the same service, and so had his father been before him. About these monastic guests he showed no curiosity at all, though he might have felt some. Those pale grey, alien eyes concealed all thought, or perhaps suggested thought's total absence.

He brought them by a grassy way to the gate of the manor enclosure, which was walled and spacious. Audemar de Clary's house sat squarely in the midst, the living floor raised well above a stone undercroft, and to judge by the small windows above there were at least two more chambers over the solar. And his ample courtyard was built round with other habitable rooms, as well as the customary and necessary stables, armoury, bakehouse and brewhouse, stores and workshops, and was populous with the activities of a large and busy household.

The groom led them to a small timber lodging under the curtain wall.

'My lady has had this chamber made ready for you. Use it as your own, she says, and the gateman will see to it you can come and go freely, to go to the church.'

Her hospitality, as they found, was meticulous but remote and impersonal. She had provided them with water for washing, comfortable pallets to rest on, sent them food from her own table, and given orders to tell them to ask for anything they might need or want that had been forgotten, but she did not receive them into her own presence. Perhaps forgiveness did not reach so far as to render Haluin's remorseful presence agreeable to her. Nor was it her house-servants who waited on them, but the two grooms who had ridden with her from Hales. It was the elder of the two who brought them meat and bread and cheese, and small ale from the pantry. Cadfael had not been deceived in their relationship, for this one was clearly father to the other, a tough, square-set man in his fifties, close-mouthed like his son, broader in the shoulders, more bowed in the legs from years spent as much on horse-back as on his own two feet. The same cold, unconfiding eyes, the same bold and power-ful shaven jaws, but this one was tanned to a lasting bronze that Cadfael recognised from his own past as having its origin very far from England. His lord had been a crusader. This man had surely been with him there in the Holy Land, and got his burnished gloss there under the fierce, remem-bered sun.

The elder groom came again later in the afternoon, with a message not for Haluin but for Cadfael. It so happened that Haluin had fallen asleep on his pallet, and the man's entrance, light and soft as a cat for all his bulk, did not disturb his rest, for which Cadfael was grateful. There was a long and unrestful night to come. He motioned to the groom to wait, and went out into the courtyard to him, closing the door softly after him.

'Let him lie. He'll need to be wakeful later.'

'My lady told us how he means to spend the night,' said the groom. 'It's you she bids to her, if you'll come with me now. Let the other brother rest, she says, for he's been mortal sick. I grant him a man's guts, or he'd never have come so far on those feet. This way, Brother!'

Her dower dwelling was built into a corner of the curtain wall, sheltered from the prevailing winds, small, but

76

enough for such occasional visits as she chose to make to her son's court. A narrow hall and chamber, and a kitchen built lean-to against the wall outside. The groom strode in and through the hall with simple authority, as one having privilege here, and entered his mistress's presence much as a son or brother of hers might have done, trusting and trusted. Adelais de Clary was well served, but without subservience.

'Here is Brother Cadfael from Shrewsbury, my lady. The other one's asleep.'

Adelais was sitting at a distaff loaded with deep blue wool, spinning the spindle with her left hand, but at their entrance she ceased to turn it, and lodged it carefully against the foot of the distaff to prevent the yarn from uncoiling.

'Good! It's what he needs. Leave us now, Lothair, our guest will find his own way back. Is my son home yet?'

'Not yet. I'll be looking out for him when he comes.'

'He has Roscelin with him,' she said, 'and the hounds. When they're all home and kennelled and stalled, take your ease, it's well earned.'

He merely nodded by way of acknowledgement, and departed, taciturn and uneffusive as ever, and yet there was a tone in their exchanges of invulnerable assurance, secure as rooted rock. Adelais said no word until the door of her chamber had closed after her servant. She was eyeing Cadfael with silent attention, and the faint shadow of a smile.

'Yes,' she said, as if he had spoken. 'More than an old servant. He was with my lord all the years he fought in Palestine. More than once he did Bertrand that small service, to keep him man alive. It is another manner of allegiance, not a servant's. As bound in fealty as ever lord is to his overlord. I inherited what was my lord's before me. Lothair, he's called. His son is Luc. Born and bred in the same mould. You'll have seen the likeness, God knows it can hardly be missed.'

'I have seen it,' said Cadfael. 'And I knew where Lothair got that copper skin he wears.'

'Indeed?' She was studying him with concentrated interest now, having gone to the trouble to see him for the first time.

'I was some years in the east myself, before his time. If he lives long enough his brown will fade as mine has faded, but it takes a long while.'

'Ah! So you were not given to the monks in childhood. I thought you had not the look of such virgin innocents,' said Adelais.

'I entered of my own will,' said Cadfael, 'when it was time.'

'So did he – of his own will, though I think it was not time.' She stirred and sighed. 'I sent for you only to ask if you have everything you need – if my men have taken proper care of you.'

'Excellent care. And for their kindness and yours we are devoutly grateful.'

'And to ask you of him – of Haluin. I have seen in what sad case he is. Will it ever be better with him?'

'He will never walk as he did before,' said Cadfael, 'but as his sinews gain time and strength he will improve. He believed he was dying, so did we all, but he lives and will yet find much good in life – once his mind is at peace.'

'And will it be at peace after tonight? Is this what he needs?'

'I believe he will. I believe it is.'

'Then it has my blessing. And then you will take him back to Shrewsbury? I can provide you horses,' she said, 'for the way back. Lothair can fetch them to Hales when we return.'

'That kindness he will surely refuse,' said Cadfael. 'He has sworn to complete this penance on foot.'

78

She nodded understanding. 'I will ask him, none the less. Well – that is all, Brother. If he will not, I can do no more. Yes, one thing I can! I am coming to Vespers tonight, I will speak to the priest, and make certain that no one – no one! – shall question or trouble his vigil. You understand, nothing must be let slip to any soul but us who already know all too well. Tell him so. What remains is between him and God.'

The master of the house was just riding in at the gate as Cadfael walked back to the lodging where Haluin lay sleeping. The ring of harness and hooves and voices entered ahead of the cavalcade, a lively sound, bringing out grooms and servants like bees from a disturbed hive to attend on their lord's arrival. And here he came, Audemar de Clary on a tall chestnut horse, a big man in dark, plain, work-manlike riding clothes, without ornament, and needing none to mark him out as having authority here. He rode in with head uncovered, the hood of his short cloak flung back on his shoulders, and his shock of crisp hair was as dark as his mother's, but the powerful bones of his face, high-bridged nose, thrusting cheekbones and lofty forehead he surely had from his crusader father.

He could not, Cadfael thought, be yet forty years old. The vigour of his movements as he dismounted, the spring of his step on the ground, the very gestures of his hands as he stripped off his gloves, all were young. But the formidable features of his face and the mastery that was manifest all about him, in the efficiency of his management here and the prompt and competent service he expected and got, made him seem older in dominance than he was in years. He had been master, Cadfael recalled, in his father's long absence, beginning early, probably before he was twenty, and the de Clary honour was large and scattered. He had learned his business well. Not a man to be crossed lightly, but no one here feared him. They approached him cheerfully and spoke with him boldly. His anger, when justified, might be withering, even perilous, but it would be just.

He had a young fellow, page or squire, riding close at his elbow, a youth of seventeen or eighteen, fresh-faced and flushed with open air and exercise, and after them came two kennelmen on foot with the hounds on leash after their run. Audemar handed over his bridle to the groom who came running, and stood stamping his booted feet as he shed his cloak into the young man's ready hands. The brief flurry of activity was over in a few minutes, the horses on their way across the court to the stables, the hounds away to the kennels. The young groom Luc came out of the stable-yard and spoke to Audemar, apparently to deliver a message from Adelais, for Audemar at once looked round towards the lady's lodging, nodded understanding, and came striding towards her door. His eye fell on Cadfael, standing discreetly aside from his path, and for an instant he checked as though to stop and speak, but then changed his mind and went on, to vanish into the deep doorway.

Judging by the time that she and her grooms and her maid had passed by in the forest, Cadfael reckoned, Adelais must have arrived here that same day, two days previously. They would have no need to halt for a night between Chenet and Elford, on horseback the distance was easy. Therefore she must already have seen and talked with her son. What she had to communicate to him now, as soon as he returned from riding, might well have to do with whatever was news this day at the manor of Elford. And what was new but the arrival of the two monks from Shrewsbury, and their reason for being here, a reason she would interpret with discretion for him? For he had been here at Elford when his sister died in Hales, for the world's ears – and her brother's also? – of a fever. That must be all he had ever known of it, a simple, sad death, such as may happen in any household, even to one in the bloom of youth. No, that strong and resolute woman would never have let her son into the secret. An old, trusted, confidential maidservant, maybe. She must have needed such a one, now perhaps dead. But her young son, no, never.

And if that was true, no wonder Adelais was taking every precaution to smooth Haluin's way to his atonement, and be rid of him as quickly as possible, warding off all enquiry, even from the priest, offering horses to hasten the departure, and pledging the two pilgrims not to reveal anything of the past to any other being, not to say one word of the import of their errand, or mention the name of Bertrade.

Something, at least, I begin to understand, thought Cadfael. Wherever we turn, there is Adelais between us and all others. She houses us, she feeds us, it is her most loyal servants who approach and wait on us, not any from her son's household. My daughter's name and fame are safe enough under the stone, she had said, let them lie quiet there. Small blame to her for making sure, and no wonder she had ridden in haste to reach Elford beforehand and be ready for them.

And go we will, he thought, tomorrow morning if Haluin is fit to set out, and she can set her mind at rest. We can find another halting-place a mile or two from here, if we must, but at all costs we'll quit these walls, and she need never see or think of Haluin again.

The young squire had remained standing to watch his lord cross to the lady's door, Audemar's cloak flung over his shoulder, his bare head almost flaxen against the dark cloth. He had still the coltish, angular grace of youth. In a year or two his slenderness would fill out into solid and shapely manhood, with every movement under smooth control, but as yet he retained the vulnerable uncertainty of a boy. He looked after Audemar with surprised speculation, stared at Cadfael in candid curiosity, and turned slowly towards the door of Audemar's hall.

So this must be the Roscelin to whom Adelais had referred, thought Cadfael, watching him go. Not a son of the house, by the cut of him and the colouring, but not a servant, either. Doubtless a youngster from the family of one of Audemar's tenants, sent here to his overlord to get his training in arms, and acquire the skills and practices of a small court, in preparation for the wider world. Such apprentice lordlings proliferated in every great barony, the de Clary honour might well be patron to one or two of the same kind.

The early evening had turned cold, and there was a biting wind rising, with a few fine needles of sleet stinging in its touch. The hour of Vespers was not far away. Cadfael went in thankfully from the chill, to find Brother Haluin awake and waiting, silent and tense, for his hour of fulfilment.

Adelais had evidently made her dispositions well. No one intruded upon their privacy, no one asked any question or showed any curiosity. The young groom Luc brought them food before Vespers, and at the end of the office they were left alone in the church to conduct their vigil as they pleased. Doubtful if any among the household wondered about them at all, being accustomed to random visitors of all kinds, with differing needs, and the devotions of a pair of itinerant Benedictines surprised no one. If monks of the abbey of Saint Peter elected to spend a night in prayer in a church of Saint Peter, that was no special wonder, and concerned no one else.

So Brother Haluin had his will, and redeemed his vow. He would have no softening of the stone, no extra cloak to ward off the cold of the night, nothing to abate the rigours of his penance. Cadfael helped him to his knees, within reach of the solid support of the tomb, so that if faintness or dizziness came over him he could at least hold fast by it to break his fall. The crutches were laid at the foot of the stone. There was no more he would permit anyone to do for him. But Cadfael kneeled with him, withdrawn into shadow to leave him solitary with his dead Bertrade and a God doubtless inclining a compassionate ear.

It was a long night, and cold. The altar lamp made an eye of brightness in the gloom, at least ruddy like fire if it gave no warmth. The silence carried hour by hour, like an infinitesimal ripple vibrating through it, the gradual heave of Haluin's breathing and the constant whisper of his moving lips, felt in the blood and the bowels rather than audible with the ear. From somewhere within him he drew an inexhaustible wealth of words to be spent for his dead Bertrade. Their tension and passion kept him erect and oblivious to pain, though pain took fast hold of him before midnight, and never left him until his rapture and his ordeal ended together with the coming of the light.

When he opened his eyes at last to the full light of a frosty morning, and laboriously unlocked his cold, clasped hands, the sounds of the customary early activity were already audible from the outside world. Haluin stared dazedly upon the waking day, returning from some place very far off, very deep within. He essayed to move, to grip the rim of the stone, and his fingers were so numbed they could not feel, and his arms so stiff they could give him no help to raise himself. Cadfael wound an arm about him to lift him, but Haluin could not straighten his stiff knees to set his better foot to the ground, but hung a dead weight on the encircling arm. And suddenly there was a flurry of light footsteps, and another arm, young and strong, embraced the helpless body from the other side, a fair head stooped to Haluin's shoulder, and between his two supporters he was hauled upright, and held so as the blood flowed back achingly into his numbed legs.

'In God's name, man,' said the young man Roscelin

impatiently, 'must you use yourself so hardly when you have already enough for any sane man to carry?'

Haluin was too startled, and his mind still too far away, to be capable of grasping that, much less answering it. And if Cadfael privately considered it a perfectly sensible reaction, aloud he said practically: 'Keep firm hold of him, so, while I pick up his crutches. And God bless you for appearing so aptly. Spare to scold him, you'd be wasting your breath. He's under vow.'

'A foolish vow!' said the boy with the arrogant certainty of his years. 'Who's the better for this?' But for all his disapproval he held Haluin warmly and firmly, and looked at him sidelong with a frown at least as anxious as it was exasperated.

'He is,' said Cadfael, propping the crutches under Haluin's armpits, and setting to work to chafe life back into the cold hands that could not yet grip the staves. 'Hard to believe, but you had better credit it. There, you can let him lean on his props now, but hold him steady. Well for you at your years, you can sleep easy, with nothing to regret and nothing to ask pardon for. How did you come to look in here so timely?' he asked, eyeing the young man with fresh interest, thus at close quarters. 'Were you sent?'

For this boy seemed an unlikely instrument for Adelais to use in shepherding her inconvenient guests in and out of Elford – too young, too blunt, too innocent.

'No,' said Roscelin shortly, and relented to add with better grace: 'I was plain curious.'

'Well, that's human,' admitted Cadfael, recognising his own besetting sin.

'And this morning Audemar has no immediate work for me, he's busy with his steward. Had we not better get this brother of yours back to his lodging, where it's warmer? How shall we do? I can fetch a horse for him if we can get him mounted.'

Haluin had come back from his distant place to find himself being discussed and handled as if he had no mind of his own, and no awareness of his surroundings. He stiffened instinctively against the indignity. 'No,' he said, 'I thank you, but I can go now. I need not trespass on your kindness further.' And he flexed his hands and gripped the staves of his crutches, and took the first cautious steps away from the tomb.

They followed closely, one at either elbow in case he faltered, Roscelin going before up the shallow steps and through the doorway to prevent a possible stumble, Cadfael coming close behind to support him if he reeled backwards. But Haluin had gathered to his aid a will refreshed and strengthened by achievement, and was resolute to manage this walk alone, at whatever cost. And there was no haste. When he felt the need he could rest on his crutches to draw breath, and so he did three times before they reached Audemar's courtyard, already populous and busy about bakery and mews and well-head. It said much for young Roscelin's quickness and delicacy of mind, Cadfael reflected, that he waited without comment or impatience at every pause, and refrained from offering a hand in help until help should be invited. So Haluin came back to the lodging in Audemar's courtyard as he would have wished, on his own misshapen feet, and could feel that he had earned the ease of his bed.

Roscelin followed them in, still curious, in no haste to go in search of whatever duties awaited him. 'Is that all, then?' he said, watching Haluin stretch out his still numbed limbs gratefully, and draw the brychan over them. 'Then where do you go when you leave us? And when? You'll not set out today?'

'We go back to Shrewsbury,' said Cadfael. 'Today – that I doubt. A day's rest would be wisdom.' By the weary ease of Haluin's face, and the softened gaze turned inward, it would not be long before he fell asleep, the best and best-earned sleep since he had made his confession.

'I saw you ride in with the lord Audemar yesterday,' said Cadfael, studying the youthful face before him. 'The lady mentioned your name. Are you kin to the de Clarys?'

The boy shook his head. 'No. My father is tenant and vassal to him, they've always been good friends, and there's a marriage tie, a while back now. No, I'm sent here to Audemar's service at my father's order.'

'But not at your wish,' said Cadfael, interpreting the tone rather than the words.

'No! Much against my wish!' said Roscelin abruptly, and scowled at the floorboards between his booted feet.

'Yet to all appearances as good a lord as you could hope for,' suggested Cadfael mildly, 'and better than most.'

'He's well enough,' the boy owned fairly. 'I've no complaint of *him*. But I grudge it that my father has sent me away here to be rid of me out of the house, and that's the truth of it.'

'Now why,' wondered Cadfael, curious but not quite asking, 'why should any father want to be rid of you?' For here was undoubtedly the very picture of a presentable son, upstanding, well-formed, well-conducted, and decidedly engaging in his fair-haired, smooth-cheeked comeliness, a son any father would be glad to parade before his peers. Even in sullenness his face was pleasing, but it was certainly true that he had not the look of one happy in his service.

'He has his reasons,' said Roscelin moodily. 'You'd say good reasons, too, I know that. And I'm not so estranged from him that I could refuse him the obedience due. So I'm here, and pledged to stay here unless lord and father both give me leave to go. And I'm not such a fool as not to admit I could be in far worse places. So I may as well get all the good I can out of it while I'm here.'

86

It seemed that his mind had veered into another and graver quarter, for he sat for some moments silent, staring down into his clasped hands with a frowning brow, and looked up only to measure Cadfael earnestly, his eyes dwelling long upon the black habit and the tonsure.

'Brother,' he said abruptly, 'I've wondered, now and then – about the monkish life. Some men have taken to it, have they not, because what they most wanted was for ever impossible – forbidden them! Is that true? Can it provide a life, if . . . if the life a man wants is out of reach?'

'Yes,' said Brother Haluin's voice, gently and quietly out of a waking dream now very close to sleep. 'Yes, it can!'

'I would not recommend entering it as a second-best,' said Cadfael stoutly. Yet that was what Haluin had done, long ago, and he spoke now as one recording a revelation, the opening of his inward eyes just as they were heavy and closing with sleep.

'The time might be long, and the cost high,' said Haluin with gentle certainty, 'but in the end it would not be second-best.'

He drew in a long breath, and spent it in a great healing sigh, turning his head away from them on the pillow. They were both so intent on him, doubting and wondering, that neither of them had noted the approach of brisk footsteps without, and they started round in surprise as the door was thrown wide open to admit Lothair, carrying a basket of food and a pitcher of small ale for the guests. At the sight of Roscelin seated familiarly upon Cadfael's pallet, and apparently on good terms with the brothers, the groom's weathered face tightened perceptibly, almost ominously, and for an instant a deeper spark flashed and vanished again in his pale eyes.

'What are you doing here?' he demanded with the bluntness of an equal, and the uncompromising authority of an elder. 'Master Roger's looking for you, and my lord wants you in attendance as soon as he's broken his fast. You'd best be off, and sharp about it, too.'

It could not be said that Roscelin showed any alarm at this intelligence, or resentment at the manner in which it was delivered, rather the man's assurance seemed to afford him a little tolerant amusement. But he rose at once, and with a nod and a word by way of farewell went off obediently but without haste to his duty. Lothair stood narrow-eyed in the doorway to watch him go, and did not come fully into the room with his burdens until the boy had reached the steps to the hall door.

Our guard-dog, thought Cadfael, has his orders to ward off any others who come too close, but he had not reckoned with having to do as much for young Roscelin. Now could there, I wonder, be some reason why that contact in particular should cause him consternation? For that's the first spark I've seen struck from his steel!

Chapter Six

A DELAIS herself paid a gracious visit to her monastic guests after Mass, with solicitous enquiries after their health and wellbeing. It was possible, Cadfael reflected, that Lothair had reported back to her the inconvenient and undesirable incursion of the young man Roscelin into a preserve she clearly wished to keep private. She appeared in the doorway of their small chamber, prayer-book in hand, alone, having sent her maid on ahead to her dower house. Haluin was awake, and made to rise from his pallet in respectful acknowledgement of her coming, reaching in haste for his crutches, but she motioned him back with a wave of her hand.

'No, be still! No ceremony is needed between us. How do you find yourself now – now that your vow is accomplished? I hope you have experienced grace, and can return to your cloister in peace. I wish you that mercy. An easy journey and a safe arrival!'

And above all, thought Cadfael, an early departure. And small blame to her. It's what I want, too, and so must Haluin. To have this matter finished, neatly and cleanly, with no more harm to any creature, with mutual forgiveness, once spoken, and thereafter silence.

'You have had little rest,' she said, 'and have a long journey back to Shrewsbury. My kitchen shall supply you with food for the first stages of the way. But I think you should also accept horses. I have said so to Brother Cadfael already. The stables here can spare you mounts, and I will send for them to Hales when I return there. You should not attempt to go back all that way on foot.'

'For the offer, and for all your kindness, we are grateful,' said Haluin in instant and hasty protest. 'But this I cannot accept. I undertook both to go and to return on foot, and I must make good what I vowed. It is a pledge of faith that I am not so crippled as to be utterly useless and unprofitable hereafter, to God and man. You would not wish me to go home shamed and forsworn.'

She shook her head over his obstinacy with apparent resignation. 'So your fellow here warned me you would argue, when I spoke of it to him, but I hoped you would see better reason. Surely you are also pledged to return to your duty at the abbey as soon as may be. Has that no force? If you insist on going afoot you cannot set out at least until tomorrow, after so hard a night on the stones.'

To Haluin, no doubt, that sounded like true solicitude, and an invitation to delay until he was fully rested. To Cadfael it had the sound of a subtle dismissal.

'I never thought that it would be easy,' said Haluin, 'to perform what I swore. Nor should it be. The whole virtue, if there is any virtue in it at all, is to endure the hardship and complete the penance. And so I can and shall. You are right, I owe it to my abbot and my brothers to get back to my duty as soon as I may. We must set out today. There are still hours of daylight left, we must not waste them.'

To do her justice, she did seem to be taken aback at such ready compliance with what she wished, even if she had not expressed the wish. She urged, though without warmth, the necessity of rest, but gave way pliantly before Haluin's

90

stubborn insistence. Things had gone as she wished, at the last moment she could afford one brief convulsion of pity and regret.

'It must be as you wish,' she said. 'Very well, Luc shall bring you food and drink before you go, and fill your scrip for you. As for me, I part from you in goodwill. Now and hereafter, I wish you well.'

When she was gone, Haluin sat silent for a while, shivering a little in the recoil from the finality of this ending. It was as he had hoped, and yet it left him shaken.

'I have made things needlessly hard for you,' he said ruefully. 'You must be as weary as I am, and I have committed you to leaving thus, without sleep. She wanted us gone, and for my part I heartily wish to be gone. The sooner severed, the better for us all.'

'You did right,' said Cadfael. 'Once out of here we need not go far, you are in no case to attempt it today. But to be out of here is all we need.'

They left Audemar de Clary's manor gates in mid-afternoon, under a sky heavy with grey cloud, and turned westward along the track through Elford village, with a chill, insidious wind in their faces. It was over. From this point on, with every step taken they were returning to normality and safety, to the monastic hours and the blessed daily round of work, worship and prayer.

From the highroad Cadfael looked back once, and saw the two grooms standing in the gateway to watch the guests depart. Two solid, sturdy figures, taciturn and inscrutable, following the withdrawal of the interlopers with light, fierce northern eyes. Making sure, thought Cadfael, that the disquiet we brought to that lady departs with us, and leaves no shadow behind.

They did not look back a second time. The need now was to put at least one safe, alienating mile between themselves and the dower house of Elford, and after that they could look for a night's shelter early, for in spite of his resolution it was clear that Haluin was haggard and grey with exhaustion, and would not get far without danger of collapse. His face was set to endure, he went steadily but heavily on his crutches, his eyes dilated and dark in their deep hollows. Doubtful if even now he enjoyed the peace he should have found at Bertrade's tomb, but perhaps it was not Bertrade who still haunted his thoughts.

'I shall never see her again,' said Haluin, to God, himself and the gathering dusk rather than to Cadfael. And it was hard to say whether he spoke in relief or regret, as at leaving something unfinished.

The first snow of a capricious March burst upon them suddenly out of the lowering sky when they were some two miles from Elford. The air was on the edge of frost, there would be no great or prolonged fall, but while it lasted it was thick and blinding, stinging their faces and confusing the path before them. The premature dusk closed down on them almost abruptly, a murky darkness out of which whirling clouds of white flakes wound about them bewilderingly, veiling even what landmarks they had on a stretch of track open, windswept and treeless.

Haluin had begun to stumble, troubled by the driven flakes filling his eyes, and unable to free a hand to draw the folds of his cowl together against the assault. Twice he planted a crutch aside from the trodden path, and all but fell. Cadfael halted and stood close, his back to the wind, to give his companion breathing space and shelter for some moments, while he considered where they were, and what he could recall of the surrounding country from their outward journey. Any dwelling, however mean, would be welcome until this squall blew over. Somewhere here, he calculated, there had been a side-path bearing north, and leading to what seemed to be a cluster of small houses and the long pale of a manor fence, the only sign of occupation within view of the road.

His recollection was accurate. Going cautiously before, with Haluin close at his back, he came to an isolated clump of bushes and low trees which he remembered clearly in this sparsely treed plain, and a little beyond these the path opened. There was even a flickering spark of torchlight, seen fitfully through the whirling snowfall, to keep them in the direct way towards the distant dwelling. Where the lord of the house showed a beacon for benighted travellers there should be a warm welcome waiting.

It took them longer to reach the hamlet than Cadfael had expected, since Haluin was flagging badly, and it was necessary to go very slowly, reaching back constantly to keep him close. Here and there a solitary tree loomed suddenly out of the spinning whiteness on the left hand or the right, only to be veiled again as abruptly. The flakes had grown larger and wetter, the hint of frost was receding, and this fall would not lie beyond the morning. Overhead the clouds were broken and torn in a rising wind, with a scattering of stars showing through.

The spark of torchlight had vanished, hidden behind the manor fence. A solid timber gatepost heaved out of the dark, the tall palisade running away from it on the left hand, the broad open gateway on the right, and suddenly there was the torch again, across a wide courtyard in a sconce jutting from under the eaves, to light the stair that climbed to the hall door. The usual encrustation of service buildings lined the stockade. Cadfael launched a shout ahead of their lurching entrance, and a man came butting his way through the falling snow from a stable door, shouting to others as he came. At the head of the steps the hall door opened on a welcome glimpse of firelight.

Cadfael brought Haluin stumbling in through the open

gate in his arm, and another willing arm took him about the body on the other side, hoisting him vigorously into the comparative shelter within the pale. A voice bellowed heartily through the snowfall: 'Brothers, you chose a bad night to be out on the roads. Hold up, now, your troubles are over. We never shut the gates on your cloth.'

There were others coming forth by then to bring in the benighted travellers, a young fellow darting out from the undercroft with a sacking hood over head and shoulders, a bearded and gowned elder emerging from the hall and coming halfway down the steps to meet them. Haluin was lifted rather than led up the steep flight and into the hall, where the master of the house came striding out of his solar to meet these unexpected arrivals.

A fair man, long-boned and sparsely fleshed, with a short trimmed beard the colour of wheat straw, and a thick cap of hair of the same shade. Perhaps in his late thirties, Cadfael thought, of a ruddy, open countenance in which the blue Saxon eyes shone almost startlingly bright, candid and concerned.

'Come in, come in, Brothers! Well that you've found us! Here, bring him through here, close to the fire.' He had taken in at once the Benedictine habits, the flurries of snow lodged in the folds, and shaken off now hissing into the steady fire in the central hearth of the hall, the crippled feet of his younger visitor, the drawn grey exhaustion of his face. 'Edgytha, have beds prepared in the end chamber, and tell Edwin to mull more wine.'

His voice was loud, solicitous and warm. Without seeming haste he had his servants running here and there on his benevolent errands, and himself saw Haluin installed on a bench against the wall, where the warmth of the fire could reach him.

'This young brother of yours is in very sad case,' said the host, aside to Cadfael, 'to be travelling the roads so far

94

from home. There are none of your order round here – barring the sisters at Farewell, the bishop's new foundation. From which house do you come?'

'From Shrewsbury,' said Cadfael, setting Haluin's crutches to lean against the bench, where he could reach them at will. Haluin sat back with closed eyes, his grey cheeks slowly gaining a little colour in the warmth and ease.

'So far? Could not your abbot have sent a hale man on his errands, if he had business in another shire?'

'This was Haluin's own errand,' said Cadfael. 'No other could have done it. Now it's done, and we're on our way home, and by stages we shall get there. Always with the help of hospitable souls like you. Can I ask, what is this place? These are parts I hardly know.'

'My name is Cenred Vivers. From this manor I take that name. This brother is called Haluin, you say? And yourself?'

'Cadfael is my name. Born Welsh, and bred up on the borders with a foot either side. I've been a brother of Shrewsbury now more than twenty years. My business on this journey is simply to keep Haluin company and see that he gets safely to where he's going, and safely back again.'

'No easy matter,' agreed Cenred, low-voiced, and eyeing Haluin's deformed feet ruefully, 'the state he's in. But if the work's done and only the way home to venture, no doubt you'll do it. How did he come by such injuries?'

'He fell from a roof. We had repairs to do, in the hard weather before Christmas. It was the slates falling after him that cut his feet to ribbons. Well that we kept him alive.'

They were speaking of him softly, a little aside, though he lay back as eased and still as if he had fallen asleep, his eyes closed, the long dark lashes shadowing his hollow cheeks. The hall had emptied about them, all the bustle of activity withdrawn elsewhere, busy with pillows and brychans and the hospitable business of the kitchen.

'They're slow with the wine,' said Cenred, 'and you must both need some warmth inside you. If you'll hold me excused, Brother, I'll go and hasten things in the pantry.'

And he was off, the flurry and wind of his passing causing Haluin's closed eyelids to quiver. In a moment he opened his eyes and looked slowly and dazedly about him, taking in the warm, high-roofed dimness of the hall, the glow of the fire, the heavy hangings that screened two alcoves withdrawn from the public domain, and the half-open door of the solar from which Cenred had emerged. The pale, steady gleam of candle-light showed from within.

'Have I dreamed?' wondered Haluin, gazing. 'How did we come here? What place is this?'

'Never fear,' said Cadfael, 'on your own two feet you came here, only an arm to help you up the steps into the house. The manor is called Vivers, and the lord of it is Cenred. We've fallen into good hands.'

Haluin drew deep breath. 'I am not so strong as I believed I was,' he said sadly.

'No matter, you can rest now. We have left Elford behind.'

They were both speaking in low voices, a little awed by the enfolding silence presiding even in the centre of this populous household. When both ceased speaking, the quietness seemed almost expectant. And in the hush the half-open door of the solar opened fully upon the pale gold candle-light within, and a woman stepped into the doorway. For that one instant she was sharply outlined as a shadow against the soft light within, a slender, erect figure, mature and dignified in movement, surely the lady of the house and Cenred's wife. The next moment she had taken two or three light, swift steps into the hall, and the light of the nearest torch fell upon her shadowy face and advancing form, and conjured out of the dim shape a very different person. Everything about her was changed. Not a gracious

96

chatelaine of more than thirty years, but a rounded, fresh-faced girl, no more than seventeen or eighteen, half her oval countenance two great startled eyes and the wide, high forehead above them, white and smooth as pearl.

Haluin uttered a strange, soft sound in his throat, between gasp and sigh, clutched at his crutches and heaved himself to his feet, staring at this sudden glowing apparition as she, brought up abruptly against the intrusion of strangers, had drawn back in haste, staring at him. For one moment they hung so, mute and still, then the girl whirled about and retreated into the solar, drawing the door to almost stealthily after her.

Haluin's hands slackened their hold, dangling inertly, the crutches slid and fell from under him, and he went down on his face in a gradual, crumpled fall, and lay senseless in the rushes of the floor.

They carried him to a bed prepared for him in a quiet chamber withdrawn from the hall, and bedded him there, still in a deep swoon.

'This is simple exhaustion,' said Cadfael in reassurance to Cenred's solicitous anxiety. 'I knew he was driving himself too hard, but that's done with now. From this on we can take our time. Leave him to sleep through this night, and he'll do well enough. See, he's coming round. His eyes are opening.'

Haluin stirred, his eyelids quivering before they rose on the dark, sharply conscious eyes within, that looked up into a circle of vague, concerned faces. He was aware of his surroundings, and knew what had happened to him before he was carried here, for the first words he spoke were in meek apology for troubling them, and thanks for their care.

'My fault!' he said. 'It was presumptuous to attempt too much. But now all is well with me. All is very well!'

Since his chief need was clearly of rest, they were left to make themselves comfortable in their small chamber, though the evening brought them a number of visits. The bearded steward brought them hot, spiced wine, and sent in to them the old woman Edgytha, who brought them water for their hands, food, and a lamp, and offered whatever more they might need for their comfort.

She was a tall, wiry, active woman probably sixty years old, with the free manner and air of authority habitual in servants who have spent many years in the confidence of lord or lady, and earned a degree of trust that brings with it acknowledged privilege. The younger maidservants deferred to her, if they did not actually go in awe of her, and her neat black gown and stiff white wimple, and the keys jingling at her waist bore witness to her status.

Late in the evening she came again, in attendance on a plump and pleasant lady, soft-voiced and gracious, who came to enquire kindly whether the reverend brothers had all that they needed for the night, and whether the one who had swooned was now comfortably recovered from his faintness. Cenred's wife was rosily pretty, brown-haired and brown-eyed, a very different creature from the tall, slender, vulnerable young thing who had stepped out of the solar, to be startled into recoil from the unexpected apparition of strangers.

'And have the lord Cenred and his lady any children?' Cadfael asked when their hostess was gone.

Edgytha was close-lipped, possessively protective of her family and all that was theirs, to the point of rendering every such enquiry suspect, but after a moment's hesitation she answered civilly enough: 'They have a son, a grown son.' And she added, unexpectedly reconsidering her reluctance to satisfy such uncalled-for curiosity: 'He's away, in service with my lord Cenred's overlord.'

There was a curious undertone of reserve, even of

disapproval, in her voice, though she would never have acknowledged it. It almost distracted Cadfael's mind from his own preoccupation, but he pursued delicately:

'And no daughter? There was a young girl looked into the hall for a moment, while we were waiting. Is she not a child of the house?'

She gave him a long, steady, searching look, with raised brows and tight lips, plainly disapproving of such interest in young women, coming from a monastic. But guests in the house must be treated with unfailing courtesy, even when they fall short of deserving it.

'That lady is the lord Cenred's sister,' she said. 'The old lord Edric, his father, married a second time in his later years. More like a daughter to him than a sister, with the difference in years. I doubt you'll see her again. She would not wish to disturb the retirement of men of your habit. She has been well brought up,' concluded Edgytha with evident personal pride in the product of her own devotion, and a plain warning that black monks cast by chance into the household should keep their eyes lowered in a young virgin's presence.

'If you had her in charge,' said Cadfael amiably, 'I make no doubt she does credit to her upbringing. Had you Cenred's boy in your care, too?'

'My lady would not have dreamed of trusting her chick to any other.' The old woman had warmed into fond fervour in thinking of the children she had nursed. 'No one ever had the care of better babes,' she said, 'and I love them both like my own.'

When she was gone Haluin lay silent for a while, but his eyes were open and clear, and the lines of his face alert and aware.

'Was there indeed a girl who came in?' he said at last, frowning in the effort to recall a moment which had become hazy and uncertain in his mind. 'I have been lying here trying to recall why I so started up. I remember the crutches dropping away from under me, but very little besides. Coming into the warmth made my head go round.'

'Yes,' said Cadfael, 'there was a girl. Half-sister, it seems, to Cenred, but younger by some twenty years. If you were thinking you dreamed her, no, she was no dream. She came into the hall from the solar, all unaware of us, and perhaps not liking the look of us, she drew back again in haste and closed the door between. Do you not remember that?'

No, he did not remember it, or only as an unconnected snatch of vision comes back out of a dream, and is gone again as soon as glimpsed. He frowned after it anxiously, and shook his head as if to clear eyes misted by weariness. 'No . . . there's nothing clear to me. I do recall the door opening, I take your word for it she came in . . . but I can recall nothing, no face . . . Tomorrow, perhaps.'

'We shall see no more of her,' said Cadfael, 'if that devoted dragon of hers has any say in the matter. I think she has no very high opinion of monks, Mistress Edgytha. Well, are you minded for sleep? Shall I put out the lamp?'

But if Haluin had no clear recollection of the daughter of the house, no image left from that brief glimpse of her, first a dark outline against candle-light, then lit from before by the ruddy glow of the torch, Cadfael had a very clear image, one that grew even clearer when the lamp was quenched and he lay in the dark beside his sleeping companion. And beyond the remembrance he had a strange, disquieting sense that it bore for him a special significance, if he could but put his finger on it. Why that should be so was a mystery to him. Wakeful in the dark, he called up the features of her face, the motion of her body as she stepped into the light, and could find nothing there that should have been meaningful to him, no likeness to any woman he had ever seen before, except as all women are sisters. Yet the sense of some elusive familiarity about her persisted.

A tall girl, though perhaps not so tall as she gave the impression of being, for her slenderness contributed to the image, but above the middle height for a girl just becoming woman. Her bearing was erect and graceful, but still with the tentative and vulnerable springiness of the child, the suddenness of a lamb or a fawn, alert to every sound and motion. Startled, she had sprung back from them, and yet she had closed the door with measured softness, not to startle in return. And her face – she was not beautiful, except as youth and innocence and gallantry are always beautiful. An oval face she had, tapered from broad brow and wide and wide-set eyes to the firm, rounded chin. Her head was uncovered, her brown hair drawn back and braided, still further emphasising the high white brow and the great eyes under their level dark brows and long lashes. The eyes consumed half the face. Not pure brown, Cadfael thought, for in spite of their darkness they had a clarity and depth and brightness perceptible even in that one glimpse of her. Rather a dark hazel shot with green, and so clear and deep it seemed possible to plunge into them and drown. Eyes utterly candid and vulnerable, and quite fearless. Young, wild, mettlesome creatures of the woods, never yet hunted or harmed, may have that look. And the pure, fine lines of her cheekbones Cadfael remembered, elegant and strong, after the eyes her chief distinction.

And in all of this, sharply defined in his mind's eye, what was there to trouble him, to pierce him like an elusive memory of some other woman? He found himself summoning up, one by one, the faces of women he had known, half the population of a long and varied life, in case some cast of features or carriage of head or gesture of hand should strike the chord that would vibrate and sing for him. But there was no match, and no echo. Cenred's sister remained unique and apart, haunting him thus only because she had appeared and vanished in a moment, and he would probably never see her again.

Nevertheless, the last fleeting vision within his eyelids as he fell asleep was of her startled face.

By morning the air had lost its frosty bite, and most of the snow that had fallen had already thawed and vanished, leaving its tattered laces along the foot of every wall and under the bole of every tree. Cadfael looked out from the hall door, and was inclined to wish that the fall had persisted, to prevent Haluin from insisting on taking to the road again immediately. As it turned out he need not have worried, for as soon as the manor was up and about its daily business Cenred's steward came looking for them, with the request that they would come to his lord in the solar after they had broken their fast, for he had something to ask of them.

Cenred was alone in the room when they entered, Haluin's crutches sounding hollowly on the boards of the floor. The room was lit by two deep, narrow windows with cushioned seats built into them, and furnished with handsome bench-chests along one wall, a carved table, and one princely chair for the lord's use. Evidently the lady Emma ran a well-regulated household, for hangings and cushions were of fine embroidery, and the tapestry frame in one corner, with its half-finished web of bright colours, showed that they were of home production.

'I hope you have slept well, Brothers,' said Cenred, rising to greet them. 'Are you recovered fully from last night's indisposition? If there is anything my house has failed to offer you, you have but to ask for it. Use my manor as you would your own dwelling. And you will, I hope, consent to stay yet a day or two before you need set out again.'

Cadfael shared the hope, but was all too afraid that

Haluin would rouse his over-anxious conscience to find objections. But he had no time to do more than open his mouth, for Cenred went on at once:

'For I have something to ask of you . . . Is either of you ordained a priest?'

Chapter Seven

ES,' SAID Haluin, after a moment of blank silence. 'I am a priest. I studied for minor orders from the time I entered the abbey, and became full priest when I reached thirty years. We are encouraged to do so now, those who enter young and are already lettered. As a priest, what is there I can do to serve you?'

'I want you to conduct a marriage,' said Cenred.

This time the silence was longer, and their concentration on him more wary and thoughtful. For if a marriage was contemplated in this house, surely provision would already have been made for a priest, and one who knew the circumstances and the parties, not a chance Benedictine benighted here by a fall of snow. Cenred saw their doubts reflected in Haluin's attentive face.

'I know what you would say. This must surely be the proper business of my own parish priest. There is no church here in Vivers, though I intend to build and endow one. And it so happens that our nearest parish church is at this moment without a priest until it pleases the bishop to name his choice, for the advowson is with him. I had meant to send for a cousin of our house who is in orders, but if you are willing we may spare him a wintry journey. I promise you there is nothing underhand in this matter, and if it is being arranged in some haste, there are sound reasons. Sit down with me, at least, and I'll tell you freely all you need to know, and you shall judge.'

With the impulsive and generous vehemence that seemed to be natural to him, he strode forward himself to support Haluin by the forearms as he lowered himself to the cushioned bench built against the panelled wall. Cadfael sat down beside his friend, content to watch and listen, since he was no priest, and here had no hard decision to consider, and the delay came gratefully to him for Haluin's sake.

'In his old age,' said Cenred, coming bluntly to the business in hand, 'my father married a second time, a wife thirty years younger than he was. I was already married, with a son a year old, when my sister Helisende was born. Those two children grew up in this house, boy and girl together, like brother and sister, and close at that. And we, their elders, have taken them for granted and been glad they should have each other's company. I have been much to blame. I never noticed when they began to be more than playmates. I never thought how childish companionship and affection could change so after years, into something more perilous by far. I do not blink away facts, Brothers, once I have seen them, and been forced to see them. Those two were left alone to play too long and too lovingly. They have slipped into an inordinate affection under my very nose, and I stone blind to it until almost too late. They love each other in a fashion and to a degree that is anathema between two so closely kin. Thanks be to God, they have not sinned in the flesh, not yet. I hope I have awakened in time. God knows I want what is best for them both, I would have them happy, but what happiness can there be in a love which is an abomination? Better by far to tear them apart now, and trust to time to take away the pain. I have sent my son to serve his apprenticeship to arms with my overlord, who is a good friend, and knows the reason and the need. And sore as he is at being banished so, my son has pledged himself not to return until I give him leave. Have I done right?'

'I think,' said Haluin slowly, 'you could have done no other. But it is a pity it went so far unchecked.'

'So it is. But when two grow up from babes together as brother and sister, that in itself is commonly enough to put away from them without grief all thought of affection after the way of marriage. I have wondered sometimes how much Edgytha noticed that I did not. She indulged them always. But never, never did she say word to me or my wife, and whether I have done well or not, I must go on.'

'Tell me,' said Cadfael, speaking for the first time, 'is not your son's name Roscelin?'

Cenred's eyes flashed to Cadfael's face, astonished. 'So it is, But how can you know that?'

'And your overlord is Audemar de Clary. Sir, we came hither directly from Elford, we have spoken with your son there, he lent Brother Haluin here a strong arm to lean on when he needed it.'

'You have talked with him! And what did my son have to say, there at Elford. What had he to say of me?' He was alert and ready to hear bitter rumour of complaint and estrangement, and to swallow that grief if he must.

'Very little, and certainly nothing you could not have heard with a quiet mind. No word of your sister. He mentioned that he had left home at his father's wish, and that he could not refuse you the obedience due. We had no more than a few minutes' talk with him, by pure chance. But I saw nothing there of which you should not be glad and proud. Consider, he is barely three miles away, and against his own wish, but he keeps true to his word. There is but one thing I remember him saying,' pursued Cadfael with sudden probing intent, 'that perhaps you have a father's right to hear. He asked us, very solemnly, whether our order could provide a worthwhile life for a man – if the life he most longed for was forbidden to him.'

'No!' cried Cenred in sharp protest. 'Not that! I would not for the world he should turn his back on arms and reputation and hide himself away in the cloister. He is not made for that! A youth of such promise! Brother, this does but confirm me in what I am asking. There is no putting off what must be done. Once done, he will accept it. As long as the loss is not final he will go on hoping and hankering after the impossible. It is why I want her married, married and out of this house, before ever Roscelin enters it again.'

'I understand your reasons very well,' said Haluin, opening his hollow eyes challengingly wide, 'but it would not be right to make them reasons for a marriage, if the lady is unwilling. However hard your plight, you cannot sacrifice the one to preserve the other.'

'You mistake the case,' said Cenred without heat. 'I love my young sister, I have talked with her openly and fairly. She knows, she acknowledges, the enormity of what threatened them both, the impossibility of such a love ever coming to fruit. She wants this terrible knot severed, as truly as I do. She wants a career of honour for Roscelin because she loves him, and rather than see it blighted through her she agrees to seek refuge in marriage with another man. This has been no forced surrender. And no wanton choice, either. I have done the best I could for her, it is a match any family would welcome. Jean de Perronet is a well-endowed, well-conditioned young man of good estate. He is due here today, so you may see him for yourself. Helisende already knows him, and likes if she cannot yet love him. That may come, for he is greatly drawn to her. She has fully consented to this marriage. And de Perronet has this one inestimable advantage,' he added grimly, 'his seat is far away. He will

108

take her home to Buckingham, out of Roscelin's sight. Out of sight, out of mind I will not say, but at least the lines of a remembered face may fade gradually over the years, as even stubborn wounds heal.'

He had become eloquent by reason of his own deep disquiet and distress, a good man concerned for the best interests of all his household. He had not remarked, as Cadfael did, the gradual blanching of Haluin's thin face, the tight and painful set of his lips, or the way his linked hands gripped together in the lap of his habit until the bones shone white through the flesh. The words Cenred had not deliberately chosen to pierce or move had their own inspired force to reopen the old wound he had come all this way to try and heal. The lines of a remembered face, surely somewhat dimmed in eighteen years, were burning into vivid life again for him. And wounds that have not ceased to fester within cannot heal until they have again broken out and been cleansed, by fire if need be.

'And you need not fear, and neither need I,' said Cenred, 'that she will not be cherished and held in high regard with de Perronet. Two years back he asked for her, and for all she would have none of him or any suitor then, he has waited his time.'

'Your lady is in agreement in this matter?' asked Cadfael.

'We have all three talked of it together. And we are agreed. Will you do it? I felt it a kind of blessing on what we intend,' said Cenred simply, 'when a priest came to my door unsummoned on the eve of the bridegroom's coming. Stay over tomorrow, Brother – Father! – and marry them.'

Haluin unlocked his contorted hands slowly, and drew breath like a man awaking in pain. In a low voice he said: 'I will stay. And I will marry them.'

'I trust I have done right,' said Haluin, when they were back in their own quarters. But it did not seem that he was asking to be confirmed in his decision, rather setting it squarely before his own eyes as a responsibility he had no intention of hedging or sharing. 'I know only too well,' he said, 'the perils of proximity, and their case is more desperate than ever was mine. Cadfael, I feel myself listening to echoes I thought had died out long ago. It is all for a purpose. Nothing is without purpose. How if I fell only to show me how far I was already fallen, and force me to make the assay to rise afresh? How if I came to life again as a cripple, to make me undertake those journeys of body and spirit that I dreaded when I was strong and whole? How if God put it into my mind to go on pilgrimage in order to become some other needy soul's miracle? Were we led to this place?'

'Driven, rather,' said Cadfael practically, remembering the blinding snow, and the small beckoning spark of the torch in the drifting dark.

'It's true, to arrive on the eve of the bridegroom's coming is very apt timing. I can but go with the burden of the day,' said Haluin, 'and hope to be led aright. These second marriages in old age, Cadfael, have sorry tangles to answer for. How can two babes playing together in the rushes of the floor know that they are aunt and nephew, and fruit forbidden? A pity that love should be spent to no end.'

'I am not sure,' said Cadfael, 'that love is ever spent for no end. Well, at least now you can be still and rest for a day or so, and all the better for it. That, at any rate, comes timely.'

And that was plainly the best use Haluin could make of this halt on the way home, since he had already tried himself very near the end of his endurance. Cadfael left him in peace, and went out to take a daylight look at this manor of Vivers. A cloudy day with a fitful wind, the air free of frost, and occasional fine drifts of rain in the air, but none that lasted long.

He walked the width of the enclave to the gate, to see the full extent of the house. There were windows in the steep roof above the solar, probably two retired rooms were available there. Haluin and his companion had been accommodated considerately on the living floor. No doubt one of those upper chambers was being prepared at this moment for the expected bridegroom. The daily bustle about the courtyard seemed everywhere to be in hand without haste or confusion; things were well ordered here.

Beyond the pale of the stockade the soft, undulating landscape extended in field and copse and sparsely treed upland, all the greens still bleached and dried with winter, but the black branches showed here and there the first nodules of the leaf-buds of spring. Faint frills of snow outlined all the hollows and sheltered places, but a gleam of sun was breaking through the low cloud, and by noon all the remnant of last night's fall would be gone.

Cadfael looked into the stables and the mews, and found both well supplied and proudly kept by servitors ready and willing to show them off to an interested visitor. In a separate stall in the kennels a hound bitch lay curled in clean straw with her six pups around her, perhaps five weeks old. He could not resist going into the dim shed to take up one of the young ones, and the dam was complacent, and welcomed admiration of her brood. The soft warmth of the small body in his arms had a smell like new bread. He was just stooping to lay the pup back among its siblings when a clear, cool voice behind him said:

'Are you the priest who is to marry me?'

And there she was in the doorway, again a shadowy form against the light, so composed, so assured that she might easily be taken for a mature and stately woman of thirty, though the fresh, light voice belonged to her proper age. The girl Helisende Vivers, not yet decked out to receive her bridegroom, but in a plain housewifely gown of dark blue wool, and with a gently steaming pail of meat and meal for the hounds in one hand.

'Are you the priest who is to marry me?'

'No,' said Cadfael, slowly straightening up from the wriggling litter and the crooning bitch. 'That is Brother Haluin. I never studied for orders. I know myself better.'

'It's the lame man, then,' she said with detached sympathy. 'I am sorry he suffers such hardship. I hope they have made him comfortable, here in our house. You do know about my marriage – that Jean comes here today?'

'Your brother has told us,' said Cadfael, watching the features of her oval face emerge softly from shadow, in every plaintive, ingenuous line testifying to her youth. 'But there are things he could not tell us,' he said, watching her intently, 'except by hearsay. Only you can tell us whether this match has your consent, freely given, or no.'

Her brief silence at that did not suggest hesitation so much as a grave consideration of the man who raised the question. Her large eyes, dauntlessly honest, embraced and penetrated, quite unafraid of being penetrated in return. If she had judged him so alien to her needs and predicament as to be unacceptable, she would have closed the encounter there and then, civilly but without satisfying what would then have been mere intrusive curiosity. But she did not.

'If we do anything freely, once we are grown,' she said, 'then yes, this I do freely. There are rules that must be kept. There are others in the world with us who have rights and needs, and we are all bound. You may tell Brother Haluin – Father Haluin I must call him – that he need have no qualms for me. I know what I am doing. No one is forcing my hand.'

'I will tell him so,' said Cadfael. 'But I think you do it for others, not for yourself.'

'Then say to him that I choose – freely – to do it for others.'

'And what of Jean de Perronet?' said Cadfael.

For one instant her firm, full lips shook. It was the one thing that still disrupted her resolute composure, that she was not being fair to the man who was to be her husband. Cenred would certainly not have told him that he was getting only a sad remainder after the heart was gone. Nor could she tell him so. The secret belonged only to the family. The only hope for this hapless pair was that love might come with time, a kind of love, better, perhaps, than many marriages ever achieve, but still far short of the crown.

'I will try,' she said steadily, 'to give him all that he is asking, all that he wants and expects. He deserves well, he shall have the best I can do.'

There was no point in saying to her that it might not be enough, she already knew that, and was uneasy about a degree of deception she could not evade. It might even be, that what had already been said here in the dimness of the kennels had re-opened a deep abyss of doubt which she had almost succeeded in sealing over. Better let well alone, where there was no possibility of rendering the load she carried any lighter.

'Well, I pray you may be blessed in all you do,' said Cadfael, and drew back out of her way. The bitch had uncoiled herself from among her puppies and was nuzzling the pail, and waving a feathered tail in hungry expectation. The ordinary business of the day goes on through births, marriages, deaths and festivals. When he looked back from the doorway the girl Helisende was stooping to fill the bitch's bowl, the heavy braid of her brown hair swinging among the scrambling litter. She did not look up, but for all that he had the feeling that she was deeply and vulnerably aware of him until he turned and walked softly away.

'You'll miss your nurseling,' said Cadfael, when Edgytha came at noon to serve food and drink for them. 'Or will you be going south with her when she's married?'

The old woman lingered, taciturn by nature but visibly in

113

need of unburdening a heart by no means reconciled to losing her darling. Within the stiff folds of her wimple her withered cheek trembled.

'What should I do at my age, in a strange place? I am too old to be of much value now, I shall stay here. At least I know the way of things here, and everyone knows me. What respect should I have in a strange household? But she'll go, I know that! She'll go, I suppose, as go she must. And the young man's well enough – if my lamb had not another in her eye and in her heart.'

'And one placed so far out of reach,' Haluin reminded her gently, but his own face was pale, and when she turned and looked at him in silence for a long moment he averted his eyes and turned away his head.

Her eyes were the pale, washed blue of fading harebells. Once, shadowed by lashes now grown thin and meagre, they might have resembled more the colour of periwinkles. 'So my lord will have told you,' she said. 'So they all say. And if there's no help, she might do much worse. I know! I came here in attendance on her mother, all those years ago, and that was no lover's match, neither, her so young, and him nigh on three times her age. A decent, kind man he was, but old, old! She had good need, poor lady, of someone from home, someone she knew well and could trust. At least they're marrying my girl to somebody young.'

Cadfael asked what had been preoccupying his mind for some little while, since no word had been said on the matter: 'Is Helisende's mother dead?'

'No, not dead. But she took the veil at Polesworth, it must be eight years ago now, after the old lord died. She's within your own order, a Benedictine nun. She had always a leaning towards it, and when her husband died, and she began to be talked about and bargained about as widow ladies are, and urged to marry again, rather than that she left the world. It's one way of escape,' said Edgytha, and set her lips grimly.

114

'And left her daughter motherless?' said Haluin, with more reproof in his voice than he intended.

'She left her daughter very well mothered! She left her to the lady Emma and to me!' Edgytha smouldered for a moment, and subdued the brief fire within lowered eyelids. 'Three mothers that child has had, and all fond. My lady Emma could never be harsh to any young thing. Too soft, indeed, the pair of them could always get their will of her. But my own lady was given to solitude and melancholy, and when it came to a new marriage, no, she would not, she took the veil gladly rather than marry again.'

'Helisende has never considered that refuge?' asked Cadfael.

'Not she, God forbid she ever should! My girl was never of that mind. For those who take to it kindly it may be bliss, but for those who are pressed into it, it must be a hell on earth! If you'll pardon my tongue, Brothers! You know your own vocation best, and no doubt you took the cowl for the best of reasons, but Helisende . . . No, I would not want that for her. Better by far this Perronet lad, if there has to be a second-best.' She had begun to gather up the platters and dishes they had emptied, and took up the pitcher to refill their cups. 'I did hear say that you've been at Elford, and seen Roscelin there. Is that true?'

'Yes,' said Cadfael, 'we left Elford only yesterday. We did, by chance, have some brief talk with the young man, but never knew until this morning that he came from this neighbouring manor of Vivers.'

'And how did he look?' she asked longingly. 'Is he well? Was he down in spirits? I have not seen him for a month or more, and I know how ill he took it that he should be sent away like some offending page from his own home, when he had done no wrong, nor thought none. As good a lad as ever stepped! What had he to say?'

'Why, he was in excellent health at any rate,' said Cadfael

cautiously, 'and very fair spirits, considering all. It's true he did complain of being banished, and was very ill-content where he is. Naturally he said little about the circumstances, seeing we were chance comers and unknown to him, and I daresay he would have said no more to anyone else who had as little business in the matter. But he did say he had given his word to abide by his father's orders, and wait for leave before he'd venture home.'

'But he does not know,' she said, between anger and help-lessness, 'what's being planned here. Oh, he'll get leave to come home fast enough as soon as Helisende is out of the house, and far away south on her way to that young man's manor. And what a homecoming that will be for the poor lad! Shame to deal so behind his back!'

'They think it for the best,' said Haluin, pale and moved. 'Even for his best interests, they believe. And this matter is hard even for them. If they are mistaken in hiding this marriage from him until it is over, surely they may be forgiven.'

'There are those,' said Edgytha darkly, 'who never will be.' She picked up her wooden tray, and the keys at her girdle chimed faintly as she moved towards the door. 'I wish this had been honestly done. I wish he had been told. Whether he could ever have her or not, he had a right to know, and to give his blessing or his ban. How was it you were brought in touch with him there, to know the half of his name but not the whole?'

'It was the lady mentioned his name,' said Cadfael, 'when de Clary came in from riding, and the young man was with him. Roscelin, she called him. It was later we spoke with him. He saw my friend here stiff from a night on his knees, and came to lend him an arm to lean on.'

'So he would!' she said, warming. 'To anyone he saw in need. The lady, you say? Audemar's lady?'

'No, our errand was not to him, we never saw his wife

116

and children. No, this was his mother, Adelais de Clary.'

The dishes jangled momentarily on Edgytha's tray. With care she balanced it on one hand, and reached to the latch of the door. 'She is there? There at Elford?'

'She is. Or she was when we left, yesterday, and with the snow coming so shortly after, she is surely there still.'

'She visits very rarely,' said Edgytha, shrugging. 'They say there's small love lost between her and her son's wife. That's no uncommon thing, either, I suppose, so they're just as well apart.' She nudged the door open expertly with an elbow, and swung the large tray through the doorway edgewise. 'Do you hear the horses, outside there? That will be Jean de Perronet's party riding in.'

There was nothing clandestine or secretive, certainly, about Jean de Perronet's arrival, though nothing ceremonious or showy, either. He came with one body-servant and two grooms, and with two led horses for the bride and her attendant, and pack-horses for the baggage. The entire entourage was practical and efficient, and de Perronet himself went very plainly, without flourishes in his dress or his manner, though Cadfael noted with appreciation the quality of his horseflesh and harness. This young man knew where to spend his money, and where to spare.

They had gone out, Haluin and Cadfael together, to watch the guests dismount and unload. The afternoon air was again clearing towards a night frost, but there were scudding clouds in the upper air, and might be further flurries of snow in the dark hours. The travellers would be well content to be under a sound roof and out of the chilly wind.

De Perronet dismounted from his flecked roan horse before the door of the hall, and Cenred came striding down the steps to meet him and embrace him, and lead him by the hand up to the doorway, where the lady Emma waited to

117

welcome him as warmly. Helisende, Cadfael noted, did not appear. At supper at the high table she would have no choice but to attend, but at this stage it was fitting that the honours of the house should rest with her brother and his wife, the guardians of her person and the disposers of her marriage. Host, hostess and guest vanished within the great hall. Cenred's servants and de Perronet's grooms unloaded baggage and stabled horses, and went about the business so practically that within a matter of minutes the courtyard was empty.

So that was the bridegroom! Cadfael stood considering what he had seen, and so far could find no fault in it except that it was, as Edgytha had said, a second-best. And a second-best was all that boy would gain. A young man of perhaps twenty-five or twenty-six, already accustomed to authority and responsibility by his bearing, and well capable of handling them. His men, these favoured ones at least, were easy with him. He knew his business as they knew theirs, and there was an air of mutual respect between them. Moreover, he was a goodlooking young man, tall and shapely, of open, amiable countenance, and by the look of him in the happiest possible humour on the eve of his marriage. Cenred had done his best for his young sister, and his best promised to turn out very well. A pity it could not have been what her heart desired.

'But what else could he have done?' said Haluin, betraying in few words the depth of his own dismay and doubt.

Chapter Eight

I N THE LATE afternoon Cenred sent his
steward to ask the two Benedictine brothers if
they felt able to join his household at supper in
hall, or if Father Haluin preferred to continue
his rest in retirement, and be waited on in his own chamber.
Haluin, who had withdrawn into a dark, inward medita-
tion, would certainly rather have remained apart, but felt it
discourteous to absent himself any longer, and made the
effort to emerge from his anxious silence, and do honour to
the company at the high table. They had given him a place
close to the bridal pair, by virtue of his office as the priest
who was to marry them. Cadfael, seated a little apart, had
them all in view. And below, in the body of the hall, the
whole household assembled in its due ranks, under the glow
of the torches.

It occurred to Cadfael, watching Haluin's grave face,
that this would be the first time his friend had ever been
called upon to be go-between for God. It was true that the
young brothers were being encouraged to aim at orders,
more now than ever in the past, but many of them would be,
as Haluin was, priests without pastoral cares, who in a long
life would probably never christen, never marry, never

119

bury, never ordain others to follow them in the same sheltered paths. It is a terrible responsibility, thought Cadfael, who had never aspired to ordination, to have the grace of God committed to a man's hands, to be privileged and burdened to play a part in other people's lives, to promise them salvation in baptism, to lock their lives together in matrimony, to hold the key to purgatory at their departing. If I have meddled, he thought devoutly, and God knows I have, when need was and there was no better man to attempt it, at least I have meddled only as a fellow-sinner, tramping the same road, not as a vicomte of heaven, stooping to raise up. Now Haluin faces this same terrible demand, and no wonder if he is afraid.

He looked along the array of faces which Haluin, being so close beside them, could see only as overlapping profiles, each briefly seen as the ripple of movement flowed along the high table, and lit deceptively by the falling glow of the torches. Cenred's broad, open, blunt-featured countenance a little drawn and taut with strain, but resolutely jovial, his wife presiding over the table with determined amiability and a somewhat anxious smile, de Perronet in happy innocence, shining with evident pleasure at having Helisende seated beside him and all but his already. And the girl, pale and quiet and resolutely gracious at his side, doing her gallant best to respond to his brightness, since this grief was no fault of his, and she had acknowledged that he deserved better. Seeing them thus together, there was no question of the man's attachment, and if he missed the like radiance in her, perhaps he accepted that as the common ground on which marriages begin, and was ready and willing to be patient until the bud came to flower.

This was the first time Haluin had seen the girl since she had startled him to his feet here in the hall, and brought him down in that crashing fall, half-dazed as he already was by the stinging wind and the blinding snow. And this stiff young figure in her best, gilded by the torchlight, might have been a stranger, never before seen. He looked at her, when chance brought her profile into clear view, with doubt and bewilderment, burdened by a responsibility new to him, and heavy to bear.

It was late when the women withdrew from the high table, leaving the men to their wine, though they would not sit here in hall much longer. Haluin looked round to catch Cadfael's eye, agreeing in a glance that it was time for them to leave host and guest together, and Haluin was already reaching for his crutches and bracing himself for the effort of rising, when Emma came in again from the solar with a flustered step and an anxious face, a young maidservant at her heels.

'Cenred, here's something strange happened! Edgytha is gone out and has not returned, and now it's beginning to snow again, and where should she be going, thus in the night? I sent for her to attend me to bed, as always, and she's nowhere to be found, and now Madlyn here says that she went out hours ago, as soon as it was dusk.'

Cenred was slow to turn his mind from his hospitable duty towards his guest to an apparently small domestic problem, surely the women's business rather than his.

'Why, Edgytha may surely go out if she so chooses,' he said good-humouredly, 'and will come back when she chooses no less. She's a free woman, knows her own mind, and can be trusted to mind her duties. If she's once missing when she's called for, that's no great matter. Why should you worry over it?'

'But when does she ever do so without saying? Never! And now it's snowing again, and she's been gone four hours or more, if Madlyn says true. How if she's come to harm? She would not stay away so long of her own will. And you know how I value her. I would not for the world that any harm should come to her.'

121

'No more would I,' said Cenred warmly, 'nor to any of my people. If she's gone astray we'll look for her. But no need to fret before we know of any mishap. Here, girl, speak up, what is it you know of the matter? You say she went out some hours ago?'

'Sir, so she did!' Madlyn came forward willingly, wide-eyed with half-pleasurable excitement. 'It was after we'd made all ready. I was coming in from the dairy, and I saw her come forth from the kitchen with her cloak about her, and I said to her that this was like to be a busy night, and she'd be missed, and she said she'd be back before she was called for. It was just beginning to get dark then. I never thought she'd be gone so long.'

'And did you not ask her where she was going?' demanded Cenred.

'I did,' said the girl, 'though it was little enough she was ever likely to tell about her own business, and I should have known she'd make a sour answer if she made any at all. But there's no sense to be made of it. She said she was going to find a cat,' said Madlyn in baffled innocence, 'to put among the pigeons.'

If it meant nothing to her, it had a meaning for Cenred and for his wife, who plainly heard it now for the first time. Emma's startled gaze flew to her husband's face as he came abruptly to his feet. The look they exchanged Cadfael could read as if he had the words ringing in his ears. He had been given clues enough to make the reading easy. Edgytha was nurse to them both, indulged them, loved them like her own, resents even their separation, whatever the church and the ties of blood may say, and much more this marriage that makes the separation final. She is gone to enlist help to prevent what she deplores, even at this last moment. She is gone to tell Roscelin what is being done behind his back. She is gone to Elford.

None of which could be said aloud, here in front of Jean

122

de Perronet, who stood now at Cenred's side, looking from face to face round the circle, puzzled and sympathetic in a domestic trouble which was none of his business. An old servant gone missing in the evening, with night coming on and snow falling, called for at least a token search. He made the suggestion ingenuously, filling a silence which at any moment might have caused him to look more narrowly at what was happening here.

'Should we not look for her, if she's been gone so long? The ways are not always safe at night, and for a woman venturing alone . . .'

The diversion came as a blessing, and Cenred seized on it gratefully. 'So we will. I'll send out a party by the most likely way. It may be she's only been delayed by the snow, if she intended a visit in the village. But this need not give you any concern, Jean. I would not wish your stay to be marred. Leave this matter to my men, we have enough in the household. And rest assured she cannot be far, we shall soon find her and see her safe home.'

'I will gladly come out with you,' de Perronet offered.

'No, no, I will not have it. Let all things here go as we have planned them, and nothing spoil the occasion. Use my house as your own, and take your night's rest with a quiet mind, for tomorrow this small flurry will be over and done.'

It was not difficult to persuade the helpful guest to abandon his generous intention, perhaps it had been made only as a courteous gesture. A man's household affairs are his, and best left to him. It is civil to offer help, but wise to give way gracefully. Cenred knew very well now where Edgytha had set out to go, there would be no question of which road to take in hunting for her. Moreover, there was some genuine call for concern, for in four hours she could have been there and back even in snow. Cenred quit his supper-table purposefully, driving the men of his following before him

123

to muster within the hall door. He bade de Perronet an emphatic goodnight, which was accepted pliantly as dismissal even from this domestic conference, and issued brisk orders to those of his servants whom he chose to go with the search party, six of the young and vigorous and his steward with them.

'What must we do?' Brother Haluin wondered half-aloud, standing with Cadfael a little apart.

'You,' said Cadfael, 'must go to your bed, like a sensible man, and sleep if you can. And a prayer or two will not come amiss. I am going with them.'

'Along the nearest road to Elford,' said Haluin heavily.

'To find a cat to put among the pigeons. Yes, where else? But you stay here. There is nothing you could do or say, if there has to be speech, that I cannot.'

The hall door was opened, the party tramped down the steps into the courtyard, two of them carrying torches. Cadfael, following last, looked out upon a glittering, frosty night. The ground was covered but meagrely, small, needle-sharp flakes out of an almost clear sky, brittle with stars and too cold for a heavy fall. He looked back from the door-way, and saw the women of the house, gentlefolk and servants alike, drawn together in mutual uneasiness in the far corner of the hall, all eyes following their departing menfolk, the maids huddling close, Emma with her smooth, gentle face wrung in distress, and pulling nervously at her plump fingers.

And Helisende standing a pace apart, the only one not clinging to her kind for comfort. She was far enough back from one of the sconces for the torchlight to show her face fully, without exaggerated shadows. All that Emma had reported to her husband, all that Madlyn had told, Helisende surely knew now. She knew where Edgytha was gone, she knew for what purpose. She was staring wide-eyed into a future she could no longer foretell, where the

124

results of this night's work hid themselves in bewilderment and dismay and possible catastrophe. She had prepared herself for a willing sacrifice, but she found herself utterly unprepared for whatever threatened now. Her face seemed as still and composed as ever, yet it had lost all its calm and certainty, her resolution had become helplessness, and her resignation changed to desperation. She had arrived at an embattled ground she believed she could hold, at whatever cost to herself, and now that ground shook and parted under her feet, and she was no longer in control of her own fate. The image of her shattered gallantry, disarmed and vulnerable, was the last glimpse Cadfael carried out with him into the darkness and the frost.

Cenred drew his cloak close about his face against the wind, and set out from the gate of the manor on a path that was strange to Cadfael. With Haluin he had turned in from the distant highway, straight towards the gleam of light from the manor torches, but this way slanted back to strike the road much nearer to Elford, and would probably cut off at least half a mile of the distance. The night had its own lambent light, partly from the stars, partly from the thin covering of snow, so that they were able to go quickly, spread out in a line centred upon the path. The country here was open, at first bare of trees, then threading a belt of woods and scrubland. They heard nothing but their own footsteps and breath, and the soft whining of the wind among the bushes. Twice Cenred halted them to have silence, and called aloud to the night, but got no answer.

For one who knew this path well, Cadfael calculated, the distance to Elford would be roughly two miles. Edgytha could have been back in Vivers long ago, and by what she had said to the maid Madlyn she had intended to return in ample time to be at her mistress's disposal after supper. Nor could she have strayed from a known way on so bright a night, and in barely more than a sprinkling of snow. It began to seem clear to him that something had happened to prevent either her errand, or her safe return from it. Not the rigours of nature or the caprice of chance, but the hand of man. And on such a night those outcast creatures who preyed upon travellers, even if any such existed here in this open country, were unlikely to be out and about their dark business, since their prey would hardly be eager to venture out in such a frost. No, if any man had intervened to prevent Edgytha from reaching her goal, it was with deliberate intent. There was, perhaps, one better possibility, that if she had reached Roscelin with her news, he had persuaded her not to return, but to remain at Elford in safety and leave the rest to him. But Cadfael was not sure that he believed in that. If it had happened so, Roscelin would already have been striding indignantly into the hall at Vivers before ever Edgytha had been missed from her place.

Cadfael had drawn close alongside Cenred, pressing forward in haste in the centre of his line of hunters, and one dark, sidelong glance saluted and recognised him, without great surprise. 'There was no need, Brother,' said Cenred shortly. 'We are enough for the work.'

'One more will do no harm,' said Cadfael.

No harm, but possibly none too welcome. As well if this matter could be kept strictly private to the Vivers household. Yet it seemed that Cenred was not greatly troubled by the presence of a chance Benedictine monk among his search party. He was intent on finding Edgytha, and preferably before she reached Elford, or failing that, in time to negate whatever mischief she had set afoot. Perhaps he expected to meet his son somewhere along the way, coming in haste to prevent that marriage that would destroy his last vain hopes. But they had gone somewhat more than a mile, and the night remained empty about them.

They were moving through thin, open woodland, over

tufted, uneven grass, where the frozen snow lay too lightly to flatten the blades to earth, and they might have passed by the slight hummock beside the path on the right hand but for the dark ground that showed through the covering of white lace, darker than the bleached brown of the wintry turf. Cenred had passed it by, but checked sharply when Cadfael halted, and stared down as he was staring.

'Quickly, bring the torch here close!'

The yellow light outlined clearly the shape of a human body lying sprawled, head away from the path, whitened over with a crust of snow. Cadfael stooped and brushed away the crystalline veil from an upturned face, open-eyed and contorted in astonished fright, and a head of grey hair from which the hood had fallen back as she fell. She lay on her back but inclined towards her right side, her arms flung up and wide as if to ward off a blow. Her black cloak showed darkly through the filigree of white. Over her breast a small patch marred the veil, where her blood, in a meagre flow, had thawed the flakes as they fell. There was no telling immediately, from the way she lay, whether she had been on her way outward or homeward when she was struck down, but it seemed to Cadfael that at the last moment she had heard someone stealing close behind her, and whirled about with hands flung up to protect her head. The dagger her attacker had meant to slip between her ribs from behind had missed its stroke, and been plunged into her breast instead. She was dead and cold, the frost confounding all conjecture as to when she must have died.

'God's pity!' said Cenred on a whispering breath. 'This I never thought to see! Whatever she intended, why this?'

'Wolves hunt even in frost,' said his steward heavily. 'Though what rich traffic there can be for them here heaven knows! And see, there's nothing taken, not even her cloak. Masterless men would have stripped her.'

Cenred shook his head. 'There are none such in these

parts, I swear. No, this is a different matter. I wonder, I wonder which way she was bound when she was struck dead!'

'When we move her,' said Cadfael, 'we may find out. What now? There's nothing now can be done for her. Whoever used the knife knew his grim business, it needed no second stroke. And whatever footprints he left behind the ground's too hard to show, even where the snow has not covered them.'

'We must carry her home,' said Cenred sombrely. 'And a sorry matter that will be for my wife and sister. They set great store by the old woman. She was always loyal and trustworthy, all these years since my young stepmother brought her into the household. This must not pass without requital! We'll send ahead to see if she ever came to Elford, and what's known of her there, and whether they have any word of chance marauders haunting these ways, perhaps on the run from other regions. Though that's hard to believe. Audemar keeps a firm hand on his lands.'

'Shall we send back and fetch a litter, my lord?' asked the steward. 'She's but a light weight, we could make shift to carry her back in her cloak.'

'No, no need to make another journey. But you, Edred, you take Jehan here with you, and go on to Elford, and find out what's known of her there, if anyone has met and spoken with her. No, take two men with you. I would not have you in any danger on the road, if there are masterless men abroad.'

The steward accepted his orders, and took one of the torches to light him the rest of the way. The small, resiny spark dwindled along the pathway towards Elford, and vanished gradually into the night. Those remaining turned to the body, and lifted it aside to unfasten and spread out on the path the cloak she wore. As soon as she was raised one thing at least was made plain.

'There's snow under her,' said Cadfael. The shrunken shape of her was dark and moist where contact had been close enough for her body's lingering warmth to melt the flakes, but all round the rim where the folds of her clothing had lain only lightly, a worn border of lace remained. 'It was after the snow began that she fell. She was on her way home.'

She was light and limp in their hands. The chill of her body was from frost, not rigor. They wound her closely in her cloak, and bound her safely with two or three belts and Cadfael's rope girdle, to give hand-holds for the servants who carried her, and so they bore her back the mile or so they had come, to Vivers.

The household was still awake and aware, unable to rest until they knew what was happening. One of the maids saw the lamentable little procession entering at the gate, and ran wailing to tell Emma. By the time they brought Edgytha's body up into the hall the whole fluttered dovecote of maids was again assembled, huddled together for comfort. Emma took charge with more resolution than might have been expected from her soft and gentle person, and swept the girls into service with a briskness that kept them from tears, preparing a trestle table in one of the small chambers for a bier, composing the disordered limbs, heating water, bringing scented linen from the chests in the hall to drape and cover the dead. The funeral ceremonies do as much for the living as for the dead, in occupying their hands and minds, and consoling them for things left undone or badly done during life. Very shortly the murmur of subdued voices from the death-chamber had softened from distress and dismay into a gentle, almost soothing elegiac crooning.

Emma came out into the hall, where her husband and his men were warming their chilled feet at the fire, and rubbing the sense back into their numbed hands.

'Cenred, how is this possible? Who could have done such a thing?'

No one attempted to answer that, nor had she looked for an answer.

'Where did you find her?'

That her husband did answer, scrubbing wearily at his furrowed forehead. 'Past the halfway to Elford by the short road, lying beside the path. And she'd been there no long time, for there was snow under her. It was on her way back here that someone struck her down.'

'You think,' said Emma in a low voice, 'she had been to Elford?'

'Where else by that path? I've sent Edred on there, to find out if she came, and who has spoken with her. In an hour or so they should be back, but whether with any news, God alone knows.'

They were both of them moving delicately about and about the heart of the matter, avoiding the mention of Roscelin's name, or any word of the reason why Edgytha should go rushing out alone on a wintry night. True, word had gone round even in the kennels and mews by then, and the entire household of Vivers was gathering uneasily, the indoor servants hovering in an anxious group in the corners of the hall, those from without prowling and peering over their shoulders, unable to withdraw to their own proper business or their normal rest until something should happen within here to scatter them. Few of all these, if any, could be in their lord's confidence in the matter of Roscelin's outlawed love, but many of them might have guessed at the undercurrents sweeping Helisende into this hasty marriage. Some reserve in speech would have to be observed in front of all this clan.

And here, to complicate matters further, came Jean de Perronet from the chamber above, where he had retired out of courtesy, but not to sleep, for he was still in his supper-table finery. And here, too, was Brother Haluin from his bed, anxious and silent. All those under the roof of Vivers that night had been drawn gradually and almost stealthily into the hall.

No, not quite all. Cadfael looked round the assembly, and missed one face. Where all others foregathered, Helisende absented herself.

By the look of his face de Perronet had been doing some serious thinking since he bowed to his host's wish, and let the search party go out into the night without him. He came into the hall with a face composed and grave, revealing nothing of what went on in his mind, took his time about looking all round the mute and dour circle of them, and looked last and longest at Cenred, who stood with his boots steaming in the ashes of the hearth, and his head bent to stare blankly into the embers of the fire.

'I think,' said de Perronet with deliberation, 'this has not ended well. You have found your maidservant?'

'We have found her,' said Cenred.

'Misused? Dead? Do you tell me you have found her dead?'

'And not of cold! Stabbed to death,' said Cenred bluntly, 'and left by the wayside. And no sign of another soul have we seen or heard along the road, though this befell no long time ago, after the snow began to fall.'

'Eighteen years she has been with us,' said Emma, wringing her hands together wretchedly under her breast. 'Poor soul, poor soul, to end like this – struck down by some outlaw vagabond to die in the cold. I would not for the world have had this happen!'

'I am sorry,' said de Perronet, 'that such a thing should be, and at such a time as this. Can there be some link between the occasion that brought me here, and this woman's death?'

'No!' cried husband and wife together, rather resisting

131

the thought already in their minds than lying to deceive the guest. 'No,' said Cenred more softly, 'I pray there is not, I trust there is not. It is of all chances the most unhappy, yet surely no more than chance.'

'There are such unblessed chances,' admitted de Perronet, but with evident reserve. 'And they do not spare to mar festivals, even marriages. You do not wish to put off this one beyond tomorrow?'

'No, why so? It is our grief, not yours. But it is murder, and I must send to the sheriff, and loose a hunt for the murderer. She has no living kin that I know of, it is for us to bury her. What's needful we shall do. It need not cast a shadow upon you.'

'I fear it already has,' said de Perronet, 'upon Helisende. The woman, I believe, was her nurse, and dear to her.'

'The more reason you should take her away from here, to a new home and a new life.' He looked round for her then for the first time, startled not to find her there among the women, but relieved that she was not there to complicate a matter already vexed enough. If she had indeed been able to fall asleep, so much the better, let her sleep on, and know nothing worse until morning. The maidservants were drifting back from the room where they had been busy making Edgytha's body seemly. There was nothing more they could do here, and their uneasy presence, mute and fearful in hovering groups, became oppressive. Cenred stirred himself with an effort to be rid of them.

'Emma, send the women to their beds. There's no more to be done here, and they need not wait. And you, fellows, be off and get your sleep. All's done that can be done till Edred gets back from Elford, no need for the whole household to wait up for him.' And to de Perronet he said: 'I sent him on with two others of my men to inform my overlord of this death. Murder in these parts is within his writ, this will be his business no less than mine. Come, Jean, with your

132

leave we'll withdraw to the solar, and leave the hall to the sleepers.'

Doubtless, thought Cadfael, watching the harassed lines of Cenred's face, he would be happier if de Perronet chose to draw off once again from all involvement, and stand apart, but there's no chance of that now. And however he hedges round the truth of why his steward has pushed on to Elford, the very name of that place has now assumed a significance there's no evading. And this is not a man who likes deception, or practises it with pleasure or skill.

The women had accepted their orders at once, and dispersed, still whispering and fearful, to their quarters. The menservants quenched the torches, leaving only two by the great door to light the way in, and fed and damped down the fire to burn slowly through the night. De Perronet followed his host to the door of the solar, and there Cenred, turning, waved Cadfael to join them within.

'Brother, you were a witness, you can testify to how we found her. It was you showed how the snow had begun to fall before she was struck down. Will you wait with us, and see what word my steward brings back with him?'

There was no word said as to whether Brother Haluin should consider this invitation as applying equally to him, but he caught Cadfael's eye, deprecating rather than recommending such a move, and chose rather to ignore it. Enough had already happened to exercise his mind, if he was to join two people whose imminent marriage was at least suspect of bringing about a death. He needed to know what lay behind these nocturnal wanderings, and withdraw from his commitment if he saw reason. He set his lips, and followed the company into the solar, his crutches heavy and slow in the rushes, and starting a dull echo as he stepped on to the floorboards within. He took his seat on a bench in the dimmest corner, an unobtrusive listener, as Cenred sat

133

down wearily at the table, and spread his elbows on the board, propping his head between muscular hands.

'Your men are on foot?' asked de Perronet.

'Yes.'

'Then we may have a long wait yet before they can be here again. Had you other parties out on other roads?'

Cenred said starkly: 'No,' and offered no further words by way of explanation or excuse. Not a quarter of an hour ago, thought Cadfael, watching, he would have evaded that, or left it unanswered. Now he is gone beyond caring for discretion. Murder brings out into the open many matters no less painful, while itself still lurking in the dark.

De Perronet shut his lips and clenched his teeth on any further questioning, and set himself to wait in uncommitted patience. The night had closed in on the manor of Vivers in hushed stillness, ominous and oppressive. Doubtful if anyone in the hall slept, but if any of them moved it was furtively, and if any spoke it was in whispers.

Nevertheless, the wait was not to be as long as de Perronet had prophesied. The silence was abruptly shivered by the thudding of galloping hooves on the hard-frozen earth of the courtyard, a furious young voice yelling peremptorily for service, the frantic running of grooms without, and the hasty stirring of all the wakeful retainers within. Feet ran blindly in the dark, stumbling and rustling in the rushes, flint and steel spat sparks too brief and hasty to catch the tinder, the first torch was plunged into the turfed-down fire, and carried in haste to kindle others. Before the listeners in the solar could burst out into the hall a fist was thumping at the outer door, and an angry voice demanded entry.

Two or three ran to unbar, knowing the voice, and were sent reeling as the heavy door was flung back to the wall, and into the brightening flurry of torchlight burst the figure of Roscelin, head uncovered, flaxen hair on end from the speed of his ride, blue eyes blazing. The cold of the night blew in with him, and all the torches guttered and smoked, as Cenred, erupting out of the solar, was halted as abruptly on the threshold of the hall by his son's fiery glare.

'What is this Edred tells me of you?' demanded Roscelin. 'What have you done behind my back?'

OR ONCE paternal authority was caught at a disadvantage, and Cenred was all too aware of it. Nor had he the past reputation of a family tyrant to fall back on, but he did his best to wrest back the lost initiative.

'What are you doing here?' he demanded sternly. 'Did I send for you? Did your lord dismiss you? Has either of us released you from your bond?'

'No,' said Roscelin, glittering. 'I have no leave from any man, and have not asked for any. And as for my bond, you loosed me from it when you played me false. It's not I who have broken faith. And as for the duty I owe to Audemar de Clary, I'll return to it if I must, and abide whatever his displeasure visits on me, but not until you render me account here openly of what you intended in the dark behind my back. I listened to you, I owned you right, I obeyed you. Did you owe me nothing in return? Not even honesty?'

Another father might well have felled him for such insolence, but Cenred had no such option. Emma was plucking anxiously at his sleeve, troubled for both her menfolk. De Perronet, alert and grim, loomed at his shoulder, eyeing the enraged boy confronting them, and already apprised of an inevitable threat to his own plans. What else could have brought this youngster haring through the night? And by all the signs he had come by the shortest road, dangerous in the dark, or he could not have arrived so soon. Nothing that had happened this night was accident or chance. The marriage of Helisende Vivers had brought about all this coil of murder and search and pursuit, and what more was to come of it there was as yet no knowing.

'I have done nothing,' said Cenred, 'of which I need to be ashamed, and nothing for which I need account to you. Well you know what your own part must be, you have agreed to it, do not complain now. I am the master in my own house, I have both rights and duties towards my family. I will discharge them as I see fit. And for the best!'

'Without the courtesy of a word to me!' flared Roscelin, burning up like a stirred fire. 'No, I must hear it only from Edred, after the damage has already begun, after a death that can surely be laid at your own door. Was that for the best? Or dare you tell me Edgytha is dead for some other cause, by some stranger's hand? That's mischief enough, even if it's no worse than that. But whose plans sent her out into the night? Dare you tell me she was on some other errand? Edred says she was on her way to Elford when someone cut her off. I am here to prevent the rest.'

'Your son refers, as I suppose,' said de Perronet, loudly and coldly, 'to the marriage arranged between the lady Helisende and me. In that matter, I think, I too have a say.'

Roscelin's wide blue stare swung from his father's face to the guest's. It was the first time he had looked at him, and the encounter held him silent for a long moment. They were not strangers to each other, Cadfael recalled. The two families were acquainted, perhaps even distant kin, and two years ago de Perronet had made a formal offer for Helisende's hand. There was no personal animosity in

Roscelin's glare, rather a baffled and frustrated rage against circumstance than against this favoured suitor, to whom he could not and must not be a rival.

'*You* are the bridegroom?' he said bluntly.

'I am, and will maintain my claim. And what have you to urge against it?'

Animosity or not, they had begun to bristle like fighting cocks, but Cenred laid a restraining hand on de Perronet's arm, and frowned his son back with a forbidding gesture.

'Wait, wait! This has gone too far now to be left in the dark. Do you tell me, boy, that you heard of this marriage, as you heard of Edgytha's death, only from Edred?'

'How else?' demanded Roscelin. 'He came puffing in with his news and roused the household, Audemar and all. Whether he meant me to hear when he blurted out word of this marriage I doubt, but I did hear it, and here am I to find out for myself what you never meant me to question. And we shall see if all is being done for the best!'

'Then you had not seen Edgytha? She never reached you?'

'How could she if she was lying dead a mile or more from Elford?' demanded Roscelin impatiently.

'It was after the snow that she died. She had been some hours gone, long enough to have reached Elford and been on her way back. *Somewhere* she had been, from somewhere she was certainly returning. Where else could it have been?'

'So you thought she had indeed reached Elford, said Roscelin slowly. 'I never heard but that she was dead, I thought it was on her way. On her way to me! Is that what you had in mind? To warn me of what was being done here in my absence?'

Cenred's silence and Emma's unhappy face were answer enough.

'No,' he said slowly, 'I never saw hide or hair of her. Nor

did anyone in Audemar's household as far as I know. If she ever was there at all, I don't know to whom she came. Certainly not to me.'

'Yet it could have been so,' said Cenred.

'It was not so. She did not come. Nevertheless,' said Roscelin relentlessly, 'here am I as if she had, having heard it from another mouth. God knows I am grieved for Edgytha, but what is there now to be done for her but bury her with reverence, and after, if we can, find and bury her murderer? But it is not too late to reconsider what was intended here for tomorrow, it is not too late to change it.'

'I marvel,' said Cenred harshly, 'that you do not charge me outright with this death.'

Roscelin was brought up short against an idea so monstrous, and stood open-mouthed with shock, his unclenched hands dangling childishly. Plainly such a notion had never entered his ingenuous head. He stammered a furious, half-inarticulate disclaimer, and abandoned it halfway to turn again upon de Perronet.

'But you – *you* had cause enough to want her stopped, if you knew she was on her way to warn me. *You* had good cause to want her silenced, so that no voice should be raised against your marriage, as now I raise mine. Was it you who did her to death on the way?'

'This is foolery,' said de Perronet with disdain. 'Everyone here knows that I have been here in plain view all the evening.'

'So you may have been, but you have men who may be used to do your work for you.'

'Every man of whom can be vouched for by your father's household. Also, you have been told already it was not on the outward way this woman was killed, but returning. What purpose would that have served for me? And now may I ask of you, father and son both,' he demanded sharply, 'what interest has this boy in his close kinswoman's

140

marriage, that he dares to challenge either her brother's rights or her husband's?'

Now, thought Cadfael, it is all as good as out, though no one will say it plainly. For de Perronet has wits sharp enough to have grasped already what particular and forbidden passion really drives this unhappy boy. And now it depends on Roscelin whether a decent face is kept on the affair or not. Which is asking a lot of a young man torn as he is, and outraged by what he feels as a betrayal. Now we shall see his mettle.

Roscelin had blanched into a fixed and steely whiteness, his fine bones of cheek and jaw outlined starkly in the torchlight. Before Cenred could draw breath to assert his dominance, his son had done it for him.

'My interest is that of a kinsman close as a brother lifelong, and desiring Helisende's happiness beyond anything else in the world. My father's right I never have disputed, nor do I doubt he wishes her well as truly as I do. But when I hear of a marriage planned in haste and in my absence, how can I be easy in mind? I will not stand by and see her hustled into a marriage that may not be to her liking. I will not have her forced or persuaded against her will.'

'This is no such matter,' protested Cenred hotly. 'She is not being forced, she has consented willingly.'

'Then why was I to be kept in ignorance? Until the thing was done? How can I believe what your own proceedings deny?' He swung round upon de Perronet, his blanched face arduously controlled. 'Sir, against you I have no malice. I did not even know who was to be her husband. But you must see how hard it is to believe that all has been done fairly, when it has not been done openly.'

'It is in the open now,' said de Perronet shortly. 'What hinders but you should hear it from the lady's own lips? Will that content you?'

Roscelin's white face tightened yet more painfully, and

141

for a moment he struggled visibly against his fear of inevitable rejection and loss. But he had no choice but to agree.

'If she tells me this is her choice, then I am silenced.' He did not say that he would therefore be content.

Cenred turned to his wife, who all this while had clung loyally to her husband's side, while her troubled eyes never left her son's tormented face.

'Go and call Helisende. She shall speak for herself.'

In the heavy and uneasy silence after Emma had departed it was not clear to Cadfael whether any or all of this disturbed household had found it as strange as he did that Helisende should not long ago have come down, to discover for herself the meaning of all these nocturnal comings and goings. He could not get out of his mind the last glimpse he had had of her, standing solitary among so many, suddenly lost and confounded on a road she had believed she could walk to the end with resolute dignity. In a situation so grimly changed she had lost her bearings. A wonder, though, that she had not, in defence of her own integrity, come down with the rest to discover the best or the worst when the searchers returned. Did she even know yet that Edgytha was dead?

Cenred had advanced into the half-lit hall, abandoning even the seclusion of the solar, since there was no longer any privacy to be found behind a closed door. A woman of the household had been killed. A lady of the family found her marriage the occasion of conflict and death. There was no possibility here of any separation between master and man, or mistress and maid. They waited with equal disquiet. All but Helisende, who absented herself still.

Brother Haluin had drawn back into the shadows, and sat mute and still on a bench against the wall, hunched stiffly between the crutches he hugged to his sides. His hollow dark eyes passed intently from face to face, reading

142

and wondering. If he felt weariness, he gave no sign. Cadfael would have liked to send him away to his bed, but there hung on everyone here a compulsion so strong that there could be no departure. Only one had resisted the pull. Only one had escaped.

'What keeps the women?' fretted Cenred, as the moments dragged by. 'Does it take so long to pull on a gown?'

But it was long minutes more before Emma reappeared in the doorway, her round, gentle face full of consternation and dismay, her linked hands playing agitatedly at her girdle. Behind her the maid Madlyn peered warily, round-eyed. But of Helisende there was no sign.

'She is gone,' said Emma, too shaken and bewildered to make many words of it. 'She is not in her bed, not in her chamber, nowhere to be found in all this house. Her cloak is gone. Jehan has been out to the stables. Her saddle-horse and harness are gone with her. While you were absent she has saddled up for herself and ridden away secretly, alone.'

For once they were all alike silenced, brother, bridegroom, frustrated lover and all. While they schemed and agonised and wrangled over her fate she had taken action and fled them all. Yes, even Roscelin, for he stood stricken and amazed, utterly at a loss like all the rest. Cenred might stiffen and frown at his son, de Perronet swing round upon him in black suspicion, but plainly Roscelin had had no part in this panic flight. Even before Edgytha's death, thought Cadfael, her secret errand and failure to return had shattered all Helisende's arduously assembled certainty. Yes, de Perronet was a decent man and an honourable match, and she had pledged herself to him to remove herself from Roscelin's path, and deliver herself and him from an unbearable situation. But if that sacrifice was to bring only anger, danger and conflict, even short of death, then all was changed. Helisende had drawn back from the brink, and cut herself free.

'She has run!' said Cenred on a gusty breath, not questioning, accepting. 'How could she do it, all unseen? And when can she have set out? Where were her maids? Was there never a groom about the stable to question her going, or at least give us warning?' He passed a helpless hand over his face, and looked round darkly at his son. 'And where would she run but to you?'

It was out now, and there was no taking it back.

'Have you hidden her away somewhere in secret, and ridden here with your false indignation to cover up the sin?'

'You cannot believe that!' said Roscelin, outraged. 'I have not seen her, nor had any word from her, nor sent her any, and you know it. I'm newly ridden from Elford by that same way your men came there, and if she had been on that path we should have met. Do you think I would then have let her go anywhere alone in the night, whether on to Elford or back here? If we had met we should have been together now – wherever that might be.'

'There is a safer way by the highroad,' said de Perronet. 'Longer, but as fast on horseback, and safer going. If she did indeed set out for Elford, she may have ridden that way. She would hardly risk the same path your men had taken.'

His voice was dry and cold, and his face set in forbidding lines, but he was a practical man, and intended wasting no energy or passion on a green boy's mistaken affections. They did not threaten his position. The match he desired was arranged and accepted, and need not and would not be abandoned. What mattered now was to recover the girl unharmed.

'So she may,' agreed Cenred, encouraged. 'So most likely she would. If she reaches Elford she'll be safe enough there. But we'll send after her by the highroad, and leave nothing to chance.'

'I'll ride back by that way,' offered Roscelin eagerly, and

144

was off towards the door of the hall with a bound, if de Perronet had not plucked him back sharply by the sleeve.

'No, not you! What we might see of either of you again, if once you met, I much mistrust. Let Cenred seek his sister, and I'm content she'll come back to speak her own mind when all this coil is over. And when she does, boy, you had best abide it, and keep your tongue within your teeth.'

Roscelin did not like being handled, nor much savour being called 'boy' by a man whose height and reach he could match, if not his years and assurance. He wrenched his arm free strongly, and stood off further affront with a blackly lowering brow.

'So Helisende be found safe and well, and let alone in very truth to speak her own mind, and not yours, sir, nor my father's, nor any other man's, overlord or priest or king or whatever he may be, I am content. And first,' he said, turning on his father between defiance and pleading, 'find her, let me see her whole and well and used with gentleness. What else matters now?'

'I am going myself,' said Cenred with reviving authority, and strode back into the solar to reclaim the cloak he had discarded.

But there was to be no more riding out from Vivers that night. Cenred had scarcely pulled on his boots again, and his grooms were no more than hoisting down saddle and harness in the stables, when there arose the purposeful stir of half a dozen horsemen riding into the courtyard, the ring of challenge and answer at the gate, the jingle of harness and dull tramping of hooves on the frozen earth.

All those within came surging to open the door and see what company this might be, so late in the night. Edred and his companions had gone on foot, and might be expected to return on foot, and here was a well-mounted troop arriving. Out went the torches into the darkness, out went Cenred, with Roscelin and de Perronet hard on his heels, and several of his menservants following.

In the yard the flickering torchlight flared and guttered and flared again on the strongly-boned countenance and massive body of Audemar de Clary, as he swung himself down from the saddle and tossed his bridle to a scurrying groom. Behind him came Edred the steward and the grooms who had been sent on with him to Elford, mounted now at de Clary's charge, along with three of Audemar's own men.

Cenred came hurrying down the steps to welcome them. 'My lord,' he said, for once formal with his friend and overlord. 'I never looked to see you tonight, but you come very timely and are more than welcome. God knows we're like to be causing you trouble enough, for we have murder here, as Edred will have told you. Murder within your writ is hard to believe, but so it is.'

'So I've heard,' said Audemar. 'Come within, and let me hear the whole tale from you. There's nothing to be done now before morning.' His eye fell on the truant Roscelin as he entered the hall, recorded the boy's grim and unrepentant countenance, and acknowledged tolerantly: 'You here, lad? That at least I expected.' Clearly the deeper reason for Roscelin's banishment was no secret from Audemar, and he had a certain easy sympathy for the boy, short of indulging his folly. He clouted him hard on the shoulder as he passed, and drew him with him into the solar. Roscelin resisted the urging, gripping his lord's sleeve urgently.

'My lord, there's more to be told. Sir,' he appealed to his father passionately. 'tell him! If she did make for Elford, where can she be now? My lord, Helisende is gone, she has ridden out alone, my father believes she must have set out for Elford – because of me! But I rode here by the rough track and saw nothing of her. Has she indeed come safely to you? Put me out of this anxiety – did she go by the high-road? Is she safe at Elford now?'

146

'She is not!' Brought up short against this new vexation, Audemar looked sharply from son to father and back again, well aware of the tensions that plagued them. 'We have just come by the highroad and never a sign of her or any woman have we seen. One road or the other, one of us would have met with her. Come, now!' he said, sweeping Cenred along with him in his free arm. 'Let's within, the few of us, and see what knowledge we can put together, to be used with good sense tomorrow by daylight. Madam, you should take some rest, all's done that you can do before morning, and I will make myself accountable from this on. No need for you to watch out the night.'

There was no question now as to who was master here. At his bidding Emma folded her hands thankfully, shared a glance of harried affection between her husband and her son, and departed docilely to such rest as she could hope to get before dawn. Audemar looked round once from within the solar, a sweeping glance amiable enough but unmistakable in its dominance, that dismissed all further attendance. His eye lit upon the two Benedictines, waiting unobtrusively on the edge of the scene, recognised them with a nod of easy reverence for their habit, and smiled.

'Goodnight, Brothers!' said Audemar, and drew the solar door firmly closed at his back, shutting himself in with the troubled Vivers household and their aspiring kinsman.

Chapter Ten

 E IS RIGHT!' said Brother Haluin, stretched on his bed in the pre-dawn twilight, wakeful still and loosed now from his long silence on the fringe of other men's chaos. 'Goodnight, Brothers, and goodbye! There will be no marriage. There can be no marriage, there is now no bride. And even if she should come back, this match cannot now go forward as if nothing had happened to cast it into such bitter doubt. When I accepted the burden – for even so it was burdensome – there was no call to question that it was for the best, grievous though it might be. There is good reason to question now.'

'I think,' said Cadfael, listening to the muted, deliberate voice, as Haluin felt his way towards a resolution, 'you are not sorry to be delivered from your promise.'

'No, I am not sorry. Sorry enough, God knows, that a woman has died, sorry that these children should suffer unhappiness without remedy. But I could not now be answerable to God for joining the girl to any man, unless I could recover the certainty I have lost. As well that she is gone, and I pray into some safe refuge. And now it only remains,' said Brother Haluin, 'for us to take our leave. We

149

no longer have any part to play here. De Clary has plainly told us so. And Cenred will be glad to see us go.'

'And you have a vow to complete, and no further cause to delay. True!' said Cadfael torn between relief and regret.

'I have delayed too long already. It is time I acknowledged,' said Haluin inflexibly, 'how small are my own griefs, and how great the part I have chosen. I made the choice for my own craven sake, now with what life I have left I will make it good for a worthier reason.'

So this journey, thought Cadfael, has not been in vain. For the first time since his flight from the world, sick with his guilt and loss, he has ventured back into the world, and found it full of pain, into which his own pain has fallen and been lost, like a raindrop in the sea. All these years he has been outwardly dutiful, keeping every scruple of the Rule, and agonised in solitude within. His true vocation begins now. Once enlightened, Haluin may well prove the stuff of which saints are made. As for me, I am unregenerate man.

For in his heart he did not want to leave Vivers, thus with nothing resolved. Everything Haluin said was true. The bride was gone, there could be no marriage, they had no excuse for remaining here any longer, nor had Cenred any further use for them. He would indeed be glad to see them go. But Cadfael would not go gladly, turning his back upon a murder unavenged, justice out of kilter, a wrong that might never be set right.

True also, Audemer de Clary was overlord here, a man of force and decision, and with such crimes as fell within his writ he must deal. There was nothing Cadfael could tell him that Cenred would not already have told him.

And what, after all, did Cadfael really know in this matter? That Edgytha had been absent several hours before she died, since there was already snow on the ground when she fell. That she must have been on her way back to Vivers, as she had intended. That she had had ample time to go as far

150

as Elford. That she had not been robbed. The murderer had simply killed and left her, not the way of footpads living wild. If not to stop her from warning Roscelin – for that would have been credible only on the outward journey – then to stop her mouth for another reason, before ever she could get back to Vivers. Yet what connection was there between Elford and Vivers except young Roscelin's banishment to Audemar's service? What other secret to fear betrayal but that of the planned marriage?

But Edgytha had never reached Roscelin, never had speech with him, nor had she gone to Audemar or any of his household. So if she had been to Elford, why had no one there seen her? And if she had not been to Elford, where had she been?

So if it was not what he along with his host and hostess had supposed, what was the cat Edgytha had gone to find, to put among Cenred's pigeons?

And in all probability he would never learn the answers to these questions, or learn what fortune awaited the lost girl and the unhappy boy, and the elders distressed and torn with concern for both of them. A pity! But no help for it, they could no longer trespass on Cenred's disrupted family and burdened hospitality. As soon as the household was astir they must take their leave and set out for Shrewsbury. No one would miss them. And it was high time they went home.

The morning came greyly, under a sky lightly clouded over but lofty, and threatening no further falls of snow. Only a few threads and traceries of white lingered along the bases of walls and under the trees and bushes, and the frost was yielding. It would not be a bad day for travellers.

The household was up and in ferment early. Cenred's servants rolled out of their brief sleep bleary-eyed and grim, well aware that there would be no rest for them that day.

Whatever else had been decided in the solemn conference in the solar overnight, whatever possible asylums had been suggested as safe havens for Helisende, it was certain that Audemar would have patrols working every road in the countryside, and enquiring at every cottage, in case some-one, somewhere, had seen and spoken with Edgytha, or seen anything of a solitary and furtive figure lurking along the path she had taken. They were already gathering in the courtyard, saddling up, tightening girths and waiting stoically for their orders, when Cadfael and Haluin, booted and girded for the road, presented themselves before Cenred.

He was deep in colloquy with his steward in the middle of the bustle in the hall, when they approached him, and he turned to them courteously but blankly for a moment, as if in these graver preoccupations he had forgotten he had ever before set eyes on them. Recollection came at once, but brought him no pleasure, only a gesture of hospitable compunction.

'Brothers, I ask your pardon, you have been neglected. If we have troubles here to deal with, don't let that disturb you. Use my home as your own.'

'My lord,' said Haluin, 'we owe you thanks for all your kindness, but we must be on our way. There is now no way I can serve you. There is no more haste, since there is no more secrecy. And we have duties waiting for us at home. We are come to take our leave.'

Cenred was too honest to pretend any reluctance to part with them, and made no demur. 'I have delayed your return for my own ends,' he said ruefully, 'and all to no purpose. I am sorry I ever drew you into so vexed a business. Believe me, at least, that my intent was good. And go with my goodwill. I wish you a peaceful journey.'

'And to you, sir, the safe recovery of the lady, and the guidance of God through all perplexities,' said Haluin.

152

Cenred did not offer horses for the first stage of the journey, as Adelais had done for the whole of it. He had need here of all the horses at his disposal. But he watched the two habited figures, the hale and the lame, make their way slowly down the steps from the hall door, Cadfael's hand at Haluin's elbow ready to support him at need, Haluin's hands, calloused now from gripping the staves of his crutches, braced and careful at every tread. In the court-yard they threaded the bustle of preparation, and drew near to the gate. Cenred took his eyes from them with relief at being rid of one complication, and turned his face doggedly if wearily upon those remaining.

Roscelin, chafing at delay, stood bridle in hand at the gate, shifting restlessly from foot to foot, and peering impa-tiently back for his father or Audemar to give the word to mount. He gave the two monks a preoccupied glance as they drew near, and then, warming, bade them a good morning, and even smiled through the grey distorting mask of his own anxiety.

'You're away for Shrewsbury? It's a good step. I hope you'll have easy travelling.'

'And you a blessed end to your search,' said Cadfael.

'Blessed for me?' said the boy, again clouding over. 'I don't look for it.'

'If you find her safe and well, and no man's wife until she so pleases, that's a fair measure of blessing. I doubt if you may ask for more. Not yet,' said Cadfael cautiously. 'Take the day's measure of good, and be thankful, and who knows but more may be added?'

'You talk of impossibilities,' said Roscelin implacably. 'But you mean me well, and I take it as you mean it.'

'Where will you ride first, to look for Helisende?' asked Brother Haluin.

'Some of us back to Elford, to make sure she has not slipped between us and made her way there, after all. And

153

to every manor around, for any word of her, or of Edgytha. She cannot have gone far.' He had truly grieved and been angry for Edgytha, but the 'she' that drove all others from his mind was Helisende.

They left him chafing and agonising, more restless than the horse that shifted and stamped to be off. When they looked back from outside the gate his foot was already in the stirrup, and behind him the rest of the hunters were gathering the reins and mounting. Back to Elford first, in case Helisende had slipped through their fingers, eluding the riders on both tracks, and come safe to shelter. Cadfael and Haluin must go in the opposite direction, towards the west. They had turned some way north from the highroad to reach the lights of the manor. They did not return that way, but turned due west at once, on a trodden path that skirted the manor fence. From the limit of the enclave they heard Audemar's hunters ride forth, and turned to watch them stream out from the gate and lengthen out into a long, many-coloured thread, dwindling into the east and vanishing among the trees of the first belt of woodland.

'And is that the end of it?' wondered Haluin, suddenly grieved. 'And we shall never know what comes of it all! Poor lad, and his own case beyond hope. All his comfort in this world must be to see her happy, if that will ever be possible without him. I know,' said Brother Haluin, in compassion untainted by any lingering self-pity, 'what they suffer.'

But it seemed that it was indeed over for them, and there was no sense in looking back. They set their faces towards the west, and went forward steadily on this untested path, with the rising sun behind them, casting their elongated shadows along the moist grass.

'By this way,' said Cadfael, taking his bearings thoughtfully when they halted to eat their midday bread and cheese and strip of salt bacon in the lee of a bushy bank, 'I think we

154

shall miss Lichfield. I judge we're already passing to the north of it. No matter, we shall find a bed somewhere before nightfall.'

Meantime, the day was clear and dry, and the country through which they made their way was pleasant, but sparsely populated, and afforded them fewer human encounters than they had met with on the direct highway through Lichfield. Having had so little sleep they made no haste, but went steadily, and took whatever rests offered along the way, wherever a solitary assart provided the hospitality of a bench by the hearth, and a few minutes of neighbourly gossip in passing.

A light wind sprang up with the approach of evening, warning them it was time to look for a night's shelter. They were in country still wasted from harsh usage fifty years past. The people of these parts had not taken kindly to the coming of the Normans, and had paid the price for their obduracy. There were the relics of deserted holdings to be seen here and there, collapsing into grass and brambles, and the ruins of a mill rotting gently into its own overgrown stream. Hamlets were few and far between. Cadfael began to scan the landscape round for any sign of an inhabited roof.

An elderly man gathering firewood in a stand of old trees straightened his bent back to answer their greetings, and peered at them curiously from within his sacking hood.

'Not half a mile on, Brothers, you'll see to your right the pale of a nunnery. They're still building, it's mostly timber yet, but the church and the cloister are in stone, you can't miss it. There's but two or three holdings in the hamlet, but the sisters take in travellers. You'll get a bed there.' And he added, eyeing their black habits: 'They're of your own persuasion, it's a Benedictine house.'

'I knew of none in these parts,' said Cadfael. 'What is this house called?'

'It's like the hamlet, called Farewell. It's no more than three years old. Bishop de Clinton set it up. You'll be made welcome there.'

They thanked him, and left him to bind up and hoist his great bundle of wood, and make off for home in the opposite direction, while they went on, encouraged, towards the west.

'I remember,' said Haluin, 'hearing something of this place, or at least of the bishop's plans for a new foundation somewhere here, close to his cathedral. But I never heard the name Farewell until – do you recall? – Cenred spoke of it, that night we first came to Vivers. The only Benedictine house in these parts, he said, when he asked where we were from. We're fortunate, it's well we came this way.'

By this time, with the twilight closing in, he was beginning to flag, in spite of the easy pace they had set. They were both glad when the path brought them to a small open green flanked by three or four cottages, and they saw beyond these the long pale fence of the new abbey, and the roof of the church above it. The track led them to a modest timber gatehouse. Both the stout gate and the grille set in it were closed, but a pull at the bell sent a succession of echoes flying away into distance within, and after a few moments brought light, flying footsteps skipping towards them from within the pale.

The grille slid open, and revealed a round, rosy, youthful face beaming through at them. Wide blue eyes surveyed their habits and tonsures, and recognised kindred.

'Good even, Brothers,' said a high, girlish voice, joyously self-important. 'You're late on the road tonight. Can we offer you a roof and a rest?'

'We were about to ask it,' said Cadfael heartily. 'Can you lodge us overnight?'

'And longer if you need,' she said cheerfully. 'Men of the Order will always be welcome here. We're off the beaten track, and not yet well known, and with the place still building we offer less comfort, I daresay, than some older houses, but we have room for such guests as you. Wait till I unbar the doors.'

She was about it already, they heard the bolt shot back and the latch of the wicket lifted, and then the door opened wide in exuberant welcome, and the portress waved them in.

She could not, Cadfael thought, be more than seventeen, and new in her novitiate, one of those superfluous daughters of poorly endowed small nobility for whom there was little to spare by way of dowry, and little prospect of an advantageous marriage. She was small and softly rounded, plain of face but fresh and wholesome as new bread, and blessedly she glowed with enthusiasm in her new life, with no apparent regret for the world she had left behind. The satisfaction of trusted office became her, and so did the white wimple and black cowl framing her bright and candid face.

'Have you travelled far?' she asked, viewing Haluin's laboured gait with wide-eyed concern.

'From Vivers,' said Haluin, quick in reassurance. 'It is not so far, and we have taken it gently.'

'And have you very far still to go?'

'To Shrewsbury,' said Cadfael, 'where we belong to the abbey of Saint Peter and Saint Paul.'

'It's a long way,' she said, shaking her head over them. 'You'll be needing your rest. Will you wait here in the lodge for me, till I tell Sister Ursula she has guests? Sister Ursula is our hospitaller. The lord bishop asked for two experienced elder sisters to come to us from Polesworth for a season, to instruct the novices. We are all so new, and there's so much to learn, besides all the work we have to do in the building, and the garden. And they sent us Sister Ursula and Sister Benedicta. Sit and warm yourselves but a few minutes, and

I'll be back.' And she was off, with her light, dancing step, as blithe in her cloistered calling as any of her secular sisters could have been in approaching a more worldly marriage.

'She is truly happy,' said Brother Haluin, wondering and pleased. 'No, it is not a second-best. So I have found it in the end, but she from the beginning. The sisters from Polesworth must be women of wisdom and grace, if this is their work.'

Sister Ursula the hospitaller was a tall, thin woman perhaps fifty years old, with a lined, experienced face at once serene, resigned and even mildly amused, as if she had seen and come to terms with all the vagaries of human behaviour, and nothing could now surprise or disconcert her. If the other borrowed instructress measures up to this one, Cadfael thought, these green girls of Farewell have been fortunate.

'You're warmly welcome,' said Sister Ursula, sailing briskly into the lodge with the young portress beaming at her elbow. 'The lady abbess will be happy to receive you in the morning, but you must be most in need now of food and rest and a bed, all the more if you have such a long journey before you. Come with me, there's a chamber prepared for chance comers always, and our own brothers are all the more welcome.'

She led them out from the lodge into a narrow outer court, where the church lay before them, a modest building of stone, with the traces of the continuing work, ashlar and timber, cords and scaffolding boards, stacked neatly under its walls, in token that nothing here was finished. But in only three years they had raised the church and the entire frame of the cloister, but for the south range, where only the lower floor which housed the refectory was completed.

'The bishop has provided us the labour and a generous endowment,' said Sister Ursula, 'but we shall be building for some years yet. Meantime we live simply. We want for nothing that's needful, and hanker after nothing beyond our needs. I suppose when all these timber housings are replaced in stone my work here will be done, and I should be returning to Polesworth, where I took my vows years ago, but I don't know but I'd rather stay here, if I'm offered a choice. There's something about bringing a new foundation to birth, you feel towards it as towards a child of your own body.'

The enclave fence, doubtless, would eventually be replaced by a stone wall, the wooden buildings that lined it, infirmary, domestic offices, guest-hall and storehouses, gradually rebuilt one by one. But already the glimpse they had into the cloister in passing showed that the garth had been grassed, and a shallow stone basin in the centre held water to attract the birds.

'By next year,' said Sister Ursula, 'we shall have flowers. Sister Benedicta, our best gardener at Polesworth, came here with me, the garth is her preserve. Things grow for her, birds come to her hand. That gift I never had.'

'And has Polesworth also provided you your abbess?' asked Cadfael.

'No, Bishop de Clinton brought Mother Patrice from Coventry. We two must go back to our own house when we're no longer needed here, unless, as I say, they let us remain for life. We should need the bishop's dispensation, but who knows, he may see fit to grant it.'

Beyond the cloister a small private court opened, and the guest-hall stood on the further side of it, close to the pale fence. The small room that awaited the first travellers was dim and full of the warmth and fragrance of wood, furnished simply with two beds and a little table, with a crucifix on the wall and a prayer-desk below it.

'Use it as your domain,' said Sister Ursula cheerfully, 'and I'll have supper brought to you here. You come too late for Vespers, but if you please to join us at Compline later, you'll hear the bell. Use our church for prayer as you wish. It is but young yet, the more good souls it harbours under its roof, the better. And now, if you have all you need, I'll leave you to your rest.'

In the blessed virginal quiet of this new abbey of Farewell Brother Haluin fell rapturously asleep as soon as he returned from Compline, and slept like a child all through the night and deep into the dawn of a soft, clear morning, free of any touch of frost. He awoke to find Cadfael already up, and preparing to go and recite the morning office and offer his private prayers in the church.

'Has the bell sounded for Prime?' asked Haluin, rising in haste.

'No, nor will for half an hour yet, by the light. We can have the church to ourselves for a while, if you're so minded.'

'A good thought,' said Haluin, and went with him gladly, out into the small court, and across it to the south door into the cloister. The turf in the garth was moist and green, the bleached pallor of winter vanished overnight. The shy mist of buds that had barely showed a few days ago along the branches of the trees now had a positive colour, grown into a tender green veil. It wanted only a few more such mild days and a glimpse of the sun, and suddenly it would be spring. In the clear shallow water in the stone bowl small birds were fluttering and shrilling, aware of change. Brother Haluin approached the little church of Farewell through evidences of hope. Certainly this first church would be enlarged or replaced later, when the abbey's immediate building needs were met, its endowment assured, and its prestige established. Yet this first edifice, small and plain as it was, would always be remembered with affection, and its supplanting a matter of regret to those, like Sister Ursula and Sister Benedicta, who had been present and served at its birth.

160

They said the office together in the dim, stony quietness, kneeling before the small spark of the altar lamp, and made their private prayers in silence afterwards. The light softened and brightened over them, the first veiled ray of the rising sun stole through the pales of the enclave and touched the upper stones of the eastern wall into pale rose, and still Brother Haluin knelt, his crutches laid beside him.

Cadfael was the first to rise. It could not be long now to Prime, and it might be an inconvenient distraction to new young sisters to have two men in evidence at their morning service, even two monks of the same order. He crossed to the south door, and stood there looking out into the garth, waiting until Haluin should need his help to rise.

There was one of the sisters standing beside the stone bowl in the centre, very slender and erect and composed, feeding the birds. She crumbled bread on the broad rim of the bowl, and held fragments of it out on her open palm, and the flurry and vibration of hovering wings span fearlessly about her. The black habit became her slenderness, and her bearing had a youthful grace that stabbed piercingly into Cadfael's memory. The poise of the head on its long neck and straight shoulders, the narrow waist and elegant, long hand offering alms to the birds, these he had surely seen before, in another place, by another and deceptive light. Now she stood in open air, with the soft morning light upon her, and he could not believe that he was mistaken.

Helisende was here at Farewell, Helisende in a nun's habit. The bride had fled her unbearable dilemma to take the veil rather than marry anyone but her unfortunate lover Roscelin. True, she could not have taken any vows as yet, but the sisters might well see fit, in her stressful circumstances, to give her the instant protection of the habit, even before she entered on her novitiate.

She had quick hearing, or perhaps she had been expecting and listening for a light footstep in the western range of the cloister, where the sisters' dortoir lay. For plainly she caught the sound of someone approaching from that direction, and turned to meet the newcomer, smiling. The very movement, measured and tranquil, in itself cast doubt on the youth he had seen in her but a moment earlier, and showed him fully a face he had never seen before.

Not a young, unpractised girl, but a serene, worn, mature woman. The revelation in the hall at Vivers came about full circle, from illusion to reality, from the girl to the woman, as then it had spun headily backwards from the woman to the girl. Not Helisende, not even very like Helisende, but for the tall white ivory brow, and the sweet and plaintive oval shape of the face, and the wide-set, candid, gallant and vulnerable eyes. In figure and bearing, yes, the very same. If she had turned her back again, she would again have become the image of her daughter.

For who else could this be but the widowed mother who had taken the veil at Polesworth rather than be harried into a second marriage? Who else but Sister Benedicta, sent here to the bishop's new foundation to help to establish a secure tradition and a blessed example for the fledgling nuns of Farewell? Sister Benedicta who could charm flowers to grow and birds to come to her hand? Helisende must have known of her move, if the rest of the household at Vivers had not. Helisende had known where to look for refuge in her need. Where should she go but to her mother?

He had been concentrating so intensely upon the woman in the garth that he had heard nothing from within the church, until he caught the tapping of crutches on the flagstones within the doorway, and swung about almost guiltily to return to his bounden duty. Haluin had somehow got to his feet unaided, and emerged now at Cadfael's side, gazing out with pleasure into the garth, where misty sunlight and moist shadow mingled.

His eyes fell upon the nun, and he halted abruptly,

swaying on his crutches. Cadfael saw the dark eyes fix and widen, their arrested stare burning hollowly into the glowing stillness of vision or trance, and the sensitive lips move almost soundlessly, forming the slow syllables of a name. Almost soundlessly, but not quite, for Cadfael heard it.

In wonder and joy and pain, and all in extremes, as one driven and wracked by religious ecstasy: 'Bertrade!' whispered Brother Haluin.

Chapter Eleven

HERE WAS no mistaking the name, and no questioning the absolute certainty with which it was uttered. If Cadfael clung to sane, sensible disbelief for one moment, he discarded it the next, and it was swept away once for all in a great flood of enlightenment. In Haluin there was no doubt or question at all. He knew what he saw, he gave it its true, its unforgotten name, and stood lost in wonder, trembling with the intensity of his knowledge. Bertrade!

The first glimpse of her daughter had struck him to the heart, the dimly-seen copy outlined against the light was so true to the original. But as soon as Helisende had stepped forward into the torchlight the likeness had faded, the vision dissolved. This was a girl he did not know. Now she came again, and turned towards him the remembered and lamented face, and there was no more questioning.

So she had not died. Cadfael grappled silently with enlightenment. The tomb Haluin had sought was an illusion. She had not died of the draught that robbed her of her child, she had survived that peril and grief, to be married off to an elderly husband, vassal and friend to her mother's family, and to bear him a daughter the image of herself in

165

build and bearing. And she had done her best to be a faithful wife and mother as long as her old lord lived, but after his death she had turned her back on the world and followed her first lover into the cloister, choosing the same order, taking to herself the name of the founder, binding herself once for all to the same discipline into which Haluin had been driven.

Then why, argued a persistent imp in Cadfael's mind, why did you – *you*, not Haluin! – find in the face of the girl at Vivers something inexplicably familiar? Who was it hiding from you deep in the caverns of memory, refusing to be recognised? You had never seen the girl before, never in life set eyes on this mother of hers. Whoever looked out at you from Helisende's eyes, and then drew down a veil between, it was not Bertrade de Clary.

All this came seething through his mind in the instant of revelation, the brief moment before Helisende herself emerged from the shadows of the west range and came out into the garth to join her mother. She had not donned the habit, she wore the same gown she had worn the previous evening at her brother's table. She was pale and grave, but had the calm of the cloister about her, safe here from any compulsion, with time for thought and for taking counsel.

The two women met, the hems of their skirts tracing two darker paths in the silver-green of the moist grass. They turned back together at leisure towards the doorway from which Helisende had come, to go in and join the rest of the sisterhood for Prime. They were going away, they would vanish, and nothing be answered, nothing resolved, nothing made plain! And still Haluin hung swaying on his crutches, stricken motionless and mute. He would lose her again, she was all but lost already. The two women had almost reached the west walk, the cords of deprivation were drawn out to breaking point.

166

'Bertrade!' cried Haluin, in a great shout of terror and despair.

That cry reached them, echoing startlingly from every wall, and brought them about to stare in alarm and astonishment towards the door of the church. Haluin tore himself out of his daze with a great heave, and went hurtling forward recklessly into the garth, his crutches goring the soft turf.

At sight of an unknown man lurching towards them the women had instinctively recoiled, but seeing at second glance his habit, and how sadly he was crippled, in pure compassion they halted their flight to permit his approach, and even came a few impulsive steps to meet him. For a moment there was no more in it than that, pity for a lame man. Then abruptly everything changed.

He had been in too much haste to reach them, he stumbled, and swayed out of balance for a moment, on the edge of a fall, and the girl, quick to sympathy, sprang forward to support him in her arms. His weight falling into her embrace swung them both about, to steady and recover almost cheek to cheek, and Cadfael saw the two faces for a long moment side by side, startled, bright, dazzled into wonder.

So now at last he had his answer. Now he knew everything there was to be known, everything except what fury of bitterness could drive one human creature to do so base and cruel a thing to another. And even that answer would not be far to seek.

It was at that moment of total enlightenment that Bertrade de Clary, staring earnestly into the stranger's face, knew him for no stranger, and called him by his name:

'Haluin!'

There was nothing more, not then, only the meeting of eyes and the mutual recognition, and the understanding, on either part, of past wrongs and agonies never before fully understood, bitter and terrible for a moment, then erased by

167

a great flood of gratitude and joy. For in the moment when the three of them hung mute and still, staring at one another, they all heard the little bell for Prime ringing in the dortoir, and knew that the sisters would be filing down the night stairs to walk in procession into the church.

So there was nothing more, not then. The women drew back, with lingering glances still wide with wonder, and turned to answer the summons and join their sisters. And Cadfael went forward from the porch to take Brother Haluin by the arm, and lead him gently, like a sleep-walking child, back to the guest-hall.

'She is not dead,' said Haluin, rigidly erect on the edge of his bed. Over and over, recording the miracle in a repetition nearer incantation than prayer: 'She is not dead! It was false, false, false! She did not die!'

Cadfael said never a word. It was not yet time to speak of all that lay behind this revelation. For the moment Haluin's shocked mind looked no further than the fact, the joy that she should be alive and well and in safe haven whom he had lamented so long as dead, and dead by his grievous fault, the bewilderment and hurt that he should have been left so long mourning her.

'I must speak with her,' said Haluin. 'I cannot go without having speech with her.'

'You shall not,' Cadfael assured him.

It was inevitable now, all must come out. They had met, they had beheld each other, no one now could undo that, the sealed coffer was sprung open, the secrets were tumbling out of it, no one now could close the lid upon them ever again.

'We cannot leave today,' said Haluin.

'We shall not. Wait here in patience,' said Cadfael. 'I am going to seek an audience with the lady abbess.'

* * *

168

The abbess of Farewell, brought by Bishop de Clinton from Coventry to direct his new foundation, was a dumpy round loaf of a woman, perhaps in her middle forties, with a plump russet face and shrewd brown eyes that weighed and measured in a glance, and were confident of their judgement. She sat uncompromisingly erect on an uncushioned bench in a small and Spartan parlour, and closed the book on the desk before her as Cadfael came in.

'You're very welcome, Brother, to whatever service our house can offer you. Ursula tells me you are from the abbey of Saint Peter and Saint Paul, at Shrewsbury. I intended to invite you and your companion to join me for dinner, and I cordially extend that invitation now. But I hear you have asked for this interview, forestalling any move of mine. I take it there is a reason. Sit down, Brother, and tell me what more you have to ask of me.'

Cadfael sat down with her, debating in his mind how much he might tell, or how little. She was a woman quite capable of filling in gaps for herself, but also, he judged, a woman of scrupulous discretion, who would keep to herself whatever she read between the lines.

'I come, Reverend Mother, to ask you to countenance a meeting, in private, between my brother Haluin and Sister Benedicta.'

He saw her brows raised, but the small bright eyes beneath them remained unperturbed and sharp with intelligence.

'In youth,' he said, 'they were well acquainted. He was in her mother's service, and being so close in the one house, and of an age, boy and girl together, they fell into loving. But Haluin's suit was not at all to her mother's mind, and she took pains to separate them. Haluin was dismissed from her service, and forbidden all ado with the girl, who was persuaded into a marriage more pleasing to her family. No doubt you know her history since then. Haluin entered our house, admittedly for a wrong reason. It is not good to turn

169

to the spiritual life out of despair, but many have done it, as you and I know, and lived to become faithful and honourable ornaments to their houses. So has Haluin. So, I make no doubt, has Bertrade de Clary.'

He caught the glint of her eyes at hearing that name. There was not much she did not know about her flock, but if she knew more than he had said of this woman she showed no sign and made no comment, accepting all as he had told it.

'It seems to me,' she said, 'that the story you tell me bids fair to be repeated in another generation. The circumstances are not quite the same, but the end well could be. It's as well we should consider in time how to deal with it.'

'I have that in mind,' said Cadfael. 'And how have you dealt with it thus far? Since the girl came running to you by night? For the whole household of Vivers is out by now for the second day, scouring the roads for her.'

'I think not,' said the abbess. 'For I sent yesterday to let her brother know that she is here and safe, and prays him to be left in peace here for a while for thought and prayer. I think he will respect her wish, in the circumstances.'

'Circumstances which she has told you,' said Cadfael with conviction, 'in full. So far, that is, as she knows them.'

'She has.'

'Then you know of a woman's death, and of the marriage arranged for Helisende. And the reason for that marriage, you know that, too?'

'I know she is too close kin to the young man she would liefer have. Yes, she has told me. More, I fancy, than she tells her confessor. You need not fear for Helisende, as long as she remains here she is safe from all harassment, and has the company and comfort of her mother.'

'She could not be in a better place,' said Cadfael fervently. 'Then, as to these two who most concern us now – I must tell you that Haluin was told that Bertrade was dead, and has believed her so all these years, and moreover, taken her death to himself as blame. This morning by God's grace he has seen her before him alive and well. They have exchanged no words but their names. But I think it would be well that they should, if you so grant. They will serve better in their separate vocations if they have peace of mind. Also they have a right to know, each one, that the other is whole, blessed and content.'

'And you think,' said the abbess with deliberation, 'that they *will* be blessed and content? After as before?'

'More and better than before,' he said with certainty. 'I can speak for the man, if you know as much of the woman. And if they part thus without a word, they will be tormented to the end of their days.'

'I would as soon not be answerable to God for that,' said the abbess, with a brief, bleak smile. 'Well, they shall have their hour and make their peace. It can do no harm, and may do much good. Do you purpose to remain here some days longer?'

'This one day at least,' said Cadfael. 'For I have one more prayer to make to you. Brother Haluin I leave to you. But there is a thing I must do, before we set off for home. Not here! Will you let me borrow a horse from your stable?'

She sat studying him for a long moment, and it seemed that she was guardedly satisfied with what she saw, for at length she said: 'On one condition.'

'And that is?'

'That when time serves, and all harm is spent, you will tell me the other half of the story.'

Brother Cadfael led out his borrowed horse into the stable-yard, and mounted without haste. The bishop had seen fit to provide stabling adequate for his own visitations, and two stout cobs for remounts should any of his envoys travel

171

this way and make use of the abbey's hospitality. Having been given a free hand, Cadfael had naturally chosen the more likely looking of the two, and the younger, a lively, solid bay. It was no very long ride he had in mind, but he might as well get out of it what pleasure he could along the way. There would be little pleasure at the end of it.

The sun was already high when he rode out at the gate, a pale sun growing brighter and clearer as the air of the day warmed into palpable spring. The fatal snow at Vivers would be the last snow of the winter, appropriately completing Haluin's pilgrimage, as the first snow had begun it.

The filigree green gauze of buds along the branches of bush and tree had burst into the tender plumage of young leaves. The moist grass shimmered, and gave off a faint, fragrant steam as the sun reached it. So much beauty, and behind him as he rode lay a great mercy, a just deliverance, and the renewal of hope. And before him a solitary soul to be saved or lost.

He did not take the road to Vivers. It was not there he had urgent business, though he might well return that way. Once he halted to look back, and the long line of the abbey fence had disappeared in the folds of land, and the hamlet with it. Haluin would be waiting and wondering, groping his way through a confused dream, beset with questions to which he could have no answer, torn between belief and disbelief, fearful joy and recollected anguish, until the abbess should send to summon him to the meeting which would make all things plain at last.

Cadfael rode on slowly until he should encounter some-one from whom he could ask directions. A woman leading sheep and lambs out to pasture at the edge of the village stopped willingly to point him to the most direct road. He need not go near Vivers, and that was well, for he had no wish to meet Cenred or his men as yet. He had nothing at this moment to tell them, and indeed it was not he who must tell what finally had to be told.

Once on the track his informant had indicated, he rode fast and purposefully, until he dismounted at the gate of the manor of Elford.

It was the young portress who tapped at the door and entered Brother Haluin's haunted solitude, later in the morning, when the sun had shed its veil, and the grass of the garth was drying. He looked round as she came in, expecting Cadfael, and gazed at her with eyes still wide and blank with wonder.

'I am sent by the lady abbess,' said the girl, with solicitous gentleness, since it seemed he might be almost beyond understanding, 'to bid you to her parlour. If you will come with me, I'll show you the way.'

Obediently he reached for his crutches. 'Brother Cadfael went forth and has not returned,' he said slowly, looking about him like a man awaking from sleep. 'Is this bidding to him also? Should I not wait for him?'

'There is no need,' she said. 'Brother Cadfael has already spoken with Mother Patrice, and has an errand he says he must do now. You should wait for his return here, and be easy. Will you come?'

Haluin thrust himself to his feet and went with her, across the rear court to the abbess's lodging, confiding like a child though half his mind was still absent. The little portress tempered her flying steps to his laboured gait, bringing him with considerate gentleness to the door of the parlour, and turning upon him on the threshold a bright, encouraging smile.

'Go in, you are expected.'

She held the door open for him, since he had need of both hands for his crutches. He limped across the threshold into the wood-scented, dimly lit room, and halted just within to make his reverence to the Mother Superior, only to stand motionless and quivering as his eyes adjusted to the subdued light. For the woman who stood waiting for him, braced and still and wonderfully smiling in the centre of the room, her hands extended instinctively to aid his approach, was not the abbess, but Bertrade de Clary.

She held the door open for him, since he had need of both hands for his crutches. He limped across the threshold into the wood-scented, dimly lit room, and halted just within to make his reverence to the Mother Superior, only to stand

Chapter Twelve

HE GROOM who came unhurriedly across the courtyard to greet the visitor and enquire his business was neither Lothair nor Luc, but a lanky lad not yet twenty, with a shock of dark hair. At his back the courtyard seemed emptied of its usual lively activity, only a few maids and manservants going back and forth about their work in a casual fashion, as if all constraints were slackened. By the look of things, the master of the house and most of his men were still out and about on the hunt for any word that might lead to the murderer of Edgytha.

'If you're wanting the lord Audemar,' said the boy at once, 'you're out of luck. He's still away to Vivers about this woman who was killed a couple of nights back. But his steward's here, if you want lodging you'd best see him.'

'I thank you,' said Cadfael, surrendering his bridle, 'but it's not the lord Audemar I've come to see. My errand is to his mother. I know where her dower apartments are. If you'll see to the horse I'll go myself and ask her woman to enquire if the lady will be good enough to see me.'

'As you please, then. You were here afore,' said the lad, narrowing his eyes curiously at this vaguely familiar visitor.

175

'Only a few days back, with another black monk, one that went on crutches and very lame.'

'True,' said Cadfael. 'And I had speech with the lady then, and she will not have forgotten either me or that lame brother. If she refuses me a hearing now, I will let her be – but I think she will not refuse.'

'Try for yourself, then,' agreed the groom indifferently. 'She's still here with her maid, and I know she's within. She keeps within, these last days.'

'She had two grooms with her,' said Cadfael, 'father and son. We were acquainted, when we stayed here, they had come from Shropshire with her. I'd willingly pass the time of day with them, afterwards, if they're not away to Vivers with the lord Audemar's people.'

'Oh, them! No, they're her fellows, none of his. But they're not here, neither. They went off yesterday on some errand of hers, very early. Where? How should I know where? Back to Hales, likely. That's where the old dame keeps, most of her time.'

I wonder, thought Cadfael, as he turned towards Adelais's dwelling in the corner of the enclave wall, and the groom led the cob away to the stable, truly I wonder how it would suit Adelais de Clary to know that her son's grooms speak of her as 'the old dame'. Doubtless to that raw boy she seemed ancient as the hills, but resolutely she cherished and conserved what had once been great beauty, and from that excellence nothing and no one must be allowed to detract. Not for nothing did she choose for her intimate maid someone plain and pockmarked, surrounding herself with dull and ordinary faces that caused her own lustre to glow more brightly.

At the door of Adelais's hall he asked for audience, and the woman Gerta came out to him haughtily, protective of her mistress's privacy and assertive of her own office. He had sent in no name, and at sight of him she checked, none

176

too pleased to see one of the Benedictines from Shrewsbury back again so soon, and so unaccountably.

'My lady is not disposed to see visitors. What's your business, that you need trouble her with it? If you need lodging and food, my lord Audemar's steward will take care of it.'

'My business,' said Cadfael, 'is with the lady Adelais only, and concerns no one beside. Tell her that Brother Cadfael is here again, and that he comes from the abbey of Farewell, and asks to have some talk with her. That she shuns visitors I believe. But I think she will not refuse me.'

She was not so bold that she dared take it upon herself to deny him, though she went with a toss of her head and a disdainful glance, and would have been glad to bring back a dismissive answer. It was plain by the sour look on her face when she emerged from the solar that she was denied that pleasure.

'My lady bids you in,' she said coldly, and opened the door wide for him to pass by her and enter the chamber. And no doubt she hoped to linger and be privy to whatever passed, but favour did not extend so far.

'Leave us,' said the voice of Adelais de Clary, from deep shadow under a shuttered window. 'And close the door between.'

She had no seemly woman's occupation for her hands this time, no pretence at embroidering or spinning, she merely sat in her great chair in semi-darkness, motionless, her hands spread along the arms and gripping the carved lion-heads in which they terminated. She did not move as Cadfael came in, she was neither surprised nor disturbed. Her deep eyes burned upon him without wonder, and he thought without regret. It was almost as though she had been waiting for him.

'Where have you left Haluin?' she asked.

177

'At the abbey of Farewell,' said Cadfael.

She was silent for a moment, brooding upon him with a still face and glowing eyes, with an intensity he felt as a vibration upon the air, before ever his eyes had grown accustomed to the dim light, and watched her lineaments grow gradually out of darkness, the chosen darkness in which she had incarcerated herself. Then she said with harsh deliberation: 'I shall never see him again.'

'No, you will never see him again. When this is done, we are going home.'

'But you,' she said, 'yes, I have had it in mind all this time that you would be back. Sooner or later, you would be back. As well, perhaps! Things have gone far beyond my reckoning now. Well, say what you have come to say. I would as lief be silent.'

'That you cannot do,' said Cadfael. 'It is your story.'

'Then be my chronicler. Tell it! Remind me! Let me hear how it will sound in my confessor's ears, if any priest takes my confession ever again.' She stretched out one long hand suddenly, waving him imperiously to a seat, but he remained standing where he could see her most clearly, and she made no move to evade his eyes, and no concessions to the fixity of his regard. Her beautiful, proud face was composed and mute, admitting nothing, denying nothing. Only the burning of her dark eyes in their deep settings was eloquent, and even that in a language he could not quite translate.

'You know all too well what you did, all those years ago,' said Cadfael. 'You executed a fearful punishment upon Haluin for daring to love your daughter and getting her with child. You pursued him even into the cloister where your enmity had driven him – all too soon, but the young are quick to despair. You forced him to provide you with the means of abortion, and you sent him word, afterwards, that it had killed both mother and child. That awful guilt

178

you have visited upon him all these years, to be his torment lifelong. Did you speak?'

'No,' she said. 'Go on! You have barely begun.'

'True, I have barely begun. That draught of hyssop and fleur de luce that you got from him – it never was used. Its purpose was only to poison him, it did no harm to any other. What did you do with it? Pour it away into the ground? No, long before ever you demanded the herbs from him, as soon as you had driven him out of your house, I daresay, you had hustled Bertrade away here to Elford, and married her to Edric Vivers. It must have been so, certainly it was done in time to give her child, when it was born, a credible if unlikely father. No doubt the old man prided himself on still being potent enough to get a child. Why should anyone question the birth-date, since you had acted so quickly?'

She had not stirred or flinched, her eyes never left his face, admitting nothing, denying nothing.

'Were you never afraid,' he asked, 'that someone, somehow, should let fall within reach even of the cloister that Bertrade de Clary was wife to Edric Vivers, and not safely in her grave? That she had borne her old husband a daughter? It needed only a chance traveller with a gossiping tongue.'

'There was no such risk,' she said simply. 'What contact was there ever between Shrewsbury and Hales? None, until he suffered his fall and conceived his pilgrimage. Much less likely there should ever be dealings with manors in another shire. There was no such risk.'

'Well, let us continue. Living you took her away and gave her to a husband. Living the child was born. So much mercy at least you had on the girl – why none for him? Why such bitter and vindictive hate, that you should conceive so terrible a revenge? Not for your daughter's wrongs, no! Why should he not have been considered a suitable match for her in the first place? He came of good family, he was heir to a

179

fine manor, if he had not taken the cowl. What was it you held so much against him? You were a beautiful woman, accustomed to admiration and homage. Your lord was in Palestine. And I well remember Haluin as he first came to me, eighteen years old, not yet tonsured. I saw him as you had been seeing him for some few years in your celibate solitude – he was comely . . .'

He let it rest there, for her long, resolute lips had parted on deliberate affirmation at last. She had listened to him unwaveringly, making no effort to halt him, and no complaint. Now she responded.

'Too comely!' she said. 'I was not used to being denied, I did not even know how to sue. And he was too innocent to read me aright. How such children offend without offence! So if I could not have him,' she said starkly, 'she should not. No woman ever should, but not she of all women.'

It was said, she let it stand, adding nothing in extenuation, and having said it, she sat contemplating it, seeing again as in another woman what she could now no longer feel with the same intensity, the longing and the anger.

'There is more,' said Cadfael, 'much more. There is the matter of your woman Edgytha. Edgytha was the one trusted confidante you needed, the one who knew the truth. It was she who was sent to Vivers with Bertrade. Utterly loyal and devoted to you, she kept your secret and abetted your revenge all these years. And you trusted in her to keep it for ever. So all was well for you, until Roscelin and Helisende grew up, and came to love each other no longer as playmates, but as man and woman. Knowing but forgetting that the world would hold such a love as poisoned, guilty, forbidden by the church. When the secret became a barrier between them, where no barrier need have been, when Roscelin was banished to Elford, and marriage with de Perronet threatened a final separation, then Edgytha could bear it no longer. She came running here in the night – not to Roscelin, but to you! To beg you to tell the truth at last, or to give her leave to tell it for you.'

'I have wondered,' said Adelais, 'how she knew that I was here within her reach.'

'She knew because I told her. All unwitting I sent her out that night to plead with you to lift the shadow from two innocent children. By merest chance it was mentioned that here in Elford we had spoken with you. *I* sent her running to you and to her death, as it was Haluin who caused you to come here, in haste to ward him off from any dangerous discovery. We have been the instruments of your undoing, who never wished you anything but well. Now you had better consider what is left to you that can be saved.'

'Go on!' she said harshly. 'You have not finished yet.'

'No, not yet. So Edgytha came to plead with you to do right. And you refused her! You sent her running back to Vivers in despair. And what befell her on the way you know.'

She did not deny it. Her face was bleak and set, but her eyes never wavered.

'Would she have come out with the truth, even against your prohibition? Neither you nor I will ever know the answer to that. But someone equally loyal to you overheard enough to understand the threat to you if she did. Someone feared her, followed and silenced her. Oh, not you! You had other tools to use. But did you speak a word in their ears?'

'No!' said Adelais. 'That I never did! Unless my face spoke for me. And if it did, it lied. I never would have harmed her.'

'I believe you. But which of them was it followed her? Father and son alike, they would die for you without question, and without question one of them has killed for you. And they are gone from here. Back to Hales? No, I doubt that, it is not far enough. How distant is your son's remotest manor?'

'You will not find them,' said Adelais with certainty. 'As for which of them did the thing I might have prevented, I do not know, I want never to know. I stopped their mouths when they would have spoken. To what end? That guilt, like all the rest, is mine alone, I will not cede any scruple of it. Yes, I sent them away. They will not pay my debts for me. Burying Edgytha with reverence is poor atonement. Confession, penance, even absolution cannot restore a life.'

'There is one amend that can still be made,' said Cadfael. 'Moreover, I think a price has been exacted from you, no less than from Haluin, all these years. Do not forget that I saw your face when he presented his ruined body before you. I heard your voice as you cried out on him: "What have they done to you?" All that you did to him you did also to yourself, and once done, it could not be undone. Now you may be free of it, if you choose to deliver yourself.'

'Go on!' said Adelais, though she knew well enough what was to come. He recognised it by the composure with which she had borne herself throughout. Surely she had been waiting here in her half-lit room for the finger of God to point.

'Helisende is not Edric's daughter, but Haluin's. There is not a drop of Vivers blood in her veins. There is nothing to stand in the way if she wishes to marry Roscelin. Whether those two would do well to marry, who knows? But at least the shadow of incestuous affection can and must be lifted from them. The truth must out, since it is out already at Farewell. Haluin and Bertrade are there together, making their peace, making each the other's peace, and Helisende their child is with them, and the truth is already out of its grave.'

She knew, she had known ever since the old woman's death, that it must come to that at last, and if she had deliberately averted her eyes and refused to acknowledge it, she could no longer do so. Nor was she the woman to delegate a hard thing to others, once her mind was made up, nor to do things by halves, whether for good or ill.

He would not prompt her. He drew back from her to leave her space and time, and stood apart, watching her disciplined stillness, and measuring in his mind the bitter toll of eighteen years of silence, of pitilessly contained hate and love. The first words he had heard from her now, even at this extreme, had been of Haluin, and still he heard the vibration of pain in her voice as she cried aloud: 'What have they done to you?'

Adelais got up abruptly from her chair and crossed with long, fierce steps to the window, to fling back the shutter and let in air and light and cold. She stood for a while looking out at the quiet court, and the pale sky dappled with little clouds, and the green gauze veiling the branches of the trees beyond the enclave wall. When she turned to him again he saw her face in full, clear light, and saw as in a dual vision both her imperishable beauty and the dust time had cast upon it, the taut lines of her long throat fallen slack, the grey of ashes in her coiled black hair, the lines that had gathered about mouth and eyes, the net of fine veins marring cheeks which had once been smooth ivory. And she was strong, she would not lightly relinquish her hold of the world and go gently out of it. She would live long, and rage against the relentless assault of old age until death at once defeated and released her. By her very nature Adelais's penance was assured.

'No!' she said, with abrupt, imperious authority, as though he had advanced some suggestion with which she was in absolute disagreement. 'No, I want no advocate, there shall no man rid me of any part of what is mine. What now needs to be told, *I* will tell. No other! Whether it ever would have been told, if you had never come near me – you with your hand for ever at Haluin's elbow, and your temperate eyes that I could never read – do I know? Do you? That is of no account now. What is left to be done, *I* will do.'

'Command me to go,' said Cadfael, 'and I will go. You do not need me.'

'Not as advocate, no. As witness, perhaps! Why should you be cheated of the ending? Yes!' she said, glittering. 'You shall ride with me, and see it ended. I owe you a fulfilment as I owe God a death.'

He rode with her, as she had decreed. Why not? He had to return to Farewell, and by way of Vivers was as good a road as any. And once she had resolved upon action there could be no delay and no denial.

She rode astride, booted and spurred like a man, she who in the common progressions of her recent years had been content to go decorously pillion behind a groom, as was fitting for a dame of her age and dignity. She rode with the lordly confidence of a man, erect and easy in the saddle, her bridle hand held low. And she rode fast but steadily, advancing upon her losses as vigorously as upon her gains.

Cadfael, riding at her side, could not but wonder whether she still felt tempted to hold back some part of the truth, to cover herself from the last betrayal. But the smouldering calm of her face spoke against it. There would be no evasion, no appeal, no excuse. What she had done she had done, and would as starkly declare. And if she repented it, only God would ever know.

184

Chapter Thirteen

HEY RODE in at the gate of Vivers an hour after noon. The gate stood open, and the turmoil within had subsided, there was no more than the normal to-and-froing in the court. Evidently the abbess's messenger had been received and believed, and whether gladly or reluctantly, Cenred had fallen in with Helisende's wish to be left alone for a while in her sanctuary. With one search abandoned, Audemar's men would be free to pursue a murderer. One they would never find! In the night and the snow, who could have been abroad to witness that knife-stroke in the woods, and put a name or a face to the slayer? Even if there had been a witness, who in these parts, apart from Audemar's own household, would recognise a groom from distant Hales?

Cenred's steward was crossing the court when Adelais reined in, and he came in haste, recognising the mother of his lord's overlord, to help her down, but she was out of the saddle before he could reach her. She let down her kilted skirts, and looked about her for any of her son's people. Cadfael had seen for himself that the hunters had not returned to Elford, nor were they in evidence here. For a moment she frowned, impatient at the prospect of having to

185

wait and contain still all that she had to say. Once resolved, it displeased her to be baulked. She looked beyond the steward's deep reverence towards the hall.

'Is your lord within?'

'He is, madam. Will you be pleased to enter?'

'And my son?'

'He, too, my lady. He came back only some minutes since, his men are still out with ours, questioning in every house for miles around.'

'Waste of time!' she said, rather to herself than to him, and shut her lips grimly on the reason. 'Well, so much the better! They are both here. No, you need not tell them I have come. That I'll do for myself. As for Brother Cadfael, this time he comes in attendance on me, not as a guest.'

Doubtful if the steward had even cast a glance at the second rider until this moment, but he did so now, speculating, Cadfael supposed, what had brought one Benedictine visitor back so soon, and in particular without his companion. But there was no time for enquiry. Adelais had set off vigorously towards the steps that led up to the hall, and Cadfael followed dutifully, as if he were indeed her domestic chaplain, leaving the steward staring after them in doubt and wonder.

In the hall the midday meal was past, and the servants busy clearing away the dishes and stacking the tables aside. Adelais walked through them without a word or a glance, straight to the curtained door of the inner chamber. A murmur of voices, dulled by the hangings, came from within, Cenred's deep tones distinguishable beneath the lighter, younger voice of Jean de Perronet. The suitor had not withdrawn, but intended to wait out his time doggedly if not patiently. Just as well, Cadfael reflected. He had a right to know how formidable an obstacle was now placed in his way. Fair is fair. De Perronet had done nothing dishonourable, fair dealing was his due.

186

Adelais swept the curtain aside and flung open the door. They were all there, in muted conference over a situation which left them frustrated and helpless, trapped in inaction, since even the gesture of sending out men to try and trace Edgytha's murderer was by this time foredoomed to be fruitless. Had any man in the region known anything, it would have been told already. And if Audemar ever thought to number over his mother's household servants, and level a suspicious finger at the missing, she would stand immovably between him and them. Wherever Lothair and Luc might now be, however confounded and chastened by her revulsion from what they had mistakenly done for her, she would not let the price be charged against them which she held to be her debt.

At the sound of the door opening they had all turned their heads sharply to see who came in, for her entrance was too abrupt and confident by far for any of the servants. Her gaze swept round the circle of surprised faces, Audemar and Cenred at the table with wine before them, Emma apart at her embroidery frame, but paying no attention to the work, rather waiting with strung nerves for events to unfold in some more comfortable form, and life to return to its level course. And the stranger – Cadfael saw that Adelais could never before have set eyes on Jean de Perronet. On him her glance halted, considering and identifying the bridegroom. Very faintly and briefly her long lips contorted in a dour smile, before her eyes passed to Roscelin.

The boy sat withdrawn into a corner where he could hold all the assembled company in his eye, as if he contemplated imminent battle, and sat prepared and armed, stiff and erect on the bench against the tapestried wall, head reared and lips tightly set. He had accepted, it seemed, however much against his will, Helisende's wish to be left in peace at Farewell, but he had not forgiven any of these conspirators who had planned to match her in secret, and cheat him of even the perverse hope he had to sustain him. His grievance against his parents extended by contagion to de Perronet, even to Audemar de Clary, to whose house he had been banished to remove the obstacle to their plans. How could he be sure Audemar had not been a party to more than that banishment? A face by nature open, good-humoured and bright now stared upon them all closed, suspicious and inimical. Adelais looked at him longer than at any. Another youth too comely for his own good, attracting unfortunate love as the flower draws the bee.

The moment of blank surprise was over. Cenred was on his feet in hospitable haste, advancing with hand out-stretched to take the visitor by the hand, and lead her to a seat at the table.

'Madam, welcome to my house! You do me honour!'

And Audemar, less pleased, half frowning: 'Madam, what brings you here? And unattended!' It suited him better that a mother of so formidable a character should exile her-self to the distant manor of Hales, and keep her own court there. Seeing them thus face to face, Cadfael found a strong likeness between the two. Doubtless there was affection between them, but once the son was grown it would be hard for these two to live together in one household. 'There was no need,' said Audemar, 'for you to ride over here, there is nothing you can do that is not already being done.'

Adelais had let Cenred's attentive hand persuade her into the centre of the room, but there she resisted further move-ment and stood to be seen clearly and alone, with an author-itative gesture freeing her hand.

'Yes,' she said, 'there is need,' and again cast a long glance round all the watching faces. 'And I am not unattended. Brother Cadfael is my escort. He comes from the abbey of Farewell, and will be returning there when he leaves us.' She looked from one young man to the other, from the favoured bridegroom to the frustrated lover, both

188

of them eyeing her warily, conscious of impending revelations, but unable to hazard at what might be coming.

'I am glad,' said Adelais, 'to find you all assembled thus. I have that to say that I will say only once.'

It could never have been a problem for her, thought Cadfael, watching, to hold the attention of everyone about her, wherever she went. In every room she entered she was at once the focal point, the dominant in every company. Now they were silent every one, waiting on her word.

'As I have heard, Cenred,' she said, 'you intended, two days ago, to marry your sister – your half-sister I should say – to this young gentleman. For reason enough, the church and the world would agree, seeing she had become all too dear to your son Roscelin, and he to her, and a marriage that would take her far away removed also the shadow of such an unholy attachment from your house and from your heir. Pardon me if I use too plain words, it's late for any others. No blame to you, knowing only what you knew.'

'What more was there to know?' said Cenred, bewildered.

'Plain words will do very well. They are close blood-kin, as you know well! Would not you have taken the same measure to ward off such an evil from your grandchild, as I intended from my sister? She is as close a charge to me as my own son, and as dear. She is your grandchild. I well remember my father's second marriage. I recall the day you brought the bride here, and my father's pride in the child she bore him. Since he is long gone, I owe Helisende a father's care no less than a brother's. Certainly I sought to protect both her and my son. I still desire the same. This is but a check on the way. Messire de Perronet has not withdrawn his suit, nor I my sanction.'

Audemar had risen from his place, and stood eyeing his mother with close-drawn brows and an unrevealing face. 'What more is there to know?' he said levelly, and for all his

189

voice was equable and low there was doubt and displeasure in it, and a woman of less implacable will might have found it menacing. She stared back at him eye to eye, and was unmoved.

'This! That you trouble needless. There is no barrier, Cenred, between your son and Helisende but the barrier you have conjured up. There is no peril of incest if they were wedded and bedded this very night. Helisende is not your sister, Cenred, she is not your father's daughter. There is no drop of Vivers blood in her veins.'

'But this is foolishness!' protested Cenred, shaking his head over so incredible a claim. 'All this household has known the child from birth. What you say is impossible. Why bring forth such a story, when all my people can bear witness she was born to my father's lawful wife, in their marriage bed, here in my house.'

'And conceived in mine,' said Adelais. 'I can't wonder if none of you thought to count the days, I had lost no time. My daughter was already with child when I brought her here to her marriage.'

Then they were all on their feet, all but Emma, shrinking appalled behind her embroidery frame, shaken by the out-cries of anger and disbelief that clashed about her like con-trary winds. Cenred was stricken breathless, but de Perronet was clamouring that this was false, and the lady out of her wits, and Roscelin had sprung to confront him, glittering, half incoherent, swinging about from his rival to Adelais, pleading, demanding, that what she said be truth. Until Audemar pounded the table thunderously with his fist, and raised an imperious voice over all to demand silence. And throughout, Adelais stood erect and unmoving as stone, and let the outcries whirl about her unacknowledged.

And then there was silence, no more exclaiming, not a sound, hardly a breath, while they stared upon her intently

190

and long, as if the truth or falsity of what she said might be read in her face if a man held still and unblinking long enough.

'Do you fully know, madam, what you are saying?' asked Audemar, his voice now measured and low.

'Excellently well, my son! I know what I am saying, I know it is truth. I know what I have done, I know it was foully done. It needs none of you to say it, *I* say it. But I did it, and neither you nor I can undo it. Yes, I deceived the lord Edric, yes, I compelled my daughter, yes, I planted a bastard child in this house. Or, if you choose, I took measures to protect my daughter's good name and estate and ensure her honourable status, as Cenred wills to do for a sister. Did Edric ever regret his bargain? I think not. Did he get joy out of his supposed child? Surely he did. All these years I have let well or ill alone, but now God has disposed otherwise, and I am not sorry.'

'If this is true,' said Cenred, drawing deep breath, 'Edgytha knew of it. She came here with Bertrade, if you are telling truth now, so late, then she must have known.'

'She did know,' said Adelais. 'And sorry the day I refused her when she begged me to tell the truth earlier, and sorrier still this day when she cannot stand here and bear me witness. But here is one who can. Brother Cadfael is come from the abbey of Farewell, where Helisende now is, and her mother is there with her. And by strange chance,' she said, 'so is her father. There is nowhere now to hide from the truth. I declare it in my own despite.'

'You have hidden from it long enough, madam, it seems,' said Audemar grimly.

'So I have, and make no virtue of revealing it now, when it is already out of its grave.'

There was a brief, profound silence before Cenred asked slowly: 'You say he is there now – her father? There at Farewell with them both?'

191

'From me,' she said, 'it can only be hearsay. Brother Cadfael will answer you.'

'I have seen them there, all three,' said Cadfael. 'It is truth.'

'Then who is he?' demanded Audemar. 'Who is her father?'

Adelais took up her story, never lowering her eyes. 'He was once a young clerk in my household, of good birth, only a year older than my daughter. He desired to be accepted as a suitor for her hand. I refused him. They – took measures to force my hand. No, perhaps I do them both wrong, what they did may not have been calculated, but done in desperation, for she was as lost in love as he. I dismissed him from my service, and brought her away here in haste, to a match the lord Edric had mooted a year or more earlier. And I lied, telling the lover that she was dead. Very blackly I lied to him, saying both Bertrade and her child had died, when we tried to rid her of her burden. He never knew until now that he had a daughter.'

'Then how comes it,' demanded Cenred, 'that he has found her out now, and in so unlikely a place? This whole wild story comes so strangely, thus out of nowhere, I cannot believe in it.'

'You had better come to terms with it,' she said, 'for neither you nor I can escape the truth or amend it. He has found her by the merciful dispensation of God. What more do you need?'

Cenred swung upon Cadfael in irritated appeal. 'Brother, as you have been my guest in this house, tell what you know of this matter. After so many years, is this indeed a true tale? And how came these three to meet again now, at the end of all?'

'It is a true tale,' said Cadfael. 'And truly they have met, by now they will have talked together. He has found them both because, believing his love dead, and having touched

192

hands with his own death a few months ago, and been spared, he turned his thoughts to mortality, and determined at least, since he could never see her again in this world, to make a pilgrimage to her grave and pray for her peace in the next. And not finding her at Hales, where he supposed she must be, he came here, my lord, to your manor of Elford, where those of your line are buried. Now, on the way home again, by the grace of God we asked lodging last night at the abbey of Farewell. There the lady who was your sister is presently serving as instructress to the novices of the bishop's new foundation. And there Helisende fled for sanctuary from too painful stresses. So they are all under one roof at last.'

After a moment of silence Audemar said softly: '*We* asked lodging last night at the abbey of Farewell' – You have said almost enough, yet add one thing more – name him!'

'He entered the cloister, long ago. He is a brother with me in the abbey of Saint Peter and Saint Paul, at Shrewsbury. You have seen him, my lord, that same brother who came to Elford with me, on crutches every step of the way. Monk and priest, the same, my lord Cenred, whom you asked to marry Helisende to the man you had chosen for her. His name is Haluin.'

Now they had all begun dazedly to believe what they could not yet fully grasp in all its implications. With glazed glances they stared within at the slow realisation of what this must mean to them. To Roscelin, quivering and glowing like a newly lighted torch, the sudden dizzy lightness and liberty of guilt and grief lifted from him, the very air of the day intoxicating as wine, the world expanded into a vast brightness of hope and joy that dazzled his eyes and muted his tongue. To de Perronet, the stinging challenge of finding himself faced with a formidable rival where he had

193

looked for no conflict, and the instinctive stiffening of his pride and determination to fight for the threatened prize with all his might. To Cenred the overturning of all his family memories, a father made to seem belittled, even senile, by his fond acceptance of such a deception, a sister abruptly withdrawn into a stranger, an interloper without rights in his house. To Emma, silent and fearful in her corner, the grief of an offence against her lord, and the loss of one she had looked upon almost as her own daughter.

'So she is no sister of mine,' said Cenred heavily, rather to himself than to any other, and as quickly repeated it with sudden anger to them all: 'She is no sister of mine!'

'None,' said Adelais. 'But until now she believed herself so. It is not her fault, never cast blame on her.'

'She is not kin to me. I owe her nothing, neither dowry nor lands. She has no claim on me.' He said it bitterly rather than vengefully, lamenting the abrupt severance of a strong affection.

'None. But she is kin to me,' said Adelais. 'Her mother's dower lands went to Polesworth when she took the veil, but Helisende is my granddaughter and my heiress. The lands I hold in my own right will go to her. She will not be penniless.' She looked at de Perronet as she spoke, and smiled, but wryly. No need to make the lovers' path too smooth by rendering the girl less profitable, and therefore less attractive in the rival's eyes.

'Madam, you mistake me,' said Cenred with muted fury. 'This house has been her home, she will still think of it as home. Where else is there for her? It is we here who are suddenly cut off, like lopped limbs. Her father and mother, both, are in the cloister, and what guidance, what care has she ever had from you? Kin to us or not, she belongs here at Vivers.'

'But nothing prevents now,' cried Roscelin triumphantly. 'I may approach her, I may lawfully ask for her, there is no barrier now. We've done no wrong, there's no shadow over us, no ban between us. I'll go and bring her home. She'll come, blithely she'll come! I knew,' he exulted, his blue eyes brilliant with vindicated joy, 'I knew we did no wrong in loving, never, never! It was *you* persuaded me I sinned. Sir, let me go and fetch her home!'

At that de Perronet took fire in his turn, with a hiss like a sulphur match flaring, and took two rapid strides foward to confront the boy. 'You leap too soon and too far, my friend! Your rights are no better than mine. I do not withdraw my suit, I urge it, I will pursue it with my might.'

'And so you may,' exulted Roscelin, too drunk with relief and delight to be ungenerous or take offence. 'I don't grudge any man his say, but on fair terms now, you and I and any who come, and we shall see what Helisende replies.' But he knew what her reply would be, his very certainty was offence, though it meant none, and de Perronet had his hand on his dagger and hotter words mounting in his throat when Audemar smote the table and bellowed them both into silence.

'Hush your noise! Am I overlord here, or no? The girl is not without kin, for she is niece to *me*. If there is anyone here who has rights in her and a duty towards her – any who has not farmed out both upon another man long since! – it is I, and I say that if Cenred so wishes, then I place her here in his fosterage, with all the rights he has exercised as her kinsman all these years. And in the matter of her marriage both he and I will take good care what is best for her, but never against her will. But now, let her be! She has asked for time untroubled, and she shall have it. When she is ready to return, I will fetch her home.'

'Content!' said Cenred, breathing deeply. 'I am content! I could ask no better.'

'And Brother . . .' Audemar turned to Cadfael. He had the entire issue in his hands now, over all matters here his

195

writ ran, and what he ordained would be done. The least damage was his design, as his mother's had been the ultimate destruction. 'Brother, if you are going back to Farewell, tell them there what I have said. What's done is done, all that waits to be done shall be in daylight, openly. Roscelin,' he ordered sharply, turning on the boy restless and glittering with the joy of his release, 'have the horses readied, we ride for Elford. You are still in my service until I please to dismiss you, and I have not forgotten that you went forth without leave. Let me have no further cause for displeasure.'

But his voice was dry, and neither words nor look cast the least shadow upon Roscelin's exultant brightness. He bent his knee in the briefest of reverences by way of acknowledging the order, and went blithely to do his lord's bidding. The wind of his flight swung the curtain at the door, and sent a current of outer air floating across the chamber like a sigh.

Audemar looked last and longest at Adelais, who stood with eyes steady and dark upon his face, waiting his judgement.

'Madam, you will ride back with me to Elford. You have done what you came here to do.'

Nevertheless, it was Cadfael who got to horse first. No one was any longer in need of him here, and whatever natural curiosity he might feel concerning the family adjustments still to be made, and perhaps less easily accomplished than decreed, must be for ever contained, since he was unlikely to pass this way again. He reclaimed his horse without haste, and mounted, and was ambling towards the gate when Roscelin broke away from the grooms who were busy saddling Audemar's horses, and came running to his stirrup.

'Brother Cadfael . . .' He was lost for a moment for words, since his wonder and happiness were beyond words.

and shook his head and laughed over his own incoherence. 'Tell her! Tell her we're free, we need not change, there's no one can blacken us now . . .'

'Son,' said Cadfael heartily, 'by this time she knows it as well as you.'

'And tell her soon, very soon, I shall come for her. Oh, yes, I know,' he said confidently, seeing Cadfael's raised brows, 'but it's me he'll send. I know him! He'd rather a kinsman he knows and can rely on, his own man, with lands bordering his own, than any lordling from distant parts. And my father won't stand between us now. Why should he, when it solves everything? What's changed, except what needed changing?'

And there was something in that, Cadfael reflected, looking down from the saddle into the young, ardent face. What was changed was the replacement of falsity by truth, and however hard the assimilation might be, it must be for the better. Truth can be costly, but in the end it never falls short of value for the price paid.

'And tell him,' said Roscelin earnestly, 'the lame brother . . . her father . . .' His voice hung on the word with wonder and awe. 'Tell him I'm glad, say I owe him more than ever can be repaid. And tell him he need never fret for her happiness, for I'll give my life to it.'

Chapter Fourteen

T ABOUT the same time that Cadfael dismounted in the court of Farewell, Adelais de Clary sat with her son in his private chamber at Elford. There had been a long and heavy silence between them. The afternoon was drawing to its close, the light dimming, and he had sent for no candles.

'There is a matter,' he said at length, stirring out of his mourne stillness, 'which has hardly been touched on yet. It was to you, madam, that the old woman came. And you sent her away with a short answer. To her death! Was that at your orders?'

Without passion she said: 'No!'

'I will not ask what you know of it. To what end? She is dead. But I do not like your manner of dealing, and I choose to have no more ado with it. Tomorrow, madam, you shall return to Hales. Hales you may have for your hermitage. But do not come back to this house, ever, for you will not be admitted. The doors of every manor of mine except Hales are henceforth closed to you.'

Indifferently she said: 'As you will, it is all one to me. I need only a little space, and may not need it long. Hales will do very well.'

199

'Then, madam, take your leave when you will. You shall have a safe escort on the road, seeing,' he said with bitter meaning, 'that you have parted with your own grooms. And a litter, if you prefer to hide your face. Let it not be said that I left you to travel defenceless, like an old woman venturing out alone by night.'

Adelais rose from her stool and went out from him without a word.

In the hall the servants had begun to kindle the first torches and set them in their sconces, but in every corner, and in the smoky beams of the lofty roof, darkness gathered and clung, draped cobwebs of shadow.

Roscelin was standing over the central fire on its flagged hearth, driving the heel of his boot into it to tease it into life after the damped-down hours of the day. He still had Audemar's cloak over his arm, the capuchon dangling from one hand. The light from the reviving flames gilded his stooping face into gold, smooth-cheeked, with elegant bones and a brow as fair as a girl's, and on his dreaming lips the softest and most beguiling of smiles bore witness to his deep happiness. His flaxen hair swung against his cheek, and parted above the suave nape of his neck, the most revealing beauty of the young. For a moment she stood apart in the shadows to watch him, herself unnoticed, for the pleasure and the pain of experiencing again the irresistible attraction, the unbearable bliss and anguish of beholding beauty and youth pass by and depart. Too sharp and sweet a reminder of things ended long ago, and for years believed forgotten, only to burn up into new life, like the phoenix, when a door opened, and confronted her with the ruin the years had left of the beloved being.

She passed by silently, so that he should not hear, and turn upon her the too radiant, too exultant blue eyes. The dark eyes that she remembered, deeply and delicately set beneath arched black brows, had never looked so, never for her. Always dutiful, always wary, often lowered in her presence.

Adelais went out into the chill of the evening, and turned towards her own apartments. Well, it was over. The fire was ashes. She would never see him again.

'Yes, I have seen her,' said Brother Haluin. 'Yes, I have spoken with her. I have touched her hand, it is warm flesh, woman's flesh, no illusion. The portress brought me into her presence all unprepared, I could neither speak nor move. She had been so long dead to me. Even that glimpse I had of her in the garth among the birds . . . Afterwards, when you were gone, I could not be sure I had not dreamed it. But to touch her, to have her call me by my name . . . And she was glad . . .

'Her case was not as mine, though God knows I would not say her burden has been any lighter. But she knew I was man alive, she knew where I was, and what I was, and for her there was no guilt, she had done no wrong but in loving me. And she could speak. Such words she offered me, Cadfael! 'Here is one,' she said, 'who has already embraced you, with good right. Now with good right embrace her. She is your daughter.' Can you conceive such a miracle? Giving the child to me by the hand she said it. Helisende, my daughter – not dead! Alive and young and kind and fresh as a flower. And I thought I had destroyed her, destroyed them both! Of her own sweet will the child kissed me. Even if it was only from pity – it must have been pity, how could she love one she never knew? – but even if it was only from pity, it was a gift beyond gold.

'And she will be happy. She can love as it best pleases her, and marry where her heart is. Once she called me 'Father', but I think it was as a priest, as first she knew me. Even so it was good to hear and will be sweet to remember.

'This hour we three have had together repays all the

201

eighteen years, even though there was so little said between us. The heart could hold no more. She is gone to her duties now, Bertrade. So must I to mine, soon . . . very soon . . . tomorrow . . .'

Cadfael had sat silent through the long, stumbling, eloquent monologue of his friend's revelation, broken by long pauses in which Haluin was rapt away again into a trance of wonder. Not one word of the abominable thing that had been done to him, wantonly, cruelly, that was washed clean away out of mind by the joy of its undoing, without a lingering thought of blame or forgiveness. And that was the last and most ironic judgement on Adelais de Clary.

'Shall we go to Vespers?' said Cadfael. 'The bell has gone, they'll all be in their places by now, we can creep in unnoticed.'

From their chosen dim corner in the church Cadfael scanned the young, clear faces of the sisters, and lingered long upon Sister Benedicta, who had once been Bertrade de Clary. Beside him Haluin's low, happy voice intoned the responses and prayers, but what Cadfael was hearing in his own mind was the same voice bleeding words slowly and haltingly, in the darkness of the forester's hay-loft, before dawn. There in her stall, serene, fulfilled and content, stood the woman he had tried to describe. 'She was not beautiful, as her mother was. She had not that dark radiance, but something more kindly. There was nothing dark or secret in her, but everything open and sunlit, like a flower. She was not afraid of anything – not then. She trusted everyone. She had never been betrayed – not then. Only once, and she died of it.'

But no, she had not died. And certainly at this moment, devout and dutiful, there was nothing dark or secret in her. The oval face shone serene, as she celebrated with joy the mercy of God, after years. Without any lingering regret; her

202

contentment was without blemish. The vocation she had undertaken unblessed, and laboured at against the grain, perhaps, all these years, surely reached its true wholeness only now, in the revelation of grace. She would not have turned back now even for that first love. There was no need. There are seasons of love. Theirs had passed beyond the storms of spring and the heat of summer into the golden calm of the first autumn days, before the leaves begin to fall. Bertrade de Clary looked as Brother Haluin looked, confirmed and invulnerable in the peace of the spirit. Henceforth presence was unnecessary, and passion irrelevant. They were eased of the past, and both of them had work to do for the future, all the more eagerly and thoroughly for knowing, each of them, that the other lived and laboured in the same vineyard.

In the morning, after Prime, their farewells made, they set out on the long journey home.

The sisters were in chapter when Cadfael and Haluin took scrip and crutches and went out from the guest-hall, but the girl Helisende went with them to the gate. It seemed to Cadfael that all these faces about him had been washed clear of every shadow and every doubt, they had all of them that stunned brightness, astonished by the good that had befallen them. Now it could be seen more clearly how like were father and daughter, so many of the marks of the years having been smoothed from Haluin's face.

Helisende embraced him without words at parting, fervent but shy. However they had spent the previous day, whatever confidences had been exchanged, she could not so quickly know him of her own knowledge, only through her mother's eyes, but she knew of him that he was gentle and of pleasing person and address, and that his eruption into her life had freed her from a nightmare of guilt and loss, and she would always remember and think of him so, with pleasure and gratitude not so far distant from love. Profit enough, even if he never saw her again.

'God keep you, Father!' said Helisende.

It was the first and the last time that she gave him that title not as a priest but as a man, but it was a gift that would last him a lifetime.

They halted for the night at Hargedon, where the canons of Hampton had a grange, in a countryside slowly being recovered out of the waste that had followed the Norman settlement. Only now, after sixty years, was ploughland being resurrected out of the scrub, and an occasional hamlet being raised where tracks crossed, or rivers provided water for a mill. The comparative security offered by the presence of the canons, steward and servants had drawn others to settle close by, and there were now assarts being hewn out of the neglected woods by enterprising younger sons. But still it was sparsely populated territory, level, lonely and in the evening light melancholy. Yet with every laboured step taken westward across this mournful plain Brother Haluin's brightness increased, his pace quickened, and his colour flushed into eagerness.

From the narrow unshuttered window in the loft he looked out westward into a night full of stars. Nearer to Shrewsbury, where the hills began to heave their fleece: towards the mountains of Wales, earth and sky balanced in harmony, but here the vault above looked immense, and the earth of men suppressed and shadowy. The brilliance of the stars, the blackness of the space between, spoke of a touch of frost in the air, but promised a fine day for the morrow.

'And you never feel,' said Cadfael quietly, 'any desire to look back over your shoulder?'

'No,' said Haluin tranquilly. 'No need. There behind me all is well. All is very well. There is nothing now for me to do there, everything where I am bound. We are sister an brother now. We ask nothing more, we want for nothing more. Now I can bring a whole heart to God. I'm glad beyond measure that he cast me down, to raise me renewed to his service.'

There was a long, untroubled silence, while he continued to stare out into the clear night with a kind of bright hunger in his face. 'I left a leaf half-finished when we set out for Hales,' he said meditatively. 'I thought to be back to complete it long before this. I hope Anselm has not given it to someone else. It was a capital N for the 'Nunc Dimittis', still wanting half the colours.'

'It will be waiting for you,' Cadfael assured him.

'Aelfric is good, but he doesn't know my intent, he might overdo the gold.' His voice was soft and practical and young.

'Leave fretting,' said Cadfael. 'Possess your soul three days more in patience, and you'll have brush and pen in hand again, and get back to work. And so must I to my herbs, for the medicine cupboards will be running low by this time. Lie down, lad, and get your rest. There are more miles waiting for you tomorrow.'

A soft wind from the west blew in through the open window, and Haluin lifted his head and sniffed the air like a high-bred horse scenting his stable.

'How good it is,' he said, 'to be going home!'

HOW TO HAVE AN OBEDIENT DOG

by

Jackie Marriott

PAPERFRONTS
ELLIOT RIGHT WAY BOOKS
KINGSWOOD, SURREY, U.K.

KT-377-459

Typeset in 10/12pt Times by County Typesetters, Margate, Kent.

Made and Printed in Great Britain by Cox & Wyman Ltd., Reading, Berkshire.

DEDICATION

To the first two dogs I owned during my adult life, Simon and Rupert, two little "terrors" who set me on the dog training road. Also, to my beloved Brumas, my first Bernese, who taught me, and gave me, so much.

THANKS

To my husband and fellow Dog Trainer, Vic, whose help and assistance has, as usual, been invaluable, and to Sandy Enzerink B.V.M.S. M.R.C.V.S. for checking the medical details and for her expertise in caring for my animals' health.

CONTENTS

big hole in the settee. You return home and your dog, thrilled to see you, comes rushing up to welcome you. You spot the ruined settee. With a face like thunder and a voice to match, you shout and scream at him, perhaps even hitting him. What have you taught him? You've taught him that when you come home, the best course of action for him to take is to run and keep well out of the way, as you're so cross when you come home. He has no way of knowing that his act of demolition, maybe done more than an hour before you returned, is the reason for your temper. How can he? He's forgotten all about it, the second he stopped chewing.

O.K. so what *should* you have done? In you come, dog rushes up to greet you. Having spotted the ruined settee, ignore it, cuddle your dog and let him welcome you home. Next, go up to the settee, *showing no sign of anger whatsoever*. Now encourage him to start chewing the settee! Sounds daft! No, because as he puts his teeth to it, that's when you correct him. Show him at that instant that what he's doing is wrong. He will immediately associate your anger with the action he is doing, i.e. chewing the settee. Apply this to anything he does which you dislike, i.e. digging holes in the garden, foraging in the rubbish bin, chewing your shoes etc., and he will instantly learn what is allowed and what isn't.

All the dog wants is to know where he stands and to be loved by you. All the time he is being good, love him to pieces. He will only want to do those things which get a favourable response from you and will not want to repeat any action which incurs your displeasure.

bothered to say "well done". It would hardly inspire you to work so hard again. Suppose there was no salary at the end of the month? I bet you wouldn't go back! Consider how you would feel if you had spent all day preparing a dinner party and not one of the guests said "thank you". Would you invite them back? Think of the dog's rewards in terms of his wages and signs of appreciation for a job well done. Reward every attempt, however small, that your dog makes to "get it right".

Boundaries

One of the earliest lessons your dog has to learn when he enters your family is where his boundaries are. By this, I mean what you are going to allow him to get away with. If you don't want him on the furniture, for example, then don't let him start. If he has already requisitioned a chair and you would rather he hadn't, then insist he removes himself, refusing to accept any show of aggression and praising him like mad when you succeed.

Don't make the mistake of treating him as you would a naughty child. There is an important difference between the two – a child has the ability to reason, a dog hasn't. You can explain to a naughty child why he is receiving punishment and he will understand. Dogs do not understand language and do not have the ability to reason, so any punishment or correction must be given *as he commits* the offence, otherwise he will not understand what the punishment is for.

I can almost hear you say "oh, but he knows when he's done wrong, he looks sad and runs away". No doubt he does know that you're angry, but I promise you that unless you actually caught him in the act, he does not and cannot know what has provoked your anger.

Let me give you an example. Suppose you have left the dog on his own and whilst you were out, he has chewed a displeases you, use your voice in a "grumbly" tone. If the misdemeanour warrants it, give him a good shake, holding him by the scruff of his neck. Don't touch him in any pleasurable way. He will immediately associate your actions with the conditioning he received from his natural mother and will understand that he has displeased you.

Reward

Rewarding your dog *should* be self-explanatory. Unfortunately, many owners find it difficult to convey genuine pleasure to their dog – a pat on the head and a verbal "good dog" is deemed to be appropriate. Others think that rewards should always be edible, with the end result being that the dog will only ever behave if food is offered.

Whenever your dog obeys you and pleases you, you must *show* him how happy you are with his compliance. Give him big enthusiastic cuddles. Stroke and touch him lovingly. Play with him. Tell him in an excited and happy voice that you are *delighted* with him.

Some people think a display of obvious affection towards their dog will adversely affect their position as number one in the "pack" order, or is somehow demeaning. Perhaps it has something to do with the traditional "British stiff upper lip"! They feel that such displays of affection will be interpreted by the dog as a sign of weakness. They may also feel they will lose control of the dog if they allow him to jump about and "go wild" for a few minutes.

Nothing could be further from reality. By showing your dog what pleases you, he will try much harder to please you in the future. As you will quickly have the ability to instil instant control when you say so, there is no danger that he will get the upper hand.

Try to imagine how you would feel if you had completed an exceptional job of work and no-one using his second priority – *affection* – and lots of it!

Correction

Throughout the book I will talk about correcting and rewarding your dog, so you have to know the right way to do both. Although I will go into correction first, do not, please, make the mistake of thinking that correction alone will train your dog – IT WON'T. All the correction in the world will be completely wasted unless you reward your dog properly.

By correction, I do not mean hitting your dog with sticks, leads, rolled-up newspapers, shoes; indeed hitting your dog with anything is counter-productive and can in some instances lead to your dog becoming aggressive. Apart from that, it is wasting a very valuable piece of training that your dog received long before you owned him.

As a new-born pup in the litter with his natural mother, he was taught from the moment of his birth what pleased his mum and what didn't. When he was naughty, she would grumble and growl, sometimes quite ferociously. If that wasn't sufficient, she would pick him up in her teeth, by the scruff of his neck and give him a very rough shake. Sometimes she would even nip him. Conversely, when he was being good, she would "stroke" him with her tongue and "cuddle" him, being very soft and gentle. She would allow him to play-fight with her, but never letting him get the upper hand, always putting him in his place when the time was right.

If you get the chance, go and watch a bitch with her puppies. She can teach you more about dog behaviour than almost anyone else. Now, I'm not suggesting that you start picking your dog up by your teeth, or start biting him! What you can do is to utilise that first basic training and adapt it to fit. When your dog is doing anything which that in his original and wild state, he was one of a group, with a leader, number two, number three, etc., in descending order. Where in the pack he stood depended on his character, physical strength and qualities of leadership.

Man has since domesticated the dog, but the very strong basic pack instinct remains and once the dog enters your family, he will look upon it as his "pack". It is entirely up to you who emerges as the leader – you, or the dog! If it is the dog, your family life could end up with the dog ruling everything, making your life and that of the rest of the family a misery. Perhaps you are already in that situation? If you are, or don't want that situation to develop, you must start now, setting yourself up as number one in the pack, with the rest of the family behind you and the dog at the bottom. I assure you that once he recognises you as "boss" and knows his place in the pack order, he will be a much happier animal.

As in all packs, there will be times when he will attempt to challenge your leadership and each challenge must be met in the same way – you are boss!

Priorities

Your dog has three basic priorities. Starting at the top, they are *food, affection* and *comfort*. Food being his most important, he will rarely, if ever, leave it for either of the other two. Comfort being the least important, he will happily leave lying down for a cuddle from you. He will quickly leave a cuddle if food is offered. You can demonstrate this with your own dog, to prove the point.

As far as training is concerned, it is not a good idea to use food as the primary inducement. Firstly, you will end up with a very fat dog and secondly you may not always have a tit-bit with you when you want your dog to comply with your wishes. So, for training purposes, you will be

1

PSYCHE OUT YOUR DOG!

Dog Logic

In an ideal world, before anyone acquired a dog, they would attend classes in canine psychology, study genetics, examine every breed for positive and negative traits and read all about the potential pitfalls of dog ownership. However, this is not an ideal world and the reasons why people get a dog are as varied as the breeds themselves.

The very best time to start training is whilst the dog is still a puppy, before he has a chance to learn any bad habits. Some of you reading this book may well be in that situation and you are the ones who should have the easiest job of all. Others may have had their dog for a few weeks or months and the problems have only just started to appear. Others still may have given a home to a "rescue" dog and perhaps, because of its previous home, the dog may have been allowed to develop many unacceptable habits, or have all kinds of phobias, both real and imaginary.

For all of you, the methods described in this book will enable you to have a happy, well adjusted and well controlled dog.

Before you start, it is as well to understand just how your dog "works". Much as you love him, you must accept that he is not blessed with human emotions, that he is an animal and a pack animal at that. By "pack", I mean recent years, owners need to train their dogs to be more socially acceptable.

Nobody likes dirty streets or dogs roaming in packs in urban areas. Nobody likes to hear about sheep being worried by dogs, or dogs left out to fend for themselves. Dogs, unlike people, have no morals; they do not know and abide by our codes of behaviour unless trained and supervised by a responsible owner. We cannot blame the errant dog, any more than we could blame a cat for following its natural instincts and killing a mouse, or a fox for killing a rabbit.

The methods used for training are basically very simple. We make as much use as possible of the natural instincts. As previously mentioned, dogs are pack animals in the wild, one dog being pack leader. This is usually the most powerful and intelligent dog. He may be challenged from time to time by subordinates and if a stronger dog wins the battle, the leader is replaced. In training dogs, we take over the role of pack leader, by inspiring respect, showing the dog we are superior to him, but also as soon as he complies with our wishes, he will receive affection and comfort.

INTRODUCTION

Why Train Dogs?

The relationship between man and dog goes back many centuries, when man discovered that dogs were more efficient hunters than himself. Over a period of time he domesticated them to help him hunt, in return providing shelter and a share of the kill. It was a partnership from which both benefited. This, combined with the dog's social needs, i.e. a pack formation requiring a leader (man), led to the forming of bonds which have lasted to the present day.

Over the centuries, dogs have been used for a variety of tasks apart from hunting. These include retrieving game, herding sheep and other livestock, guard duties, guiding blind people and, more recently, as ears for the deaf. Dogs that were good at certain jobs were used for breeding and as a result the distinctive breeds developed.

Nowadays, large numbers of dogs are kept purely as pets and do not have any specific duties, other than being a companion. Those dogs which were developed for working, however, need to use and develop their basic instincts. Training can either encourage this, or, where the instincts are undesirable, channel them into activities which are acceptable in society. Training is essential for the big, strong breeds, but is also beneficial for smaller breeds, to improve nervousness or subdue aggression.

Well cared for, healthy dogs, are not carriers of disease nor are all dog lovers cranky or eccentric. However, because of the enormous amount of adverse criticism over

LIST OF ILLUSTRATIONS

2

INFORMAL TRAINING

By informal training, I mean all those things which you want to teach your dog *not* to do, as opposed to formal training, which is teaching him things which you want him to do. Informal training can start from the moment he enters your house.

Possessiveness with Food

Having said earlier that food is his most important priority, an early and vital part of your establishing yourself as the leader is by showing him that he can only have his food at your discretion and command. Give him his dinner, let him eat for a few seconds, then take his bowl away from him. Use an appropriate sound each time you do so, such as **leave** or **stop**, and keep the bowl for a few seconds. Provided he did not show any sign of aggression as you removed the bowl, tell him "good boy", give it back and allow him to continue eating. Repeat this two or three times during each meal for a few days, then once or twice a week for a few weeks.

Any sign of aggression, however slight, must be corrected very firmly and immediately. Some dogs are never possessive with food, but you may find that if your dog came from a large litter, the way he obtained his share was by threatening his brothers and sisters. If such action achieved the desired result, i.e. getting more food, he may well try that with you. If you don't sort this out very early on, this possessiveness will transfer to other things, such as bones, toys, furniture and so on, perhaps even to members of the family.

And what happens if he has been allowed to get his most important priority, food, by showing aggression? Later, at any stage of his training which he doesn't want to comply with, he may attempt to repeat the aggressive action, which previously got him what he wanted.

Coming when Called – Early Training

Although this will be covered more fully in Chapter 3, you can start to formulate this exercise before ever putting a collar and lead on your dog. Food being the dog's first priority, use it to "condition" him to come when called.

Make sure he is in another part of the house whilst you prepare his dinner. When you are ready, have the bowl in your hands, holding it at chest height. Signal your dog to come, by calling his name and giving him the sound **come**, said with a very pleasant tone. His sense of smell will have already "told" him what is going on and he will no doubt come rushing to you. As he arrives at your feet, don't allow him to jump up for the bowl, but tell him to **sit**. Keep the bowl at chest height and do not give it to him yet. He will probably sit more than willingly; in fact at this stage he would probably walk across the ceiling if you told him to, such is his desire for food! Once he has sat, tell him to **wait** and place the bowl on the floor in front of him. Any attempt to get the bowl must be stopped; if necessary hold his "scruff" to restrain him. Make him wait at least five seconds, then tell him "go on then, good boy" and allow him to eat his food.

Now, quite easily and without any need for harsh correction, you have started the build-up to three separate exercises - coming when called – sit – wait – all of which

Fig. 1. Dinner is served!

you will be teaching formally later on. What you will have succeeded in doing is to start a very pleasant association in your dog's mind with returning to you when called to the sound of **come**, sitting when told to the sound of **sit** and waiting when told to the sound of **wait**, all being rewarded not only with a verbal sound from you, but with his dinner too!

Make sure that you give him the verbal reward clearly, plus some gentle stroking, as later on you won't be using his dinner bowl as a reward, so you want him to understand that praise is verbal as well as edible!

House Training

Although some of you will have progressed beyond this problem, I am including a section on it, firstly for those who have young puppies and secondly for those who are experiencing problems with a previously clean dog.

There are many different methods for teaching a dog to be clean and most people have their own "pet" theory. Like everything you want your dog to learn, you can teach him to be clean on command, by giving him a sound to go with the action! If you are having difficulties with house training, I suggest you start again from scratch and try my methods.

The "old wives tale" of rubbing the dog's nose in it is not only most unpleasant for all concerned and completely illogical, but more importantly it doesn't work. Likewise, it is no good "putting" your dog outside in the garden and hoping he will relieve himself. He may well do so, but he will not be learning anything.

Dogs need to go to the toilet at certain regular times, such as on waking, after a meal, after playing. Make sure that at all these times you immediately *take* him into the garden, staying out there with him, even if it is cold, wet and dark. As soon as he starts to relieve himself, give him a command to go with his action. I use "hurry up", but you can use any words you like, provided you keep them short.

Remember too, that you will eventually be giving him this same command when he is outside, with other people around, so do choose something sensible! Reward him profusely as he finishes, lots of "good dog, clever dog", etc.

If he always receives that praise when he relieves himself outside, he will quickly learn to associate the action with the reward. Any accidents indoors should be ignored. You may be able to stop him just before he squats, in which case quickly but *calmly* take him outside. Don't panic him, or he will forget what his original intention was.

With young puppies, you should take them outside at least once an hour to begin with. Again, with young puppies, you can start training them to paper if you prefer, although it does take a little longer to get them clean this way. Cover an area of the floor with the newspaper and take the puppy to it at all the relevant times, giving the same commands and praise as you will when he is outside. Over a few days, gradually reduce the area of paper, moving it slowly towards the back door. Move it progressively over the back doorstep and outside.

Make a point of putting the puppy on his lead sometimes when you take him out to be clean in the garden. He has to learn to relieve himself whilst being confined on a lead and some dogs get quite confused if previously they have only ever been running free when they want to relieve themselves. If you don't put them on the lead occasionally, it can take a long time to get the idea through to them that sometimes they have to remain on the lead and still go to the toilet.

GETTING CLEAN THROUGHOUT THE NIGHT. Getting the dog clean through the day is relatively easy, but the long period during the night can be a problem.

This could be for a variety of reasons. Sometimes, the young dog has simply not yet learnt to control himself and here you can try using the newspapers on the floor just for night-time use. It could be that he is "asking" to go out and has been unable to attract your attention. If this is the case, it may be worth setting your alarm clock a couple of times during the night, just for a week or two, so that you can let him out. Admittedly this will mean a broken night's sleep for you, but if the end justifies the means, so be it. Perhaps he has learned that if he stands by the back door, he is let into the garden, but of course at night-time nobody can see him as everyone's in bed.

It may be worth investing in a little D.I.Y. here, which can help solve the problem. Get a thin flat piece of hardboard and buy an ordinary battery-operated door-bell, complete with wire. Fix up the bell outside your bedroom door, running the wire to the back door, to floor level. Attach the bell push towards the edge of the board and connect up the wire. Place the board, bell push side down, on the floor by the back door, if possible under the floor covering. When you put pressure on the board, the bell should ring. When your dog next goes to stand by the back door, asking to go out, he will stand on the board and hey presto! he will have operated the bell, alerting you that he wants to go outside. I have used this with several of my puppies, to great effect.

Sometimes it may just be a matter of altering his feeding times. If he is normally fed his last meal of the day around 6 p.m. his natural bodily functions will decree that he will want to relieve himself at about 3 a.m. Try either bringing his last meal forward, or leaving it until much later. Also, to ensure that his bladder is empty before he goes to bed, pick up the water bowl at 5 p.m. Obviously, if he has been playing energetically, allow access to the water for a short while to satisfy his thirst, then remove it again.

ONLY GOING TO THE TOILET IN THEIR GARDEN. There are some dogs who, having grasped the idea of going to the toilet in the garden, seem to think that it is the *only* place they can go. You take them out for a walk, but they "hang on" until they return home. Maturity usually tends to solve this particular snag, but in the meantime it can be quite a problem, especially if you are taking the dog out for the day, or going away on holiday. You must persevere with the training, encouraging him all the time he is outside, giving him the command he has learnt in the garden.

If necessary, stop him going into the garden at all for a few days. On every occasion when he normally wants to go to the toilet, put him on his lead and take him out to the park or wherever, giving him his command and, eventually, nature should take over! This may be time-consuming but it will pay dividends in the end.

In view of the enormous amount of publicity which has been given to the problem of dogs fouling public areas, it can sometimes be a positive advantage if your dog prefers his own back garden! Do try and be a thoughtful dog owner when you are out exercising your dog. No-one, dog owner or non-dog owner, likes stepping in dog excreta, so always take a few plastic bags with you so that you can clear up after your dog. Plastic bags are not cumbersome and are very simple to use. Just place your hand inside the bag, scoop up the "deposit", turn the bag inside out using your other hand, seal it and place it in the nearest litter bin. Your hand will not come into contact with anything unpleasant and your dog will not be causing any offence by leaving little "presents" behind him!

ACCIDENTS CAUSED BY EXCITEMENT. This seems to be more common with young animals and usually affects bitches more than males. Usually the dog doesn't want or intend to be dirty, but gets so excited that he simply cannot help himself. First of all, DO NOT PUNISH THE DOG, you will only make matters worse, as the dog will become so nervous of your reaction that he will relieve himself through fear. To try and overcome the situation, be very calm when you first greet your dog – not cool, but controlled, and immediately go through to the garden with the dog, where you can greet him properly and any "accident" will not matter.

Usually they grow out of this problem, but if it persists, it may be something physical and a trip to the vet may be necessary.

HABITUALLY DIRTY DOGS. With some dogs it becomes a habit to urinate and defecate wherever they choose. It may be that they have never been properly house trained, or because they have a very strong territorial instinct and feel the need to mark out their territory.

In the first case, where the dog has simply been allowed to become dirty, you must go right back to the basic training, as you would for a young puppy. If he is a "territory marker", he may be urinating on the furniture, especially in a strange house. Obviously, if you can catch him "in the act", a quick correction may save the day – and the sofa! It doesn't seem to make any difference even if the dog has just relieved himself outside – the instinct to leave his mark is so strong. If the problem only occurs when you take him to strange houses, the only answer may be not to take the dog in.

If the problem is happening in the dog's own home, then try moving the furniture, as often dogs tend to do it in the same spot and by putting a piece of furniture on that spot, you may break the habit. There are products you can buy which have a smell and taste repugnant to the dog. Sprayed over the relevant area this may help to stop the dog dirtying that spot.

There is a theory that with male dogs who urinate indoors, having them castrated can be the answer. It does work sometimes, but castration is *not* the answer to every training problem, as some people tend to think. It most certainly should not be contemplated until the dog is completely mature and then only after discussing it thoroughly with your vet.

There is now available a course of injections which can simulate temporarily the result of castration and is worth considering before you have your dog operated on. If the injections work, there is a good chance that the castration will too, but if they don't work, the chances of castration working are remote. In Chapter 5, page 117, I go into the advantages and disadvantages of both castrating male dogs and spaying the females, so please read as much as possible about the likely outcome of such operations, before you take such a step.

BACKWARD STEPS. It is quite common for dogs who have previously "got the idea" of being clean to revert to being dirty again, usually when they are around four-to-five months old. This generally coincides with them starting to teethe and is only a passing phase. Understanding and patience are required and a few days' repetition of initial house training will usually sort the problem out.

Likewise, some bitches become dirty indoors just before they start their season. It is basically because their hormones are "having a sort out" and is only temporary, so do be patient. Emotional upset within the family, moving house, or indeed any change in the normal routine can get the dog's "wires" crossed temporarily. This especially applies to "rescue" dogs, who may have undergone quite an emotional trauma and are having difficulty adjusting to a new home and new routine. Do be really patient, treat the dog as you would a young puppy and the problem will soon be solved.

Routine

Because any upset in routine can cause possible problems with house training, it is important that you establish early on a regular routine for your dog. All the important things in his life should happen in a regular pattern, such as eating, walking and sleeping, allowing his head and his body to get into a "system". Imagine the effect on his stomach if you fed him at 8 a.m. on one day and at 2 p.m. the next. His stomach would soon get very upset, as would his sleeping and toilet routine.

The same thing happens if there is no regularity in his life and no consistency over what he is and is not allowed to do. He can only adapt into the human way of life if he has a regular timetable, i.e. feeding, sleeping, exercise, playing, being left, etc. Even though it is not ideal for you to leave your dog all day whilst you go to work, he can adjust to long periods of being alone – although of course you will have to make sure that the time he does spend with you is as full and interesting as possible.

As well as the routine of the household, you should get him into a regular routine of being brushed and "looked at". Examining your dog may sound strange, but if you get him used to his ears being checked, his teeth, eyes, feet, etc., all being held and examined, it will make your job, and that of the vet, much easier when the dog is unwell and in need of attention. It is very difficult, for example, to bandage up a cut paw when the dog won't let you near his feet!

Get used to the look and feel of him when he is healthy, so that you will quickly be able to spot when something is wrong. For those of you who have a female dog, make sure you know what her intimate parts look like, so that you will be able to see the difference when she starts her season. If you don't know how to tell when she is in season, by the time you do notice, it may be too late – she may already be pregnant!

Leaving the Dog Alone

At some stage, you are going to have to leave your dog alone, whether it is to go to work, or just to the shops. If you have first taught him that being left is part of his routine and there are times when he can't come with you, he will soon accept the situation. Don't just go out and expect him to behave, teach him first what you expect.

Decide where you are going to leave him, either confined in one room, or in the garden, or with the run of the house. Make sure that there is nothing lying around on which he could hurt himself, or which is accessible for chewing. If you are leaving him in the garden, obviously make sure it is totally secure.

When you have decided on an area, arrange a practice session by pretending to go out. Do all the things that you normally do when you really go out, such as collecting up your bag, putting your coat on, shutting doors, etc. Begin by teaching him an association with a set of sounds which he will learn mean that he is to remain at home, you are going out, but you *are* coming back. I usually say "just going over the road, won't be long" every time I leave my dogs, whether I'm going out for ten minutes or a couple of hours. They now associate those sounds with me going, then a period of being left alone, then me coming back, as I have done every time after I have given them those sounds.

So, decide on what you're going to say, say it and leave the house. Stand outside the door, very quietly. Any sound of barking, scratching, whining, etc., must be dealt with *instantly*. Rush back indoors, grumble and say "Bad dog", enforcing your displeasure with a shake if necessary. Don't touch him or speak to him in any pleasant way at all, but don't shout and scream at him either. Immediately you have chastised him, leave him again. Only when he has been quiet for five minutes do you go back in, this time full of love and praise, thus teaching him that being quiet gets a lovely reaction, i.e. loads of affection, whereas to disturb the peace provokes a most unpleasant reaction from you. Slowly, over a period of several days, increase the length of time you leave him, until he has been quiet for half an hour without your having to correct him. Then you can start going out properly for short periods of time, gradually increasing the amount so that you can eventually trust the dog to be left for as long as necessary within your household routine.

HOWLING AND CHEWING. Sometimes the silence of an empty house can distress the dog and may start him howling or barking. Sometimes, because of the silence, dogs can hear noises outside more easily, thereby provoking them into barking. Try leaving the radio on when you go out, as the sound of human voices may soothe the distressed dog and mask the external sounds for the barking dog. Some dogs learn to be very destructive when they are left alone and young puppies, particularly, like to chew, especially when they are losing their baby teeth. In this instance, leave them something they *can* chew which is not going to matter. I have found that a pile of empty cardboard boxes, the sort you can get from the supermarket, provide a dog with endless amusement, as they can demolish them beautifully! Of course, you must remove any staples or wire first.

By leaving the boxes for him to chew, you are getting two distinct benefits. Firstly, he is not damaging the furniture or the carpets and all you have to clear up when you return are pieces of cardboard. Secondly, you will not inadvertently be teaching him to chew anything precious, as you would if you gave him an old slipper or shoe to play with. If you do actually give him an old shoe to demolish, you can hardly be surprised when he chews up your best pair – how is he supposed to know the difference between old ones and new ones?

For puppies who are teething, I have found that an old saucepan or frying pan comes in useful – and no, not for hitting him with! When he's teething, he wants something cold and hard with which he can ease his painful gums, so you can see that such an article is ideal. Obviously, make sure there are no sharp edges or loose screws on which he could harm himself and don't use the non-stick variety, as this could poison him. One word of warning here – if they try to carry it around in their mouths, watch out for your shins, as a clout from a metal pan really hurts – and I speak from very painful experience!

Dogs who Steal

It is quite natural for a dog to take things in his mouth – after all, he doesn't have hands! Unfortunately, it is often the owners who inadvertently teach their dogs to steal. A fairly typical reaction to seeing your dog wandering around with your best pair of socks in his mouth, is to chase after him and shout at him to leave them. He runs away and it turns firstly into a game and secondly into a way of challenging your authority and getting you to lose your temper. This all culminates in him stealing at every opportunity.

What you *should* do is to encourage him to bring whatever he has in his mouth to you, by praising him and telling him what a clever dog he is, saying "good boy, come and bring it here". When he does come up, all pleased with himself, reward him and tell him to **give**, holding your hands level with his mouth and taking the article as he opens his mouth. As you are going to be ever so nice when he brings it to you, he will enjoy your reaction so much that he will not want to run away. He may even end up actively seeking things out to bring to you.

You will probably end up with the sofa piled high with

socks, clothes, shoes, slippers, shopping bags, etc., but at least they will not have been hidden or destroyed. He will have learned a valuable lesson in what pleases you, plus you will have the added bonus of laying down the groundwork for the retrieve exercise. Retrieving is not necessary for the average pet to learn, but if you want to do obedience competitively later on, you will have already done some basic training towards it.

Jumping up

Why do dogs jump up? Usually because they are pleased to see you and jumping up gets them closer to you, especially your face. Think about your reaction when the dog jumps. You probably touch him with your hands to push him off. Or to "get it over with", you stroke him, say "hello" and are generally pleasant.

Either way, as far as he is concerned his action of jumping has received a favourable response from you, i.e. you have touched him and spoken to him. So he will repeat the action which gave him that response – he will jump up again.

So, how do you stop it? Initially, you will need to enlist the help of a friend, who is going to be a very silent assistant. Put the dog on his lead and get your friend to hold him. You then go out of the front door, wait a few minutes then come back in. Your assistant is not going to restrain the dog from coming to greet you; he will simply be holding the end of the lead at this stage.

As the dog launches himself at you, keep your hands well away from him. Give him the verbal command **off**, at the same time bringing your knee up to deflect the dog. Simultaneous with your command of **off** your assistant will jerk the lead downwards, putting pressure on the collar and causing the dog to return to the floor, quicker than he would do naturally. Any attempt to jump up again must be corrected in exactly the same way. Once the dog has all four feet on the ground, go down to his level and reward him lavishly, stroking him and telling him what a good dog he is.

Remember, your helper must remain silent, only being there to enforce your verbal command. Repeat the exercise until your dog makes no attempt to jump at you when you come in the door, not forgetting to reward him every time.

You can then change the situation around, with you holding the lead and your friend coming in the door, who will do exactly as you have done previously.

You may think that once the lead is removed, the dog will start leaping up again, but if the timing of you and your assistant is correct, the dog will associate the sound of the command with the extra, uncomfortable correction provided by the lead. After a few sessions of practice, you will find that the verbal command is quite enough. Very soon he will make no attempt to jump up, as he will have learnt that the quickest way to get you to touch and speak to him is by remaining on the floor, whereas jumping up does not get the reaction he wants.

Finally, please do not use the word **down** for this exercise. This word is going to mean something completely different during later training and you do not want to confuse the dog. Each sound is to mean one thing and one thing only.

Barking

The dog which barks unnecessarily is a pain to live with and agony to live next door to! Some dogs bark because their guarding instinct is very strong and they feel it necessary to alert you to every little noise. Some bark because they are nervous and the sound of their own barking gives them confidence. Some bark because they like the reaction it provokes in you and some bark simply because they haven't been taught not to. It is quite normal for a dog to bark if someone comes to the door or if he hears a strange noise during the night. Continuing to bark after an acceptable time is what you want to deter.

In most cases, the way to stop a dog barking is to teach him to bark on command! This may sound very strange, but it does work. At the same time as teaching him to bark, you are also teaching him when *not* to bark.

For the dog to learn this exercise, you again need to enlist the help of a friend, so that you can set up the situation. You should be sitting relaxing, then your helper, at a pre-arranged time, should come to the door and ring the bell. Your dog will then naturally bark and as he does so, give him the command **speak**. Allow him to bark for five seconds, then command him **quiet**, giving him lots of fuss when he does. Don't attempt to answer the door until the dog is silent. Then go to the door, open it, speak to your friend on the doorstep, as you would a casual caller, then close the door.

Go back and sit down again and after an interval of about ten minutes, repeat the whole process again. Alternate between talking to your friend on the doorstep and inviting him in, to simulate what would sometimes happen, i.e. someone coming to the door, then being invited into the house.

Try to repeat this over a few days, building up the association with the dog that he is allowed to bark for just a few seconds when that doorbell rings, but he must stop when you say so, the door never being opened until he has stopped barking. You are also getting him to associate the sound of your command **speak** with his barking.

Why must the door *never* be opened until he is silent? If you allow him to continue to bark whilst you open the door, he will associate that it is his action of barking which gets the door open, resulting in future problems. If he is the type of dog who imagines there is someone at the door and barks often unnecessarily, the only way you will get him to be quiet is to go and open it. You may even end up in a situation of the dog training you – every time he wants attention, he will bark to provoke you into getting up to answer the door to an imaginary caller.

Having taught him to bark on the command **speak**, you will then be able to get him to bark if ever you feel in a threatening situation – when you're out for a walk, perhaps, and are approached by a suspicious character, or if you should hear a strange noise in the middle of the night. You can also apply the same training if your dog barks every time the telephone rings. Arrange for a friend to telephone you and don't answer until the dog is quiet. On these occasions though, don't practise by giving him the **speak** command, as you don't want him barking every time the phone rings. Simply correct him for barking unnecessarily at the telephone.

DOGS WHO BARK BECAUSE THEY LIKE THE REACTION IT PROVOKES: Sometimes it is your action in response to the dog barking which can actually make the situation worse. In an attempt to shut the dog up quickly, you tend to rush to answer the door or the telephone and in the process get the dog even more excited. If you think you may be guilty of this, then deliberately do not answer the door, etc., having previously arranged with a friend either to telephone or ring your doorbell. If you show no sign of agitation with the ringing noise, you will take the excitement out of the situation.

You may have fallen into the trap of shouting at the dog each time he barks – or even taken to chasing after him to get him to be quiet. As far as he is concerned, the whole thing turns into a game, at the same time he has learned how to provoke you and get you to lose your temper, thus challenging your authority as pack leader.

He may be the type of dog who simply stands in the garden, head thrown back, barking like crazy and waiting for some reaction from you. If you recognise this situation, indulge in what I call "negative" training. As it is your reaction which excites and stimulates him, you are going to show no reaction whatsoever. It isn't easy to ignore a barking dog, but you need to give an Oscar-winning performance of complete indifference! Don't speak to him, don't look at him, read the newspaper, pretend to be asleep, show no reaction *at all*. The dog will then probably become curious as to your lack of interest and will come over to you enquiringly. When he does, give him a calm, gentle pat, tell him "good dog", etc., and carry on reading. As far as he is concerned, it's no fun if he can't get you to react, so he will shut up.

After a few minutes of silence, make a point of going over to him and fuss and play with him. You are thereby conditioning the dog that noise gets no reaction from you, but when he is silent he gets the attention he wants.

THE NERVOUS, HYSTERICAL BARKER. If you have the type of dog who rushes out into the garden, barking at unseen terrors, or simply rushes out barking because he likes the sound of his own voice, shock tactics can sometimes work.

Have ready a plastic jug filled with cold water. When he starts his ear-splitting routine, sidle up to him very casually and throw the water over his head. Don't speak as you do it, but praise him like mad the second he stops. Better still, if you can arrange to "bomb" him with the water from an upstairs window, or from an unobserved position, without him realising where the water has come from, it can be far more effective. Once again, he will have received a most unpleasant reaction to his barking, which should prove quite a deterrent in the future.

This method can also be applied if you have a dog who barks whilst travelling in the car. Substitute for the jug a water pistol or plant spray. When the barking starts, aim the jet of the spray between his eyes, again saying nothing as you do it, but praising like mad when he stops. It is obviously much safer if someone else is driving the car at the time!

Car Travel and Travel Sickness

Many dogs develop a fear of car travel and become sick during the journey. Unfortunately we as dog owners inadvertently contribute towards this.

Usually the very first experience a dog has with a car is when you collect him from the place where he was bred. The trauma of leaving his mum, brothers and sisters, plus the people he has become used to, is compounded by being put into a moving machine, possibly for several hours. The car thus becomes an upsetting place, associated with being taken away from his first family.

Then, he settles in with you and more than likely his very next trip in the car is to the vet for a check-up and his first inoculations, again compounding his opinion that cars are most unpleasant places to be, this time associated with having an injection. The car has turned into a monster and his dislike of it increases. Fortunately, most dogs do grow out of this phobia as they mature, but some retain their hatred.

There are various things which you can do to help him overcome this fear and reinstate the car as a place of pleasure. Use his highest priority, food, and start to give him one of his daily meals in the car, whilst it is parked outside your home. His love of food should overcome any reluctance to enter the car, coupled with lots of encouraging sounds from you.

When you have done this for a few days, set aside half an hour, when you can take your dog to the car and sit in there with him, again whilst the car is stationary. Turn the radio on, talk calmly and lovingly to him all the time. When you've done this a few times, start the engine, letting it run for a few minutes, still talking all the time to the dog. Don't try and rush any stage.

When he seems calm being in the car while it is stationary, yet with the engine running, plan a short trip, either to the park (assuming he has had all his inoculations), or to visit someone whom the dog is fond of. Slowly, build up the association that nice things happen when he is in the car, gradually increasing the time spent in the car and the distance travelled.

If he is prone to being sick, make sure that he travels with an empty stomach. For the very nervous dog, the type who tries to charge around in the car, restrain him by attaching his lead to a strong bracket inside the car, putting him in the down position. Leave him enough room so that he can turn his head, but not so much that he can sit up and move about.

Dogs who will not remain still are not only very dangerous in a car, but the tearing about only succeeds in winding them up further. In very extreme cases you can obtain tranquillisers from the vet, but try not to rely on these permanently.

Strange Sights and Sounds

As soon as you bring a new puppy into your home, start accustoming him to as many different sights and sounds as possible. This applies equally to older dogs as well, which you have given a home to, as you have no way of knowing what might frighten them. Get them used to all the usual domestic noises, such as the washing machine, vacuum cleaner, hair dryer, etc. Deal with any show of fear as it arises, being very calm, patient and loving. As soon as the dog has had all his inoculations, make a point of taking him along roads which have heavy traffic, accustom him to pedestrian crossings, level crossings, etc. Take him across pedestrian bridges and under pedestrian subways. If he shows apprehension at any of these things, don't avoid them, but make a point of taking him to them regularly. For example, if he is showing fear of heavy traffic, take the time to stand on the pavement with him – obviously well back from the edge of the road – talk calmly to him all the time, stroke him and if necessary, give him the odd tit-bit. Don't baby him, or try and avoid taking him past any of his "terrors". You will only make matters worse. If you are too sympathetic, it will only convince him that there really is something to be frightened of. He needs to get his confidence from you, so adopt a gentle but chivying attitude, be kind, lots of fuss, but don't try to protect him.

If your puppy is still small, don't be tempted to pick him up. Apart from not curing his fear, you could be setting up a situation when he will ask to be carried – easy enough when he only weighs a few pounds, but a full grown labrador or similar is not so easy to pick up! Likewise, if you have a small dog, which is easy to carry, please don't. However tiny they may be, they are *dogs*, and as such should be treated like dogs, not children.

Make a point of taking the dog to crowded, noisy places. An ideal venue to socialise your dog is the local pub. The combination of crowds of people, juke boxes and fruit machines will all help to make him completely bomb-proof. Of course, another advantage of taking him to the pub is that it gives you a perfect excuse for "popping down to the local"! Don't forget to take the dog though!

Getting your Dog used to Children

If you have children in your family, make sure they understand that the dog is *not* a toy. Most dogs brought up with children are incredibly tolerant towards them and will put up with treatment that they would never accept from an adult. Provide the dog with a place of safety to which he can retreat when he's had enough. If all the children understand that when the dog takes himself off to his basket, for example, he is to be left alone, the dog will willingly put up with all kinds of things, as he knows he can escape whenever he wishes. Don't let the children torment or degrade the dog, however tolerant he may be. They must be taught to respect the dog, in the same way that the dog must respect them.

If you haven't any children at home, get the dog used to other people's children as soon as possible. Dogs who are nervous or aggressive towards children can be quite a handicap. Children can be quite unkind to dogs, prodding and poking them, shouting and rushing about, so make sure that the children to whom you introduce your dog have themselves been properly trained! At the first meeting, use food as an inducement and have the child give the dog a tit-bit, thereby giving a pleasant association to the dog in connection with children.

Finally, however well behaved your dog is around children, it is most unwise to leave a dog alone with young children. Anything could happen, from the children letting the dog out onto the road, to their provoking the dog so much that he ends up biting them. The dog cannot speak and his only answer to cruel treatment, however unintentional it may be, is to use his teeth.

Young babies especially should never be left alone with any dog. As far as the dog is concerned, babies make funny noises and smell very interesting, arousing his basic natural instincts and curiosity, which could have disastrous consequences. Having said that, don't immediately get rid of the dog if a new baby comes along. Just be sensible and vigilant and the two of them will happily co-exist.

Dog Training Clubs

As soon as your puppy is old enough, join a dog training club. More and more clubs are coming around to the opinion that the earlier a puppy starts his training the better and will let you join as soon as the puppy has had all his inoculations. As well as the advantage of getting help with training problems, it is an excellent way of socialising your dog with people and other dogs.

Clubs usually advertise in the local paper, library and vets' waiting rooms. Go along and watch a couple of times before joining, to assess whether it is the right club for you. Are the instructors continually telling the members to praise their dogs? Are they explaining *why* the dogs do certain things, as well as how to deal with each problem? Are the dogs working happily, tails wagging? If so, these are all good indications that the instruction and training is on the right lines. Talk to the other members, find out about the social aspect of belonging to the club. Use your common sense and you will soon work out whether it's a good club.

Dogs who Eat their Droppings

Almost without exception, when a dog eats his own waste matter, or indeed that of another animal, the owner is appalled and revolted, thinking perhaps that they have a perverted dog on their hands.

The correct term for this practice is coprophagia and it is quite common, not only amongst dogs but many other animals as well. Young puppies often exhibit this behaviour, much to the distress of their owners. A bitch with her litter naturally cleans up after her pups, but this does not mean she is always going to do it, even after her pups have gone to their new homes.

Coprophagia is usually a behavioural problem, but I would always advise owners to take their dogs for a check-up at the vet's first, to ensure that there is no physiological reason why the dog is doing this, especially so in the case of an adult dog who suddenly starts. There are various medical reasons for this behaviour. They are: vitamin or mineral deficiency/pancreatic insufficiency/malnutrition/a low roughage diet/parasitic burden/hyperthyroidism.

Obviously, if the cause is medical, then treatment will cure the problem. If no medical reason is found, then corrective training should help resolve the problem. You approach this in the same way that you would teach him not to chew the furniture, dig holes in the garden, demolish slippers, etc. Showing no anger at all, you put him in his training collar and lead, take him up to the droppings and encourage him to attempt to eat them (I know it's unpleasant). As he goes to eat them, correct him, both with the collar and verbally, saying firmly **no** or **leave**, rewarding him each time he refrains. Repeat this several times until he shows no interest whatsoever in eating the droppings, remembering to reward him profusely for his compliance.

Sometimes, dogs start eating their droppings simply out of boredom, particularly if the dog is left alone for long periods of time. Breaking the boredom will often break the habit. Try to rearrange your schedule so that the time he is left is reduced. If that is not possible, ask if a neighbour or friend could pop in to see the dog, breaking up the time span of being alone. Leave him harmless things to play with, not slippers or rubber balls, but empty cardboard boxes which he can demolish.

Another canine companion would obviously be an

answer, but it is hardly fair on another dog, just getting him as companionship for the first one. The second dog will require attention and training and if you are away from the house for long periods of time, he is not going to get the consideration from you that he deserves. A cat can sometimes provide company for a lonely dog, but a cat is not generally a social animal and will more than likely go off and do his own thing, leaving the dog alone again. Really, the only answer is not to leave the dog for so long in the first place.

Obviously, if the dog is eating his own droppings, then clearing them up as soon as they are deposited will prevent it.

Rolling

Rolling in animal droppings, or indeed other foul smelling substances, is another example of how our dogs unwittingly offend us. We think of it as dirty, disgusting behaviour. To a dog though, it is a normal, instinctive part of his canine personality.

One of the most commonly accepted reasons for this behaviour is that, in dog language, the stronger and more pungent he smells, the more superior he appears to another dog. This desire to smell more powerful than other dogs reverts back to when dogs were wild creatures running in packs. The pack leader would wish to impress on his subordinates that he was still top dog. Or perhaps a dog lower in the pecking order would attempt to challenge the pack leader, so to give him added courage, he would first roll in strong smelling animal droppings.

Although our pet dogs have been domesticated for centuries, the desire and instinct to cover themselves in, to us, evil smells is still very strong, even though they may not know why they are doing it. It could occur because you are still having a tussle with your dog as to who is boss, so the dog reverts to his instinctive behaviour in an attempt to impress you.

Our reaction to our smelly dogs is firstly to reject them, not wanting them to get near us and secondly, to bath them as soon as possible to get rid of the smell. This can in turn merely heighten the desire for the dog to repeat his rolling actions as soon as he gets the chance.

As with everything that we wish to deter the dog from doing, you can, through corrective training on the lead, show the dog that you do not like this behaviour. The bad news, though, is that in my experience, a determined "roller" will generally remain so.

3

FORMAL TRAINING

Formal training is the process of teaching your dog to perform certain actions in response to certain stimuli. It means putting a collar and lead on the dog and conditioning him to respond instantly to your command.

Types of Collars and Leads

The first step is to select the right collar and lead. I would recommend you use a good quality leather lead, at least three feet long, with a strong trigger type clip for attaching the lead to the collar. Rope and nylon leads do not have the same flexible quality as leather and they can "burn" your hands if pulled through quickly. As to collars, there are many types available:

TRAINING CHAINS. The training chain, or choke chain as it is commonly called, is only needed in a minority of cases, where the dog is exceptionally strong or aggressive. It most certainly should not be used for young puppies.

Correctly fitted around the dog's neck and properly used, chains are perfectly safe and will not choke the dog. If you feel that your dog needs a chain collar, ensure you get the right size and type. The close-welded link variety are best, as they run freely through the metal rings at each end, as opposed to the open link type which tend to jam up. As to size, you will need a suitable thickness in

Fig. 2. (Left) Incorrect and (right) correct adjustment for a chain collar.

keeping with the size of your dog's neck and a suitable length so that when it is around his neck, and adjusted so that it fits snugly (but not tightly), there is about a hand's width of chain left, before it connects to the lead.

To put the collar on correctly, sit the dog by your left leg, with you standing next to him and both of you facing the same direction. Form the collar into a circle, by threading it through one metal ring. With the end that is going to attach to the lead uppermost, slip the chain over the dog's head. Attach the lead to the free ring and to check that you have put it on correctly, use the lead to tighten the collar, then relax the pressure. The collar should slacken instantly. If it doesn't, then the collar is on "upside down".

DOUBLE ACTION TRAINING COLLAR. In my experience, this is the best type of training collar, suitable for the majority

Fig. 3. A chain collar with a suitable leather lead.

of dogs, including puppies. It is made of flat nylon, which is formed into a circle using a connection of a small length of chain, each end of the chain attaching to the nylon via a metal ring, with a third metal ring in the middle of the chain, for attaching the collar to the lead.

These collars are adjustable and come in various sizes, so they are suitable for the smallest of breeds to the largest. Make sure that you get the type with two adjusters on it – you can buy them with only one adjuster, but these tend to slip and consequently need adjusting frequently.

When the collar is fitted around the dog's neck and the lead is attached, pull the lead gently so that pressure is applied to the collar and check that the two metal rings are not meeting. If they are, it means that there will be no "give" in the collar and it will remain tight whether or not you are applying pressure via the lead. Use the adjusters so that when you do tighten the collar, at least half an inch of chain separates the two rings. That way, there is sufficient slack in the collar to relax it once pressure from the lead is stopped.

Fig. 4. A double action training collar showing (left) incorrect and (right) correct adjustment.

ROPE AND NYLON SLIP COLLARS. These collars are quite satisfactory once you have achieved control over your dog, but are not recommended to begin your training. They tend not to release very quickly; they keep the pressure on the dog's neck even after you have slackened the lead. This could have an adverse effect and actually hinder the training.

ORDINARY LEATHER COLLARS. You should not try to teach my methods of training using an ordinary collar. These collars only put pressure on the front part of the dog's neck and could end up choking him. Once the dog is controlled and no longer needs collar correction, they are perfectly adequate but until then should only be used as an identification collar, carrying your name and address.

When using the training collar, remove all other collars from around the dog's neck, or they could interfere with the action of the training collar.

There are other types of training collars and training equipment, but they do not suit the type of training that I advocate.

How to use the Collar and Lead

Having obtained the right kind of collar and lead and adjusted them correctly, how are you going to use them to train your dog? Although I have so far discussed only putting pressure on the dog's neck, it is most important that you do not rely totally on the lead to control your dog.

The collar, via the lead, is used in conjunction with your hands and your voice. Initially, you will be giving the dog verbal and visual signals, *backed up* with a *momentary* pressure on the collar, which must be relaxed the instant the dog complies. The pressure is applied by a "snatch" type of action, not a pull or a tug. If you try to pull on the lead, the dog will simply pull back and you will end up having a tug of war – with him coming out the winner. The neck is used to absorb the pressure, as it is the strongest part of his anatomy. The sensation the dog feels is uncomfortable but it does not hurt him. The dog is going to learn that by instantly obeying your commands, all pressure is removed, followed immediately by lavish praise and fuss from you.

Although I have previously mentioned that you must not rely on the lead to control your dog, there should never be a time when you take him out of the house or garden without being attached to you, via the lead, however well-trained he eventually becomes. Apart from being an offence to have your dog off a lead on a main road, it is incredibly stupid and potentially very dangerous to allow him to walk free on *any* road. There is always a chance that he could be startled into doing something unpredictable, or be frightened into dashing into the road. As well as risking his life, he could also endanger the life of other animals, or worse still, other humans.

If, like me, you are a car driver, you may well have experienced the dilemma of seeing a dog walking along off the lead, with the owner several yards away. You have your foot hovering over the brake pedal, wondering if he's about to dash into the road. As the driver of a potentially lethal machine, you may well be put into the position of swerving or braking to avoid the dog, and in the process hit some innocent pedestrian, or at the very least damage someone else's property.

Dog owners are now held responsible for any damage their dogs cause, even indirectly, and it could be a very expensive lesson to learn, both for the owner's pocket and his conscience.

Tones of Voice and Visual Signals

As your voice is one of the most important training aids you are going to use, do remember that your dog does not understand the English language. He hears "sounds" not words, so in theory you can use any word you choose to fit any action, as long as you are consistent. However, it is more realistic for us to use a word that makes sense to us, so we use the word **sit** to get the dog to sit, etc. The tone of the word must be decisive. You don't need to bellow like a sergeant-major, but your voice should convey determination and authority, with you "telling" your dog, rather than "asking" him. Each command must also sound different for each separate action.

After each command you will be rewarding your dog, so use lots of excited, loving sounds, such as "good dog", "super dog", "clever dog" etc., all said in a really happy voice. *Show* him with your hands that you are pleased with him, stroke him lovingly, play with him, let him see that his action of compliance has really pleased you. Praise and reward are *vital* to his learning. Reward every effort, however small.

Some exercises will eventually lead to your controlling your dog when he is some distance away from you, so you will be teaching a visual command as well as a verbal one. If you only train with verbal commands you could, for example, have quite a problem getting your dog back to you when he is 200 yards away and the wind is blowing your voice back in the opposite direction. Or suppose you lose your voice – does that mean you also lose control over your dog? Some dogs become deaf as they grow old. Must that mean he can then do as he pleases, because he can no longer hear you?

By giving him audible and visual signals, he has an even better chance of understanding what you want him to do, so that you are not totally dependent on the lead for control.

Getting the Dog to Pay Attention – Watch

By necessity, this has to be the first lesson. Even if you do everything perfectly, all the signalling and commands will be wasted if the dog is not watching you to begin with. You will be incorporating this exercise into all the others you will be teaching, getting him to "watch" you before giving him any other command.

The aim is to get him to watch you and nothing else, for at least twenty-five seconds at any one time, without moving his head away *at all.* Lack of attention is one of the biggest problems which everyone has when they start training, so it is worth spending time teaching him to watch, before you progress to any of the other exercises. The verbal aids you use are his name, which he should know better than any other sound, and the command

watch me. You can start teaching him when there are no other distractions and on the occasion when your dog has deliberately chosen to come and seek your attention.

At some time, perhaps when you are sitting watching television, your dog comes over to you, nudges your hand with his nose and "asks" you for attention. When this happens, gently guide him around so that he is sitting leaning against your left leg. With your right hand under his chin and your left hand on the top of his head, stroke and tickle his head, into your left leg and upwards so that you have eye contact. At the same time, tell him **good boy**, **watch me**. All the time he is gazing up at you, continue to reward him, repeating the command **watch me**, speaking to him in a soothing voice and telling him how good he is. The second his attention wanders, stop stroking and change your voice to a commanding tone, telling him **watch me** again. Although at this early stage you are not giving him any forcible compulsion to watch, you are building up a very pleasant association with the sound of **watch** and the action of watching. Do this over a couple of days, then you can go on to the next stage.

Having laid the foundations, the next stage is to put him on his collar and lead, and teach him to watch, even when there are distractions going on around him. Sit him by your left leg, with you and he facing the same direction. Hold the lead in your right hand and shorten the lead until your right hand is just a few inches away from his collar. With your hand under his neck, give the collar a little "check", turning his head into your leg and tilt his chin up, so that he is looking directly at you. At the same time, use his name and give the command **watch me**. Your left hand should be placed on the top of his head, stroking and turning his head into your leg at the same time. Keep stroking and verbally rewarding all the time he is watching, until his attention wanders, then stop all stroking and repeat the collar and verbal command.

When he has watched for ten seconds, release him from the exercise and allow him to play. By releasing him, I mean making it clear to the dog that he is off duty and work has finished until you command him again. I teach my dogs a release command, namely **that'll do** and they know that when they hear that sound, they can relax and play. Allow him to play, with you participating, for at least two minutes, then get him back under control and repeat the whole process again. You can, if you wish, also teach him a command that means "back on duty", by saying, "work" or something similar, but if you teach him from the outset that when you tell him **watch me**, he is on duty, that should be sufficient for him to know that he is about to be commanded to perform some action.

Do the whole exercise three or four times for the first day, with two-minute play breaks between each session. On the second day, repeat as before; this time making him watch for fifteen seconds. Continue over three or four days until he will watch for twenty-five seconds without being distracted.

Coming When Called – The Recall

Verbal Command – Dog's name followed by **come**.

Visual Signal – Arms outstretched, either side of your body.

You should have already built the groundwork for this exercise by calling your dog each time you feed him, as suggested in Chapter 2. You will have started to condition the dog to return to you when he hears the sound **come**, by being rewarded for obeying – albeit so far because he wants his dinner!

Now you are going to start teaching him, on the lead, that he must come to you when he hears that sound, even if he doesn't want to. The lead is there to use as an added compulsion if he should ignore the verbal command.

Hold the lead in your right hand and with the dog on your left, walk forward a few paces, letting the dog get in front of you. Then run backwards, calling your dog as you go and stretching your arms out as far as you can, bearing in mind you're holding the lead.

Being attached to the lead he can hardly fail to respond, but if he hesitates even for a fraction of a second after you call him, give him a quick check on the lead, repeating the verbal command. As soon as he starts to respond, praise him verbally and take all pressure off the collar. After running backwards a few paces, stand still and let him catch up with you and then praise him like mad. The visual signal will at this stage obviously be slightly abbreviated, because you are still holding the lead and are at close quarters to your dog, but do give as much of the signal as you can, remembering that later on you will be expecting him to return from a distance. Therefore he must start learning it now. Repeat the exercise two or three times, giving full signals each time and loads of praise when he reaches you. When you have practised the above for two or three days, make the lead longer by attaching a piece of rope or cord to the end, thereby allowing you to get a further distance from your dog before you call him. Let him "wander" around at the end of the lead, enjoying his walk, then stand still and call him, gathering in the excess lead as he comes to you. Remember, full hand, voice and if necessary, lead signals, each time you call him, and *full* praise *every* time he comes back.

Repeat this several times over a few days and when he has complied instantly with your command, you can then let him off the lead. To give you more confidence, choose a nice, safe enclosed area for the first time. If you've taught him properly, he'll come back, so don't worry.

When he comes to your call, praise and praise and praise him, cuddle him, play with him, be really excited. He'll *really* want to come back each time if you make it so enjoyable for him to do so.

There are a few pitfalls still to be avoided. Don't get into the habit of only calling him back when the walk is ended and you are about to return home. If you do, he will very soon come to associate that being called back means the end of his freedom and he will become more and more reluctant to come back to you.

Make a point of calling him to you throughout the walk, always to lots of fuss – that way he won't get to learn *which* call signifies the end of the walk. Likewise, when the walk is ended, don't always call him from the same spot in the park. They quickly learn the route of their walk and if you put him back on his lead at the same spot each time, he will again associate that place with the end of his walk and will soon start to ignore your call.

POSSIBLE PROBLEMS. Your dog may have already learned that once he is off the lead, he can do as he likes and goes very conveniently "deaf". Interesting diversions such as other dogs, people playing football, fascinating smells, etc., are far more compelling than coming back to you when you call. Don't fall into the trap of chasing him, as all this will do is turn the whole thing into a game and your dog is much faster on his feet than you. *Don't*, when he does eventually honour you with his presence, tell him off. Your logic tells you that you are punishing him for keeping you waiting. His "understanding" tells him he is being punished for coming back. Even if you've been trying to get him back for over an hour, reward him like mad when he does come, otherwise next time he'll keep you waiting two hours!

There are things you can do to encourage the reluctant

dog. One: walk away from him pretending indifference. Two: sit on the grass, study something on the ground with great interest. Three: pretend to have something in your hands (you *can* have a tit-bit hidden away in this instance).

Dogs are incredibly curious and he may come back, firstly to check why you're not running after him and secondly, to see what you are finding so interesting. When he does, don't make a grab for him, as he will no doubt manage to evade you. Give him a warm welcome, but continue to be "pre-occupied". Once it's obvious that he's going to settle back with you, calmly take hold of his collar, give him a big fuss, so he will associate pleasure with being restrained, then *let him go again*. If you don't, he will once again connect coming back to you with his fun being curtailed, therefore ensuring that he definitely won't return next time you call. If he is showing interest in someone else and prefers to remain with them rather than come back to you, enlist their help. Ask them to be very unwelcoming towards him. Get them to stamp their feet and shout at him. You, meanwhile, will be ever so welcoming, calling him pleasantly. He will soon decide that it's much better to come back to you rather than stay with those nasty people.

If the problem is really persistent, you may need to go back to basic training. Put him back on a long lead and let it trail on the ground. Once you have decided he is to return to you, you can tread on the trailing lead, to prevent him running away. It's not the ideal answer, but unfortunately there are some dogs who quickly learn that once they're off the lead, there's precious little you can do about it – another good reason for starting the training early.

The following exercise, the **down,** can sometimes help with a persistent "non returning" dog, so study it well, it may be the answer.

Down on Command and Down Stay

Verbal Command – Dog's name and **down**.

Visual Signal – Right arm raised above your head, lowering to floor level.

As with every exercise, you teach your dog, on the lead, to lie down on command, with the eventual aim that he will drop on command from 100 yards away. The **down** is the most submissive action that your dog can make for you. If taught correctly, it will assist you greatly in all aspects of gaining control over your dog.

You may have noticed that when two strange dogs confront one another, one dog will sometimes lay down, often rolling right over onto his back. This action is understood by the other dog as a sign of his own dominance, the underdog having recognised the other as his superior.

Similarly, when two dogs are fighting, the conflict often ends before any damage is done, by one dog giving in to the other by rolling over on his back, acknowledging that the other is stronger and thus pack leader. Therefore, each time you command your dog to lie down and he complies, you are compounding your authority over your dog.

Before you begin teaching him on the lead, you can already have started to condition him to the sound of **down** with the action of lying down, by cheating a little. Every time you see your dog about to lie down naturally, give him the verbal command **down**, telling him "good boy" as he does. By doing this, you're not teaching him to lie down when you say so, but you are teaching him a sound to go with the action.

To teach him to lie down when *you* say so, start with your dog, on the lead, sitting on your left side, against your leg, with you and him both facing the same direction, as shown in fig. 5.

Fig. 5. Ready to start the *down* exercise.

Hold the lead in your right hand and gather up the slack until your right hand is about six inches from the collar. Slide the collar around so that it is under the dog's neck. The lead and hand signal, given together at this stage, is applied by a gentle jerk straight downwards, at the same time you give the verbal command **down**. The action of your right hand will dip the dog's head downwards. As you give the verbal and lead commands, place your left hand, palm downwards, just behind the dog's shoulders and push gently downwards and backwards.

As soon as the dog goes down, take all the pressure off the dog's collar and shoulders and go down to his level and reward him. If he should make any attempt to get up again at this stage, correct him immediately, repeating all signals. Don't worry if he rolls over on his back – as mentioned previously this is a sign of complete submission.

Keep the dog on the floor for about ten seconds, remaining there with him, all the time praising and stroking him. Then release him, using the release command you have taught him during the "watch" exercise, i.e. **That'll do**, and let him get up and play.

Fig. 6. Place your left foot on the lead . . .

Repeat the exercise three or four times, each time using full signals, staying there with him each time, then releasing and rewarding. The visual signal you are teaching, i.e. the right hand raised and then lowering to the floor, is obviously abbreviated at this stage because of the close proximity to your dog, but you are building up the association of the verbal and visual signal with the required action.

The next stage is to get the dog to remain on the floor whilst you stand up. Command the dog to lie down then carefully place your left foot on the lead, about nine inches from the collar. You should still be holding the end of the lead in your right hand. As you stand up, give him the verbal command **stay**.

When teaching the **stay** command, do not use your dog's name. Use of his name in this context could actually encourage him to move, which is the opposite of what you want.

If he should try to move as you rise, your left foot standing on the lead will apply the pressure to the collar which previously was given with the right hand. Make sure your left foot is not too close to the collar, pinning his head to the floor, just sufficient distance away to allow his head to move, but not enough to allow him to get up. Your left hand can still be used to apply pressure behind his shoulders if he should try to get up rear end first.

Any sign of movement on his part must be corrected immediately, giving full signals – **down . . . stay** – and all the time he remains where he should be, verbally reward him. When he has remained down for ten seconds, go down to his level, praise and release him, again allowing him to play.

It is important that you do not allow him to anticipate his reward by starting to rise as you go down to him. If you let him do this, he will gradually start getting up earlier and earlier, eventually not staying down at all. He must learn to associate that he only gets rewarded whilst he is lying down for this exercise, thus making it unlikely that he will move.

STAYING DOWN AT A DISTANCE. When you have practised for two or three days getting him to stay down whilst you stand up, you can then progress to the next stage – leaving him in the down, whilst you move to the front of him.

Fig. 7. The visual *stay* signal.

This is where you bring in the visual **stay** signal, as well as the verbal command. The signal is given with the left hand, which is placed in front of the dog's face, palm facing towards the dog. You will also start to establish "foot" signals as well. Every time you require your dog to remain in a position while you move away, you will always set off on your right foot first. Your feet are, after all, much nearer to your dog than your face and you will find that if you consistently position your feet in the same pattern when doing a particular exercise, your dog will pick up the additional signal very quickly. So, command the dog to lie down, tell him **stay** and place your left foot on the lead, again about nine inches from the collar, holding the other end of the lead in your right hand. Repeat the verbal command **stay**, plus give the visual command as well. Now start to move your right foot

Fig. 8. How you should move away from the *stay* position.

slowly backwards and forwards, in front of his face, keeping the left foot still. This is to get him used to the idea of your moving whilst he remains still, in the down position.

When he has remained still for ten seconds, take a small step with your right foot, turning to face him, so that you are now standing in front of the dog, right up close to his front feet. You will obviously have had to move your left foot as well, but do this very carefully, sliding it around with the lead still underneath.

Take care not to put any pressure on the collar as you move your foot, otherwise your dog may move. Stay in front for about ten seconds, then step back to the side, right foot moving first, stand still next to him for a couple of seconds, then go down to him, reward him lavishly and release him.

Always wait a few seconds after returning back to his side, before going down and releasing him, to prevent him from anticipating the end of the exercise and his reward.

Whenever you move around your dog, move positively. Don't hover, as any sign of uncertainty could be misinterpreted by your dog and could be used as an excuse to move. When he is happily staying down for ten seconds with you standing close in front of him, you can then dispense with keeping the left foot on the lead. Gradually increase the distance, taking one pace at a time, always facing the dog, so that after a few days' practice you can get to the length of the lead away, without the dog moving. Then you can start leaving the lead on the floor, out in front of the dog, without holding the end.

If you have the lead out in front of the dog, where you will be standing, you can quickly take hold of it if the dog should need correcting. Over a period of several days, build up the distance and time, so that after about two weeks you can leave him for a distance of five yards for two minutes. Don't try and be too clever, marching off twenty yards away and leaving him down for ten minutes. One, your dog will quickly get very fed up and two, if he should try to move, you will be too far away to do anything about it. Five yards' distance for two minutes is quite enough for normal purposes.

THE "QUICK" DOWN. To get your dog not only to lie down but to "drop" into the down instantly, is most important for several reasons. Firstly, if at any time during his training he starts to challenge you, you can instantly re-enforce your control. Secondly, however excited he becomes, during play times, you will have a very effective stop switch. Thirdly, and perhaps most importantly, it could be a potential life-saver.

You could get into a situation when, perhaps, you trip and let go of the lead, or the lead breaks, and the dog is frightened and runs into the road. If you can get him to lie down and remain still, he will not be nearly such a hazard to oncoming traffic – a stationary dog being much easier to avoid than one who is running about. Finally, if you have been experiencing trouble getting your dog to come back when called, if you can instil the **down** into him and get him to drop at a distance, you will at least have regained control and be able to go and collect him.

To teach him the quick **down**, put him on his lead and play very excitedly with him for a few seconds, then give him the **down** command, pushing him instantly into the position. Keep him down for a few seconds, then praise and release, then play again. The object is to get him to drop before you can push him down – in other words, for him to avoid the correction by going down before you can push him. Practise this until your dog is literally throwing himself into the position.

Sit and Sit Stay

Verbal Command – Dog's name and **sit**.

Visual Signal – For **sit**, right hand raising up and in front of dog's face.

For **stay**, as you have done in the **down . . . stay**.

Sit is a very basic exercise and one which you have probably already started teaching, with varying degrees of success. You may have found that you can get him to sit, but he springs back up before you want him to. Or he may sit, but not beside you where you want him, either sitting in front of or behind you. So, assuming you have already started building up the association of the word **sit** with the action required, it is probably best if you start back at square one, ensuring that each time, the dog sits immediately and in the position and place you want.

With the dog by your left leg, both of you facing the same direction, hold the lead in your right hand. The length of the lead at this stage depends on the size of your dog and how tall you are. The ideal length is so that, when he is sitting by your side, with you holding the lead in your right hand and with your arm hanging down and resting just above your right thigh, the dog's collar is slack. But the instant you apply pressure by using your right hand on the lead, the collar will tighten.

If you find that you have to lift your right arm right up above your head to put pressure on the collar, then the lead is too long. Using the verbal command **sit**, apply pressure to the dog's collar by raising your right hand up and across your body, in front of the dog's face. The pressure and direction of the signal will lift your dog's head up slightly. At the same time, you will apply gentle pressure, with your left hand, on the dog's rear end, by his left thigh, pushing down and at the same time in towards your leg. *Do not* push on the top of the dog's back as you could well damage his spine. As soon as the dog has sat, take all the pressure off the collar, remove your left hand and reward him. If he should try to move, repeat all commands and signals. Correct him every time he tries to move, making sure you always put him back in the original spot each time. As with every other exercise, he will soon learn that when he remains sitting in the right position he is rewarded, whereas any movement on his part meets with determined correction from you.

Fig. 9. Correct way to position the dog to sit.

SIT . . . STAY. Once he has learned that **sit** means to sit on one spot, the next stage is to teach him to **stay** on that spot while you move away from him. The visual signal for the sit . . . stay is exactly the same as for the down . . . stay. There are, however, three main differences between the sit . . . stay and down . . . stay.

Firstly, do not put your left foot on the lead before starting to move with the right foot. You could well put pressure on the lead via your foot and you have been teaching him that pressure on the collar in a downwards direction means that he is to lie down – the exact opposite of what you are teaching now.

Secondly, before you start moving to the front of the dog, slide the collar around so that the part attaching to the lead is on the TOP of his neck. This is so that when you are in front of your dog, you will easily be able to repeat the lead/hand signal, if he should try to move.

Fig. 10. Correct positioning of collar and lead for the *sit, stay*.

Thirdly, the most important difference is the way you release your dog from the sit . . . stay. When you return back to his side, you are going to make him move *backwards*. You are going to "condition" him that the *only* way he ever moves from this exercise is by going backwards first. Thus it is highly unlikely that he will break the stay, by moving himself backwards then coming

Fig. 11. *Sit, stay,* from the front.

forwards – I've never seen a dog do it yet! It may sound strange, but I assure you it works. So, having told the dog to **stay**, move to the front of him (right foot first), and stay there for ten seconds, as you did for the down . . . stay.

Fig. 12. The *sit-stay* signal from the front without the lead.

Return to the side of your dog, wait a couple of seconds, then physically move the dog backwards, by stepping back yourself, gently guiding the dog back with you, giving him his release command **That'll do**, praise and reward him. Do that *every* time you release him from the sit . . . stay, until you will eventually be able to dispense with any pressure on the collar to move him backwards – he will do it automatically. When you give him the release command, do sound excited, so that he continues to enjoy his training.

As in the down . . . stay, gradually build up the time and distance over a couple of weeks so that he is rock steady at each stage before going on to the next.

Wait

Verbal Command – Dog's name and **wait**.

Visual Signal – One sweep of the left arm, starting from the side of your left leg, over in front of the dog's face – like the pendulum swing of a clock.

Fig. 13. The hand signal for *wait*.

Having taught your dog that **stay** means "stay where I tell you until I come back to you", you now need to teach him that **wait** means, "wait where I tell you until I give you further commands". For example, **wait** whilst the door is opened before he jumps out of the car; **wait** whilst the front door is opened properly, rather than trying to push through it half opened; **wait** while you put his dinner on the floor, etc.

Some people teach the **stay** to cover all these things, plus staying in one place, but I firmly believe this confuses the dog, giving him one command to mean two different things and expecting him to know which one you mean. It also encourages him to break the **stay** exercise, as he will be continually on edge, waiting for further commands. If you have taught him that **stay** means he *never* moves until you return to his side, there can be no doubt in his mind whatsoever. With the **wait**, you are teaching him that he is to wait until given further instruction.

A word of caution before you start. Please don't practise the **stay** and **wait** exercises one after the other. You don't want to give your dog any chance of becoming confused. Even though the command is different, at the beginning there is a risk that he may try and anticipate your wishes.

To begin, start with the dog in the normal position, beside your left leg. Remember to leave him right foot first, give him the verbal and visual **wait** commands and step to the front of him. Remain there for a couple of seconds, then repeat the verbal command and back away from him, until you are at the end of the lead (fig. 14). Stand still and call him to you, rewarding him as he comes.

If he should move before you call, correct him very gently by putting him back on the exact spot again. Don't be too harsh with the correction, as, if you over correct, it may put him off moving and make him hesitant when you call him next time. All the time he remains sitting and

Fig. 14. Dog waiting.

waiting, tell him gently what a good dog he is – don't get too excited at this stage, otherwise again it may encourage him to move before you want him to.

By telling him gently that he is good for waiting, he will understand quicker what he is supposed to be doing. Repeat this two or three times over a couple of days and then start incorporating the **wait** command whenever the situation is appropriate. Getting out of the car is usually

Fig. 15. Hand signal for *come*.

Fig. 16. The dog responds.

where this exercise is most beneficial – there are few things worse, or potentially more dangerous, than a dog which leaps out of the car the instant the door is open. By teaching him the **wait** exercise properly, you will be able to open the car door and know he will not move until you tell him to.

Stand

Verbal Command – Dog's name and **stand**.

I'm sure that some readers are wondering why on earth they should teach their dog to stand on command and what practical purpose it would serve. Well, how about when you brush your dog? What about when he comes back from a muddy walk and you have to dry him? Think about when you have to take the dog to the vet – it's much easier for the vet to examine him if he's standing nice and still. I'm sure you can think of other occasions within your own lives when it would be very convenient if he stood still on command.

Fig. 17 The "stand".

The **stand** is the gentlest of all exercises to teach and also one of the easiest. The verbal command **stand** is given very gently, unlike all other commands you have been using and is delivered in a "sing-song" type of voice. It must sound completely different from the authoritative commands of **sit** and **down**. The aim is to teach him that on receiving the verbal and visual commands, he will stand up, keeping his front feet still and moving his back feet *backwards*.

Start as always with the dog on your left, in the sit position. Slide the collar under his neck and gather up the lead in your right hand, until your hand is just a couple of inches from his collar. The direction you signal the collar is directly out in front, gently pulling his head forward, but not making him walk forward. Your voice says **stand** at the same time.

The dog will not yet understand what he is supposed to do, so you are going to assist him into the position with your left hand. Place your hand between the dog and your left leg. Put your hand under his tummy and gently lift him up and backwards, tickling his tummy as you lift. As soon as he is up, take all the pressure off the collar, but leave your right hand on his chest, to prevent him moving forwards and leave your left hand tickling his tummy. He will no doubt remain in that position very willingly, as he is receiving such lovely inducement to do so. Eventually you will want him to stand solely on the verbal command, so don't make the mistake of relying on the lead and your hands to make him stand – give him the **stand** sound each time you assist him into the position.

You might think that it would be much easier for you to place your left arm *over* the dog to lift and tickle, rather than placing it between you and the dog. What you will find, if you do that, is that your dog will tend to lean towards the arm that is tickling, with the result that he will be leaning away from you, rather than leaning towards you, which is what you want.

You may also find that once he stands, he starts to walk forward. This is because you are putting too much pressure on the collar as you pull forwards, plus you are not putting your hand on his chest quickly enough. Perhaps, too, you have your lead too long to begin with.

You may also find that as soon as you have positioned the dog into the stand, he immediately goes to sit again. You could be causing this, by pulling up on the lead, which, as the dog has already learned, means **sit**. Do be careful, therefore, not to put any upward pressure on the collar once he has stood.

Finally, you may find this exercise easier to begin with if you kneel down to the dog's level to give the signal – especially if you have a small dog.

Walking to Heel

Verbal Command – Dog's name and **heel** or **close** (choose one and stick to it).

I suspect that some readers may have jumped straight to this section, as it is probably the one thing that causes more problems than any other. However, if you have skipped the previous pages, it would be in your own interest to go back and read them first. Everything taught so far has been designed to get overall control of your dog, culminating in making this exercise easier to teach.

You will be teaching your dog to walk on his lead, by your left leg, with his shoulder level with your knee and without pulling or jumping up. You will be using your voice, hands and lead to show him where he should be. As with all exercises, your voice and hands will be the prime form of correction and reward. Don't rely on the collar, via the lead, to keep the dog in the correct place.

Start with your dog sitting, against your left leg. Hold the lead in your right hand and hang your right arm down naturally, so that it is resting on the front of your right thigh. The lead should be just long enough so that with the dog sitting beside you, there is no pressure on the collar, but should he move from the sit position, the collar will tighten. This is shown in fig. 18. Don't have the lead so short that the collar is permanently tight.

Fig. 18. Prior to starting *heel* work.

You will be using the lead to give a directional signal, via the collar, across your body to your right hand. With young puppies you should keep any collar correction to an absolute minimum, as their necks are still growing. Use your voice and hands as the main stimuli.

Decide which verbal command you are going to use and stick to it. If you decide upon **heel**, try to pronounce it "heyall", otherwise, it tends to sound rather flat. If you decide to use **close**, pronounce it as "clowss".

You will be stepping off with your *left* foot first, as in this exercise you want him to accompany you. (In the **stay** and the **wait**, you stepped off right foot first, as he was to remain behind.) Give him full commands – his name, **watch me** and the heel command, signalling the collar with a quick snatch and step off, taking one pace only, then stopping and telling the dog **sit** as you stop.

Fig. 19 Dog walking by handler's left leg.

Taking one pace only will not have given him much chance to pull, but it will give you the opportunity to show him what all the signals mean. There is no point galloping off for several yards at this stage. So, for the first lesson, it will be one pace at a time. Reward the dog every chance you get. By rewarding, I mean that every second or fraction of a second that he is walking with you and not pulling, take all the pressure off the collar and tell him that he's doing what you want. Use your left hand to fuss him under the chin when he's walking nicely.

Fig. 20. Dog walking nicely, gets reward.

Practise the whole exercise, one pace at a time, for no more than two minutes, then release the dog, take his lead off and have a good romp with him. After a couple of minutes' play, put him back on the lead, set him up again in the sit position by your left leg and repeat the whole process for a further two minutes, after which more playtime. This is quite enough for the first lesson. Leave the training for at least a couple of hours then put him back on his lead, ready for the next stage. This time you will be taking two paces at a time for a further two minutes, again another play break of two minutes, then another two minutes' training. You will have then done enough for the first day.

Always let him have a good romp between each session – don't try and short-cut the process by leaving it out. You want him to enjoy learning and walking on the lead. Far

Fig. 21. Walking to *heel,* lead at correct length.

too many dogs are seen being dragged along the road, tails down, faces miserable, so don't let your dog become like that. Make the training fun.

The next day, start off by taking two paces at a time, then slowly progress until you are walking about ten paces before stopping. Correct him every time he pulls, with a rapid snatch on his collar, reward him every time he is in the right place and all the time he remains there. Use your left hand to encourage him, patting the front of your left leg, not the side, or you will find he will hang back to be near your hand. Again, with your left hand, stroke his head and body, gently pull and tickle his ears, fuss him

Fig. 22. Walking to *heel,* lead too long.

under his chin, etc. All pleasant and enjoyable things to encourage him to be with you, rather than pulling.

When he is walking nicely, tell him what a clever, good dog he is at every opportunity. Again, train for only two minutes at a time, then release him and let him have his playtime.

PROBLEMS SO FAR. You may have found that as soon as you stepped off, the dog was out in front, at the end of the lead, before you could signal him via the collar. This is probably because you have the lead too long, as in fig. 22, and therefore cannot get the signal through to the collar in time. Remember what you are trying to teach your dog.

Fig. 23. Walking to *heel,* lead too short.

Every time he tries to pull, the correction must be instant and repetitive. Every attempt he makes to walk without pulling, however slight, must be rewarded with a slack collar and lots of reward.

You may actually be causing the dog to pull, by having the lead too short and the collar too tight. Any attempt to hang on to him via the lead will result in him fighting you and the restriction, as shown in fig. 23. When it comes to pulling power, your dog will win every time – by holding him back, you cause him to set his neck and you cannot give the rapid *tighten then slacken* signal on an already tight lead.

If he tries to pull hard, off-balance him by taking a sideways step, to the right, signalling the collar at the

Fig. 24. Lead held incorrectly, left hand positioned half way up.

same time. Work hard on the **watch** exercise too. If he is paying attention to you, he will not be getting out of position, because the act of watching will put his head in the correct place, by your left leg.

You may be holding the lead with your left hand as well as your right, perhaps with the left hand half way up the lead, as shown in fig. 24, attempting to stop the dog getting in front of you. This ties up your left hand, when you should be using it to reward and encourage the dog and also when you want him to sit. It is a counter-productive action. When you apply the signal with your right hand, the first object that the signal connects with is your left hand and not, as you want, the dog's collar.

Perhaps you are trying to hold the lead just in your left hand. Again, you need that hand for positioning the dog, plus you will find that you cannot give the lead signal in the correct direction – across your body to your right – but instead you are pulling the lead back, behind the dog.

You could be walking at the wrong pace for your dog, therefore not allowing him to get into his natural stride and making him walk unevenly. If you walk too fast, you either end up leaving him behind, or he tries to race you. Too slow and you give him more chance to be distracted. Try to get a happy medium and both of you will find it easier.

Perhaps you have the opposite problem from pulling – the dog is lagging behind you and hanging in his collar. Although you still need to correct such action, use lots of encouragement to get him walking in the correct place, both verbally and with your hands.

It may be necessary to take all pressure off the collar. Turn and face him, run backwards and call him. As soon as he is willingly walking towards you, turn around and walk alongside him, talking to him in an excited voice.

The odd tit-bit can be used as an occasional added inducement. Basically, he needs to find his feet, so keep the pressure off the collar, tell him he's doing it right and soon he'll be walking properly.

Don't bore the dog by endlessly marching about. A few minutes' practice every day is quite enough, making sure the training is happy and interesting and rewarding at every opportunity. Change direction frequently, especially if the dog isn't paying attention. A change of direction, done smartly, will give you a good opportunity to signal your dog and, even better, a chance to reward him afterwards for responding to your commands.

Try practising heelwork on the spot, without moving forwards. With the dog sitting beside you, give him full signals and do a quarter turn to your right. Repeat several times, commanding the dog each time and positioning him in the **sit** after each turn. Turn about on the spot, turning away from the dog again with full signals. All this will help get the message through to the dog. When he receives the heel commands, he must always move with your left leg.

GETTING THE DOG TO RETURN TO HEEL FROM ANY POSITION.

There will be times when your dog manages to position himself in the wrong place, just as you want to start walking with him. You have probably been "scooping" him back to your left side with your hands, which will only have made him want to sit incorrectly even more. He likes being touched and so repeats the action which makes you touch him!

Using the commands which, by now, will be meaning **heel** to the dog, you are going to show him how to get there on his own, without your having to touch him. Obviously you will use exactly the same signals as you have been using to teach him to be by your left leg, as this is where you want him to be.

To show him how to move into the correct position, he must first of all be in the wrong one. For the purpose of teaching, start with him sitting in front of you – something which happens very easily if you are too slow with the **sit** command when you come to a halt.

To set this up, incorporate the **wait** command which you

Fig. 25. Ready to return to the *heel* position.

have already taught him. Start with him sitting by your left leg, command him to **wait** and step around to face him, close to his front feet, as in fig. 25. Now you are going to stand still and he is going to move around behind you, going past your right leg and ending up on your left-hand side.

Gather the lead up in your right hand, give him the verbal **heel** command and, at the same time, apply a little

(b)

(a)

Fig. 26. Being guided round behind the handler.

pressure to the collar by giving it a little tug. This is to get him up and moving towards your right leg. See fig. 26(a). As soon as his head is level with your right leg, you must change the lead over into your left hand. Reach your left arm around behind you and take the lead from your right hand, at the same time giving the lead another gentle tug, accompanied with another verbal **heel** command. Guide

(a)   (b)

Fig. 27. Coming to the right position; completing the exercise.

the dog around behind you (fig. 26(b)), until his head becomes level with your left leg, change the lead back into your right hand, completing the dog's positioning at the same time (fig. 27(a)), and telling him to **sit** (fig. 27(b)).

Now, all that is a great deal more complicated to write down than actually do! Follow the pictures carefully and you will see it is quite simple really. It helps if your dog can see your face as he is coming around behind you. Once he is up and moving, turn your head around to your left, so that you can see him coming and greet him as he comes around. Remember to keep your feet still. You must remain stationary; he is moving to you, not you to him.

If you are having trouble getting the initial movement from your dog (i.e. getting him up from the sit position), you can, just to start with, take a step back with your right foot as you give him the first heel signal on the collar. This gives you a little more "impetus". As soon as he is up and moving, you must put your right foot level with the left one. Don't leave it out behind you, or your dog will have to walk out and around you to get to the heel position, making him go very wide and giving you more trouble in controlling him.

When you've practised this exercise a few times and your dog understands what you want, start getting him to come to heel from any direction. Again using the **wait** command, start with him sitting by your left leg, tell him **wait** and step forward one pace, stand still and call him up to heel, using full commands and signals. Again, with him sitting by your left leg, take a step sideways, away from him, then call him to heel, this time continuing to walk forwards as he comes to you.

If you are determined and patient, it will not be long before your dog is walking beautifully on the lead. Be consistent, be very pleasant and loving when he does it right and he will soon "give in" and actually enjoy his confinement on the lead.

4

THE AGGRESSIVE DOG

Sadly, some dogs are, or become, aggressive. It is difficult to generalise over possible cures without seeing and assessing each individual case, but I will go into some of the causes and suggest ways to cope.

If you have a dog who likes to bite, be it other dogs, strangers, family members or even yourself, you may possibly have already thought about muzzling him, re-homing him, or even having him put to sleep.

A muzzle, or some other kind of head restraint, may well stop him from biting, but it won't teach him *not* to, nor help you to find out why he wants to bite in the first place. Re-homing him is simply passing on the problem to somebody else, which is hardly very fair to them or to the dog. The last resort, having the dog painlessly destroyed, should only be considered when you have explored every possible avenue available to you.

What makes a dog aggressive? It could be anything from bad treatment in a previous home, accidental mistreatment, or poor basic training, through to poor breeding or medical ailments.

Bad Treatment in a Previous Home

If you have a "rescued" dog, you may well not have been given the real reason why the dog needed a new home, either by a previous owner or the rescue kennels, even if they knew the true reason in the first place.

People who mistreat dogs fall into two groups – those who are deliberately cruel or those who are cruel through ignorance. The result however is the same, a dog who is confused, who will use aggression either to protect himself, or to get his own way.

Despite the bad treatment and subsequent confusion, the dog will still feel insecure when he leaves his "family" and enters a new one. At first he may behave gratefully and, depending on the basic nature of the dog, this period may be very short, or last for ages. Provided that you are consistent in what you will allow him to do and what you will not permit, in a fair and logical way, the dog should settle in with his new family and will know where he stands. However, if his treatment in the previous home was not consistent, or indeed was deliberately cruel, at some stage he will try to test you, in an attempt to establish his position within the new pack.

If, in the past, he has used aggression, either to defend himself or to get what he wants, he will repeat that behaviour to see what reaction he gets. All shows of aggression *must* be dealt with swiftly and firmly.

Use the training collar, if he is wearing one, or if not take him very firmly by the scruff of his neck. You can do this either one-handed, placing your hand on the top of his neck, or, more effectively, by facing the dog and using both hands, one either side of his neck. Shake him *very* hard, lifting his front legs off the ground in the process. If the dog is small enough, lift his whole weight off the ground. Grumble at him, saying **no** or **leave** in a very authoritative voice. Don't shout or scream, as this will simply wind him up and make him even more agitated. Make sure he is in no doubt whatsoever that you are displeased with him. Do not stop the correction until the dog has ceased all display of aggression and is showing signs of contrition.

The most important thing to remember in any such confrontation is that *you* must win. If necessary, finish the incident by forcing the dog to lie down at your feet, putting the dog into a submissive position, at the same time giving you the opportunity to praise him for obeying a command, i.e. **down**. This will also further support your position as pack leader.

Don't assume that this display of dominance on your part will lead to the dog being frightened of you, or indeed that you are being cruel. However sympathetic you may be to the dog's feelings, you must correct aggressive behaviour immediately. You cannot afford to give the dog any ground whatsoever in this matter. He will most certainly not feel sorry for you when he bites, simply seeing your acceptance of such behaviour as a sign of your weakness and his dominance.

Most good dog training clubs include an exercise within their courses which will teach you this technique for correcting your dog, for use as and when necessary.

It should be possible for you to identify what situations are going to elicit such bad behaviour. Once you have established the trigger, you can set up a situation which you can be in control of, in order to teach the dog what you expect. It may be a particular type of person, place or thing which the dog associates with cruel or unkind treatment.

As an example, let's use the case of a dog whose previous owner used to beat him. Suppose the owner also had a motor-bike and consequently wore a crash helmet. The dog therefore has a remembered association between people wearing crash helmets and pain. You may have owned the dog for some time, but during that time the dog has not come into contact with anyone wearing a helmet. Then one day an innocent visitor arrives at your house by motor-bike and enters your home, either wearing or carrying the helmet. Suddenly, your previously placid, friendly dog becomes a snarling, biting maniac. Exit one visitor, hopefully not hurt, but definitely unimpressed! Your next step is to borrow a crash helmet. Start to treat it as an extension of yourself, carrying it around with you, leaving it beside your chair when you sit down. Be very calm and casual about it, not making any direct reference to the helmet as far as the dog is concerned. Of course, any aggressive displays must be corrected in the way previously described. Once the dog is used to you walking around with the helmet, start wearing it for a few minutes, several times a day. When he accepts that, leave the helmet by the dog's bowl, until he accepts it completely and ignores it.

The next stage is to set up a dummy situation, of a visitor wearing the helmet and arriving at your house. Enlist the help of a member of the family, or a friend whom the dog knows and likes. Make sure the visitor has plenty of dog-type tit-bits in his pocket. Invite the visitor in, sit him down and talk calmly to him and the dog. Provided there has been no sign of aggression from the dog, the visitor is to offer the dog a tit-bit, talking to him very calmly and quietly. He must not make any sudden moves, or try to touch the dog at this stage.

The slightest hint of aggression must be dealt with by you, not the visitor. When all has been calm for about ten minutes, the visitor can start to stroke the dog, again offering more tit-bits.

Once the dog is totally at ease with the visitor, tell him to remove the helmet and place it on the floor beside him. Try putting a tit-bit inside the helmet, encouraging the dog to seek it out. Repeat this whole procedure two or three times over a couple of weeks, using different people each time.

What you are showing the dog is that the situation, i.e. a person wearing a helmet, is no longer a threatening one for him and nothing dreadful is going to happen, so long as he behaves himself. If he does misbehave, you are going to correct him. All the time he is good, he receives affection and reward, in the shape of stroking and tit-bits.

Eventually, people wearing crash helmets will only provoke pleasant associations for the dog – you may even end up with him actively seeking out people wearing helmets. However, that's another problem!

Apply this type of therapy to whatever is provoking the dog into defensive aggressive behaviour. Remember, correct all shows of aggression, reward all acts of submission.

Accidental Mistreatment

This could range from you accidentally treading on your dog's foot, to touching the dog where he has an injury of which you were unaware. Such occasions will stick in your dog's mind as an experience which he will not want repeated.

Let's assume that you have accidentally stepped on your dog and he flies out at you, perhaps even biting you in the process. You may well be inclined to forgive him because it was your fault. However, he will remember that not only did it hurt him when you trod on him, but that you allowed the aggressive retaliation which followed. After that, any time anyone steps near his feet, he will repeat the behaviour which you accepted and he will try to bite.

So, as previously described with the helmet situation, he must learn that aggressive behaviour will not be accepted and that, because you once trod on his foot and caused him pain, the same thing is not going to happen every time someone steps near him.

Put the training collar on the dog and attach the lead.

Command him to lie down by your side. Get a member of the family to approach the dog gradually, one step at a time. Any grumbling or snapping must be corrected instantly. All the time he lies there quietly, speak to him in a soothing tone, occasionally stroking him. Don't allow him to back away from the feet, as that way he will not only be avoiding them, but also your correction. Take plenty of time over this stage – if necessary do it over several days, five minutes twice a day, say, for a week.

Once the dog is happy with the feet approaching him slowly and eventually standing still beside him, get the person to move slowly around the dog. They can now start to give the odd tit-bit as an added reward for his good behaviour. Assuming your helper is wearing soft shoes or slippers, have them start gently stroking the dog with their feet. Progress from this to placing a tit-bit on his foot. This will not encourage the dog to eat feet! The opposite will happen, feet will become pleasant objects, not painful ones.

When you have achieved all this, change places with your helper and repeat the whole process, this time getting the dog used to *your* feet being close to him and touching him. Start walking more quickly towards him. Don't forget to reward the dog verbally all the time he shows no sign of aggression. You don't want him to get into the habit of only tolerating feet near to him if food is offered. Get every member of the family to go through this procedure, as well as any friendly visitors, so that eventually feet will no longer hold any fear for him.

Incorrect Basic Training

Dogs do not naturally know right from wrong. Unfortunately many owners unintentionally allow their dogs to become aggressive, by permitting certain behaviour. This is especially so with young puppies, when signs of aggression are allowed because "he's only a baby". It can also happen when you give a home to a rescued dog. You try to compensate him for the trauma he has gone through, by being too soft and feeling sorry for him.

In the same way, dogs who are not given the opportunity to socialise with other people and/or dogs, will often show aggressive tendencies when they do eventually come into contact with people and dogs they do not know.

It is obviously better for all concerned to socialise the dog properly. By socialise, I mean regular interaction with other people, dogs, other animals, places, etc. During this socialising time you can teach the dog, using the corrective methods previously described, the type of behaviour you expect and the behaviour which you will not tolerate.

Introduce the dog properly to the world outside his home. Then he will not feel threatened by other people or dogs. There is often a tendency for under-socialised dogs to be protective towards their owners. Most dogs, once they are secure with those they know well, will assume that strangers are equally trustworthy, unless those strangers show warning signs to the contrary.

Some people, either deliberately or through ignorance, may tease the dog into aggressive behaviour. Children, especially those who have not been taught to respect animals, often end up the victim of their own actions, when a dog retaliates against constant teasing.

Other people may be genuinely afraid of dogs, giving off confusing "vibes" to the dog, which could cause him to act in an aggressively defensive manner.

You are responsible to and for your dog, so you must correct any aggression he shows, be it to humans or animals. Depending on the circumstance, whether or not the dog is reacting to deliberate provocation, you must show him that such behaviour will not be tolerated. If the provocation is deliberate, you can of course take the provoker to task. If the subject of the dog's aggression has innocently sparked off the situation, try to explain, in a reasonable manner, what the action was which initiated the dog's behaviour.

When you have corrected the dog, command him to lie down, or sit, at your feet, so that you can finish the incident by rewarding the dog for obeying your instruction. Assuming that the dog is on a lead at the time, do make sure that once he has complied with your wishes, all pressure via the lead is taken off the collar. A tight lead can indicate to the dog that there is something to be on guard against. In the same way, tightening the lead in an attempt to stop him showing aggression in the first place will probably provoke him further, into an aggressive display. It can also make the dog feel safe, as by hanging on to him, you are effectively keeping him out of trouble. The dog then feels that you are protecting him, which encourages aggressive displays, as you are not going to let him get hurt.

With the dog either sitting or lying down at your side, with the lead slack, the dog recognises that you are in control and that there is no need for him to act defensively.

If you have been guilty of continually keeping your dog out of trouble when he exhibits aggressive behaviour, this could lead to him resenting others coming close to you, as you are his protector. The intervention of another person can threaten his security, which results in his being over-protective. He will resent anyone attempting to sit next to you and either through aggression, or persistent attention-seeking behaviour, will try to undermine the other person, until they remove themselves.

Human nature being what it is, displays like this are often misinterpreted as the dog seemingly being devoted to you, which is very good for your ego. Because it appears that the dog wants you all to himself, you are inclined to tolerate the behaviour and, worse, condone it by getting the other person to move away. It is up to you to show the dog that, much as you love him, you will not tolerate such intervention between you and another person.

Sometimes, the dog is allowed to develop possessive feelings towards food, toys, furniture or territory.

It is a popular misconception that it is natural for a dog to growl at anyone who ventures near whilst he is eating his food or chewing on a bone. If the dog is permitted to get away with intimidating behaviour over something as important to him as food, he will almost certainly use aggression to achieve lesser goals.

The method described at the beginning of the book when feeding puppies can be used just as effectively with an adult dog, and you must persist until the dog realises he only gets these things because you let him.

The more confident your approach when taking food or bones from him, the quicker he will respond in an acceptable fashion. Quick, firm correction, using the dog's collar or, if he isn't wearing one, his scruff, followed by praise when he submits, will re-enforce your position of pack leader.

The same method should be used if the dog shows possessive traits with his toys. He must be taught that he owns nothing and only has access to toys, etc., if you say so.

It is most important that you and other members of the family are consistent with permission and denials. For instance, if you do not want the dog to play with slippers, but another member of the family gives him a slipper to play with, this will confuse the dog over what is and is not acceptable behaviour. It will also undermine your authority with the dog, making future confrontations harder to deal with.

This also applies to territory and furniture. Either the dog is allowed on the settee or he is not. Either he is allowed in the bedrooms, or he is not. He must not be allowed by some members of the family, yet corrected for being there by others. He will become very confused by this and a confused dog is potentially an aggressive dog. You *can* train him, for example, that he is only allowed on the furniture when he is invited, but first he has to learn that he is only there because you say he can be.

Don't make the mistake of thinking that if others allow him to have, or do, things which you don't, that he will love them more and you less. A dog is much more secure when he knows exactly where his place is and is also much more secure when he can instantly recognise who is the leader of his "pack".

Last in this category of poor basic training comes the dog who likes to mouth or bite your hands. Although this is often done in play, without any aggression, it can lead to aggressive displays, is anti-social and is also painful for the recipient.

Once again, this has probably come about because you, or perhaps the dog's previous owner, allowed such behaviour to continue unchecked when the dog was a pup. As far as he is concerned, there is nothing wrong with him taking your hand in his mouth and he does not know how much it hurts you.

You may have already tried slapping his nose, or wrenching your hand away, but both of these reactions can actually encourage him to try and catch your hand.

To correct this behaviour, you can use the corrective methods already described, but there is a far more effective alternative which, if applied properly, will stop the dog ever wanting to put his teeth near your hand again. This should not be attempted by the amateur with a dog which may be really vicious. In this circumstance, seek proper professional guidance.

A strong word of caution before you start – please apply the correction *exactly* as described and study fig. 28 very carefully before you attempt it. It is a physical type of correction and you must be very sure that you do not damage your dog's mouth in the process.

Fig. 28. Stop him mouthing or biting your hand!

When your dog tries to take your hand in his mouth, quickly position your hand palm upwards and close it over the dog's lower jaw. It is the lower jaw where the leverage action is. If you hold that, rather than the upper jaw, the dog cannot close his mouth over your hand.

Squeeze the jaw firmly, at the same time turning the flaps of his mouth inwards, towards his teeth. *Do not jerk or pull the jaw, either upwards or downwards.* As you apply the squeezing pressure, the dog will feel discomfort and will probably yelp. As he yelps, so *must you!* You must make the same sound that he makes when he feels the discomfort, so that at any time in the future, should he attempt to take hold of your hand, you repeat the sound which he made when last in that uncomfortable situation. The remembered discomfort will be sparked off by the sound of your yelp and will deter him from continuing with the attempt to bite your hand.

After you have yelped, remove your hand from his mouth immediately and then straightaway offer him your hand again, saying softly **gently**. If he should try to mouth it, repeat the whole process. If he doesn't, stroke him gently around his mouth and head. You want him to understand that your hands can be rewarding as well as correcting, not something to be wary of, provided of course that he is not trying to bite them.

It may take two or three sessions for the dog to learn this exercise, but most of them learn it very quickly.

If you wish, you can actively encourage him to lick, rather than bite, your hand. Whenever he voluntarily licks you, give him the sound **gently**, so that he learns to associate that sound with his action of licking, which can help considerably when teaching him not to mouth your hand. I know some people dislike their dogs licking them and it is entirely a matter of personal choice whether or not you encourage it.

Being Bitten by Another Dog

If your dog has been intimidated, attacked or bitten by another dog, he may make a point of avoiding that particular dog, dogs of that particular breed, or indeed all dogs. However, it can affect him the other way – he might actively want to attack that dog, breed type or all dogs.

Both these reactions are understandable and naturally

you will have great sympathy with the dog's feelings. In the first instance, if you allow him to avoid the dog and over-protect him, you could actually make him more nervous. Of course, if the attacker is a known aggressive dog, not being properly controlled by the owner, it is common sense for you to avoid it and take whatever action you deem appropriate to prevent the situation happening again.

If it was just a one-off incident, over-protection by you will lead to him being even more wary. Seek assistance from a dog training club, where they will help you to regain the dog's confidence.

For the dog who begins to respond in an aggressive fashion to *all* other dogs, you must correct him quickly. To the dog, he sees his actions as getting in first, before the other dog can attack him. This will end up with him trying to attack innocent dogs and before long he will become known as "that aggressive dog whose owner can't control him". Your walks with the dog will turn into a nightmare, with people keeping their dogs away from yours and you having to keep the dog on a lead all the time. Proper socialising, with appropriate correction and reward, should sort this out.

Leaving his Natural Mother at the Wrong Age

Sometimes, either through ignorance on the part of the breeder, or circumstances such as the bitch dying, puppies are taken from their natural mother too early. The ideal age for a pup to leave his mum is between seven to nine weeks, which is the crucial man-bonding time. Leaving mum and his litter brothers and sisters before this time means that he misses out on vital parts of his formative education and development.

The bitch teaches her pups what behaviour is acceptable, by admonishing them very firmly when they step out of line. She shows them, by example, how to interact with humans, what to be wary of and what things and situations are harmless.

Leaving his litter brothers and sisters too soon, he will not have completed learning the rules of behaviour when encountering other dogs. By play fighting in the litter, he learns how to moderate his behaviour so as not to cause discomfort, by experiencing early on what over-boisterous behaviour provokes in his litter mates. He learns the correct postures and signals to use when encountering another dog. If this learning is curtailed by leaving the litter before seven weeks old, he will not recognise these signals when he meets his first strange dog and may react in an aggressive fashion. Likewise, because *he* will be giving out confusing signals to the strange dog, that dog may act aggressively, because he is confused by the behaviour he is encountering.

This particularly applies when pups are orphaned at birth and hand-reared by humans. They tend to form a very deep attachment to the person who rears them, which in turn can lead to the pup being very possessive towards people. Not having had the benefit of another canine's teaching in proper dog behaviour, they are inclined to feel antagonistic towards other dogs, as they feel themselves to be human rather than canine.

The reverse can happen if the pup stays with his mum too long, i.e. beyond nine weeks. Because he remains in a dog-oriented environment beyond the man-bonding time, he will relate more easily with dogs than with people, resulting in him being uneasy in human company, which could show itself as either very nervous behaviour or in displays of aggression.

If any of the above applies to your dog, you must pay great attention to socialising him, being scrupulously clear with your correction and reward. It would be very helpful if you could befriend someone who has a docile female dog, as she can help with showing your dog, in canine language, what behaviour is acceptable. Joining a dog training club could well help with finding a suitable companion for this purpose.

You may never achieve complete success in your attempts to mix your dog with other dogs and people, but you should achieve a level at which your dog can co-exist with both.

Poor Breeding

Although the majority of breeders are very selective, there are unfortunately many people who breed from unsuitable stock, often for very dubious reasons.

Some people breed from their bitch in the mistaken belief that it will "be good for her to have a litter". Even worse are those who breed from a bitch who has a poor temperament because they think it will improve it. Others breed simply with an eye to making money from the sale of the litter and, worst of all, are the puppy farmers, who over-breed their bitches, without giving a thought either to temperament, or to the health of the bitch or her pups.

Some of these people may well check the bitch and prospective stud dog for genetic faults, but do not give the same attention to the temperament of the prospective parents. Their offspring will inherit character traits from them both. Often the bitch is bred from far too early, without being given the chance to mature properly, either mentally or physically. As already mentioned, a bitch teaches her pups much by example and if she is nervous or immature, she will pass her own fears and phobias on to her offspring.

Inexperienced or ignorant breeders often fail to give correct advice to new owners, particularly when the owners find the dog showing character traits which they cannot understand, and ask for help. If poor breeding could be the reason why your dog is showing aggressive signs, you will need patience, positive training and the help of a good dog training club, to help you get the best from your dog.

Choosing a Breeder

Whilst on the subject of breeding, if you are reading this book prior to getting your puppy, do make sure that you choose the breeder very carefully. Don't be tempted to buy the puppy which gazes at you appealingly from the nearest pet shop window. Although there are good pet shops, there are also plenty who do not enquire too deeply into the origins of their stock. It is also advisable to avoid the one-off private breeder, who may fall into one of the categories previously mentioned, or at best will not have the expertise needed to raise a litter properly.

The safest way to obtain a puppy is either by personal recommendation, or, once you have decided on the particular breed you want, obtain a list of registered breeders from the Kennel Club.

Before you go and see the puppies, find out about any genetic defects which can occur in your chosen breed. Ask the breeder if both the bitch and the stud dog have been tested for these defects. For some conditions, such as hip dysplasia, there are schemes for submitting the results of such tests to a veterinary panel, who "award" points depending on the severity of the defect. Ask your local vet to explain the scoring system to you, so that you are fully aware before you go and see the puppies.

Often, the breeder does not own the stud dog, so it may not be possible for you to see him. However, when you do eventually go to see the puppies, make sure you see the bitch as well. If the breeder does not let you see her, *do not buy one of the puppies*. Most breeders are only too happy to let you see their stock, so any reluctance on their part to let you see the mother of the puppy you intend to buy should be viewed with the greatest suspicion.

You should be able to observe the bitch with her pups, when you will have the chance to study her temperament, bearing in mind the important part it plays in the development and character of your chosen pup. It is understandable if she shows some apprehension should you touch her puppies – when you want to start picking them up, the breeder will probably remove her from the room.

If she shows any other displays of nervousness or aggression, please think very carefully before buying one. To see a litter of puppies is a wonderful sight and it is easy to get carried away, letting your heart rule your head and not paying sufficient attention to the character of the bitch. A bad decision at this stage though could mean the beginning of years of trauma and heartache for you and your family.

Assuming that the bitch's temperament is all that it should be and the pups are obviously healthy and well adjusted, you then have to choose one! It is not necessarily a good idea to go for the biggest and boldest pup in the litter. He has become like that by pushing and bullying his brothers and sisters, having found that he gets a bigger share of food and attention that way. Although this need not be a fault, if you do pick this bossy puppy, you must be prepared for him to try that behaviour out on you, so if you are of a gentle and quiet disposition, this pup may not be the right one for you.

In the same way, the quietest pup in the litter will not adapt very easily if you have a noisy home full of boisterous children!

It is very much a matter of personal choice, but do try to use common sense if possible. Personally, I'm a great believer in instinct when it comes to selecting a puppy, but then not everyone's instincts are the right ones!

Medical Ailments

You may have read all the categories previously mentioned, yet still cannot "fit" your dog into any one of them, so cannot understand *why* your dog is being aggressive.

If this is the case, it would be advisable to have your dog thoroughly checked over by your veterinary surgeon. Simple things, such as ear infections, bad teeth, blocked anal glands, etc., can cause your dog to be bad tempered. Once treated, you may find that his aggressive behaviour ceases.

Unfortunately, there are more serious conditions, such as brain tumours, which cause the dog to act irrationally. Obviously in such cases, your vet is the best person qualified to give an opinion as to the dog's future.

5

KEEPING YOUR DOG HEALTHY

With luck, your dog will lead a long and healthy life. A few sensible precautions on your part will increase the chances of your dog doing just that. You also have a responsibility to ensure that your dog does not spread disease to other dogs or indeed to humans.

Regular Inoculations

With the system currently in operation in this country, killer diseases which can affect dogs have been closely controlled and in some cases almost eradicated.

The most lethal of them all, rabies, has been so far excluded from the UK and Ireland by the quarantine laws. Quarantine means long separation from our dogs, which is not very pleasant, but it is infinitely better than bringing in a disease which could have such awful consequences on domestic animals, wild life and humans.

It is up to all of us to act responsibly to ensure that rabies never reaches this country and to report any known instances of quarantine evasion to the authorities immediately.

The four main diseases which can be controlled by regular inoculation are distemper, hepatitis, leptospirosis and parvo virus. This last disease, parvo virus, is relatively new. It particularly affects young puppies and elderly dogs and is quite virulent in some parts of the country.

All dogs must be inoculated against these diseases, to lessen even further the chance of an epidemic. Puppies are usually inoculated at around eight weeks and again at twelve weeks, with a further booster against parvo virus at between 18 to 20 weeks. After that, yearly booster inoculations are essential, so that the dog has continual protection throughout his life. Until puppies have received their second inoculation at twelve weeks, they should not be mixed with other dogs.

Worming

There are two groups of worms which can affect dogs, namely the nematode group and the cestode group. These are more commonly known as roundworms and tapeworms. Signs of worm infestation in the dog are abnormal hunger, diarrhoea, anal itching, poor growth and loss of condition.

The unwormed dog can pass worms to other dogs, via the worm eggs. The eggs are passed by the dog in his faeces. These eggs are then moved around by the wind, rain and on the soles of people's shoes. The eggs can then adhere to passing dogs, sticking to their feet and coat. The dog can then ingest the eggs when licking himself, thus the life cycle of the egg continues, resulting in worm infestation.

It is also possible for these eggs to be ingested by humans, especially children. By touching infested ground, or by stroking a dog who has the worm eggs attached to his coat and then putting their hands in their mouths, people can ingest the eggs. The cycle of the egg is then altered and in rare circumstances can lead to blindness and mental retardation. This disease is called Visceral Larvae Migrans and is caused by the egg of the roundworm Toxocara Canis.

There is also a strain of tapeworm, which, if ingested during its development stage, can affect humans, causing a disease called Hydatidosis, which affects the liver and lungs. Fortunately, cases of this disease are extremely rare.

All this unpleasantness can be avoided if all dog owners abide by the following simple rules:

1. All puppies should be wormed before leaving the breeder, at three weeks and five weeks of age. They should be wormed again twice more by the time they reach 13 weeks. Thereafter they should be regularly wormed every six months throughout their lives.

2. Bitches who are about to be bred from should be wormed prior to mating and again after the puppies are weaned.

3. All faeces should be removed daily from the garden and burned or hygienically disposed of. Always remove any faeces your dog leaves behind when out on exercise.

4. Always wash your hands after handling your dog, before consuming food.

By following these simple procedures, you can be assured that you have taken all possible steps to prevent your dog passing the infection to other dogs or humans.

Fleas

Dog fleas are quite indiscriminate and will infest the clean, healthy dog just as much as the dirty, neglected animal. The flea lives on the dog, sucking blood, and its bites can cause extreme irritation. Some dogs also become allergic to the saliva which is injected into the skin when the flea bites. As well as the irritation caused, fleas are also the intermediate host of the tapeworm.

Fleas can be seen quickly moving over the dog's skin and are particularly partial to the base of the dog's tail and behind its ears. Flea droppings look like specks of grit and are especially visible on the dog's stomach. Fleas like warmth and will lay their eggs in the gap between the carpet and the skirting board, between the floorboards, in the pile of fitted carpets and in the dog's bedding and basket. After the eggs hatch, the larvae stage can remain dormant for anything up to one year, if the temperature is not warm enough.

The adult fleas spend only a short time actually on the dog, just long enough to feed, mate and then they jump off, either onto the floor, another dog or cat, or, worse still, onto you.

At one time, flea infestations were confined to the warmer summer months, but nowadays, with more and more homes being centrally heated, the larvae can hatch all year round, jumping on to the next passing host, after hatching. Flea spray preparations can be obtained from your vet and regular treatment of the dog, his bedding and all carpet edges, as well as regular use of the vacuum cleaner, will keep the problem at bay.

Exercise

It is impossible to generalise over how much exercise you should give your dog. Some need a five mile walk daily, whilst others only need a short run around the park. As a very rough guide, medium to large breeds such as Alsatians, Retrievers, Labradors, Collies, etc., should have at least one *good* walk every day, supplemented with shorter walks on the lead. The very large heavy breeds, such as Newfoundlands, Pyreneans and St. Bernards, should not be run for miles and miles – they are quite content to have shorter, more sedate regular exercise, although they can walk a fair distance at a gentle pace. With the smaller breeds, it very much depends on the type of dog – some small dogs can run for hours, whilst others can only take exercise in short bursts. Find out from the breeder, or the vet, exactly how much your particular dog should have. With very young puppies, especially those who are going to grow into big dogs, exercise should be very moderate during the first few months, as their young bones are forming all the time and could be damaged through over exercise.

Grooming

Whether your dog has a short or long coat, he should be brushed regularly, to keep his coat healthy, clean and tangle-free. The shorter-coated dog should be brushed at least once a week, whilst the dog with a longer coat needs brushing daily to keep it in tip-top condition. A few minutes spent every day is far better than half an hour once a week. When you are brushing your dog, it is also a good time to check him over and examine him.

Bathing

It is really a personal choice as to how often you bath your dog, but regular brushing should be sufficient most of the time. Obviously, if your dog has rolled in something unpleasant, or during a heavy moult, a bath may be necessary. It is also a good idea to bath a bitch once she has finished her season, to get rid of any "interesting" smells which may remain. On these occasions, do use a proper, good quality dog shampoo and rinse the coat thoroughly.

Where possible, bath your dog on a warm, sunny day,

so that after you have removed the excess water with a towel, your dog can stay outside and dry his coat properly. If it is a cold or wet day, dry as much as possible with a towel, then use a hair drier, or let him lie in front of a warm, but not hot, fire. Make sure that his joints are dried thoroughly, to prevent any future problems with rheumatism.

Swimming

Many dogs enjoy swimming and it can be very good exercise for them. If you do allow your dog into the sea, you must rinse his coat well in fresh water when you return home, as the salt and the sand can cause skin irritation. Also, please be considerate if you take your dog onto the beach. It can be very annoying for other beach users to have a dog running through their possessions and having to avoid the little "piles" which dogs can leave behind them!

Heat Stroke

Most dogs do not enjoy being exposed to hot sun. Their body temperature is higher than ours and their tolerance of heat is lower. During the summer months, it is best to restrict the dog to light exercise during the heat of the day, leaving strenuous exercise either for early morning or evening. Make sure they always have access to both shade and water.

Never leave a dog unattended in a car during warm weather. Even with the windows open, the temperature can soar within minutes, causing the dog extreme distress, which can lead very quickly to collapse and death. I did an experiment with my own car, to see what the temperature was inside, on a hot, sunny day. The car, an estate, was parked on the roadside, with a small amount of shade being cast on it. The outside temperature was 80° Fahrenheit.

With all the windows fully opened, the sunroof and the tailgate open, after ten mintues the temperature inside the car was the same as outside, i.e. 80°.

With the windows half open, the sunroof open and the tailgate shut (as you may possibly leave the car when popping into a shop), within ten minutes the temperature inside the car was 98°.

With windows, sunroof and tailgate all shut, the temperature inside the car reached 122° within ten minutes. So, you can see that even with leaving windows opened, the dog would very quickly be overcome by the heat and lack of air circulation.

However, if you ever come across a dog which is unfortunate enough to suffer from heat stroke, you must take action fast. The signs are panting, profuse salivation, vomiting and general weakness. Quickly move the dog to a cool, airy place and apply cold water and/or ice packs to the head, neck and shoulders and seek veterinary assistance immediately.

Feeding

Nowadays, the choice of what to feed your dog is very extensive, ranging from fresh meat, canned meat, all-in-one dried foods, to various forms of processed food. What you decide upon is basically a personal matter between you and your dog, but don't allow him to become a fussy eater. If he turns his nose up at what you provide, don't immediately rush out and buy something different. Assuming he is not ill and provided that the food is not stale, leave the bowl down for a couple of minutes and if he hasn't eaten it, pick it up again. Try him once more, half an hour later and if he still doesn't eat, remove the bowl, keep the food fresh and give it to him for his next meal. Dogs are not stupid. He will not starve himself. He can actually survive for several days without food, provided he has access to fresh water. Obviously, if your dog has previously been a good, unfussy eater and suddenly goes off his food, something is wrong and you should take him to the vet. This is particularly so with young puppies.

All dogs are different – some gulp their food down ravenously, whilst others pick delicately, taking a long time to clear their dishes. However, if you have the type of dog who will only eat best steak, then that's because *you* have let him choose. After all, I'm sure you'd rather eat steak than fish fingers, given the choice, but cost dictates that you can't!

If you decide to feed your dog fresh meat, give it to him raw and don't waste all the essential vitamins by boiling them out during cooking. You may not like the look of raw meat, but I assure you your dog will – and the taste! In the wild, dogs didn't carry their primus stoves around with them to cook their kill on! Their teeth and stomachs are designed for eating and digesting raw meat, so please, don't cook it.

Don't feed him solely on meat and biscuits. Substitute the biscuit with bran occasionally – particularly if your dog is putting on weight when he shouldn't. Bran is a very good filler and will make him feel replete without putting on unwanted weight. Feed him vegetables too, raw if possible.

If you are having temperament problems with your dog, either with aggression, or hyper-activity, have a look at his diet. There has been some research done, which has shown that a reduction in the protein content of the dog's diet can have a calming effect on such dogs, over a period. Basically, too much protein can over-fuel the dog, in the same way as extra oats charge-up a horse. If you feel your dog fits into one of these categories, try changing to a food high in cereals and feed white meat rather than red – in fact choose a blander diet overall.

Once your dog is past puppyhood and is on a balanced diet, there is no need to give him any liquid other than water to drink. Milk is not necessary and can in fact upset the stomach. Too much milk is also a big factor in dogs becoming overweight.

Don't be tempted to feed your dog "human" food as tit-bits. Chocolate designed for us to eat is not suitable for your dog. It contains refined sugar, which the dog cannot digest. The fact that he will eat it if offered is quite irrelevant – he'll get all kinds of things that aren't good for him.

If you must give your dog tit-bits, either buy a proprietary brand of dog treats, or give him apples or a small piece of cheese. Apples contain natural sugar, which the dog can digest and most dogs love cheese, which does no harm in small quantities.

As regards to the amount you should feed, a rough guide is to feed ½ oz of total food per pound of target bodyweight. For example, if your dog should weigh 30 lbs, then he should have no more than 15 oz of total food per day. Like people, dogs have varying metabolic rates and some dogs may get overweight given the average quantity of food per day. With growing puppies, the diet will obviously not be the same as for a full-grown dog – if you have not obtained a diet sheet from the breeder, get advice from your vet. As dogs grow old, their food requirements may change, so again, get advice from the vet.

Castration

Earlier in the book, I briefly touched on the subject of castrating a male dog and the possible outcome of such action. Apart from the obvious fact that castrated males cannot reproduce, it can, in certain cases, help with behavioural problems. But castration is not the answer to every training problem. It does not stop them forever sniffing the ground, sniffing other dogs or sniffing humans in places that we wish they wouldn't! It will not stop them recognising the difference between male and female dogs and it will not stop them cocking their legs. Neither will it automatically stop them from running off, or attempting to mount bitches.

Having listed the things which castration will probably not help, there are some occasions when it can have positive results. If your dog is very sexually possessive, for example with one particular member of the family, or with a female dog who lives in the same house, and this possessiveness culminates in shows of aggression, then castrating the dog can have beneficial results. It does not work overnight, however, and can take anything up to six months before you see any improvement. You should not rely on the operation to stop the problem on its own and you should train the dog at the same time, preferably with the help of a good training club, so that the combination will produce the required results.

As I mentioned in the opening chapter, injections simulating castration can be tried first, to assess their reaction before taking the step of having your dog operated on.

If you are contemplating having your dog castrated, please wait until he is properly mature. A dog neutered while still a puppy will not develop properly, either physically or mentally. Once you have had him castrated, watch his weight carefully, as the act of castration, which prevents the circulation of the hormone testosterone, can result in an increase of fat, due to a lowered metabolic rate. Any sign of weight increase should be dealt with immediately – too much weight causes numerous health problems and can kill your dog.

Spaying

If you have a female dog, she will come into season roughly twice a year, starting any time after five or six months of age. The term "season" means that, for three to four weeks at a time, her body will go through the process which, if allowed, will culminate in mating and the production of puppies. I know that some people are of the opinion that it does a bitch good to allow her to have a litter. I have not seen any evidence to prove this theory.

In my opinion, unless you have an exceptional specimen of a particular breed and know that you can get good homes for all the puppies, to breed from a bitch, just because it's natural, is very irresponsible. Even worse are those people who breed from their bitch to make money from the sale of the puppies. Dog breeding should be left to the knowledgeable specialist. Indeed, if the laws regarding breeding were tightened up and revolting places like puppy farms and dog supermarkets were closed down, we would see a dramatic reduction in the number of unwanted dogs, pedigree and non-pedigree alike, sitting in rescue centres up and down the country.

Before any bitch is bred from, she should firstly be at least two years old and have had tests to see whether she carries any genetic abnormalities, with the chosen stud dog also tested in the same way. It is the responsibility of the breeder to ensure that all puppies go to a good home and they should also be prepared to take back any puppies who cannot be kept by their new owners.

Dog breeding takes planning – it is not just a case of putting any old bitch to the nearest male dog and letting them do what comes naturally.

So, assuming that you are not going to breed from your

bitch, you have two choices. You can ensure that each time she comes into season, for the entire length of the season, that she is kept away from all male dogs and only exercised on the lead, well away from all other dogs. Or you could put her into kennels each time she has a season, which could prove very costly.

The alternative is to have her spayed – that is to remove her ovaries surgically and in some cases part of the uterus, thus stopping the seasons and making it impossible for her to reproduce. The operation itself is very common and should ideally be done after the bitch has had her first season, preferably mid-way between the end of the first one and the beginning of the second.

You can have her spayed before she ever has a season, but I would strongly advise against this. Although physically possible, I have seen the mental result of bitches being spayed before they have had a season. Many of them get mentally screwed up at around the time when their season would have been due.

The fact that some vets will perform the operation before the bitch has had one season does not, to me, make it right. After all, the vet doesn't have to live with the mental effect that it can have on the bitch. I also like to know that my bitch has developed normally, allowing her to go through the process of one season first, before being spayed.

6

INTRODUCING A SECOND DOG

Nowadays, many families are becoming multi-dog. They start with one, then get another as company for the first one and so on. Normally, second and subsequent dogs join the family without many problems, but there are things which you can do to aid the acceptance process.

Generally speaking, if you already have a male dog, it is better to choose a female as the second dog. There is less risk of fighting between male and female, whereas male dogs can be very territorial and resent another male dog intruding on their territory. Naturally, care must be taken with a male and female dog in the same household when the bitch comes into season, but having her spayed after the first season will resolve that problem. There *is* a slight possibility that once your male dog has a female dog for a companion, he may become a little possessive towards her, by showing aggression to other male dogs who approach his bitch.

Whichever sex you decide upon, try and arrange for their first meeting to be on neutral territory, in case the first dog should show any territorial aggression towards the newcomer. Obviously, if the new dog is a young puppy, you will have to bring the pup straight home, but make sure that the first dog's favourite and most loved member of the family is not the one who carries the puppy indoors. Usually, whatever sex the new puppy is, the original dog will make allowances, and will recognise it as a baby, who offers no threat to his position within the family.

Whether it's a puppy or an older dog, both dogs will adjust more easily if you accept that between them, *they* will work out who is going to be boss dog over the other. Don't try and use human logic by assuming that the dog who was in the house first should be number one dog. It may turn out that way, but if it doesn't and you interfere and upset the natural order of things, you could end up with a very unpleasant situation. By watching their behaviour towards one another, you will quickly see which dog is showing signs of subservience. The underdog will possibly lie down when the other approaches and sniffs him. He may allow the other dog to take his food – here you *should* interfere, by feeding the two dogs separately, or you will end up with one very overweight dog! Boss dog will demonstrate his superiority by pushing the other out of the way when affection is in the offing. He will always try to be first out of the door when going for walks and first into the car when going for a ride. He may well threaten the other dog verbally, to instil his dominance.

Don't try to treat the two dogs as equals – in their world equality does not exist, remember their basic instincts. Once the pecking order has been established, don't be tempted to compensate the underdog by cuddling him more than the boss dog, or feeding him an extra tit-bit. This will merely antagonise the boss dog, who will then punish his subordinate for what he considers to be liberty-taking and getting above his position.

Always allow boss dog to be first through the door, after you. Feed him first, welcome him first when you come in. You are not showing favouritism by doing this –

you're simply accepting the natural order which both dogs recognise.

If you have an elderly dog and are bringing a young puppy into the household, you must obviously take care that the boisterous behaviour of the youngster does not harm the old dog. The youngster will obviously want to play and here you can shield the older dog a little, by getting on to the floor and playing with the pup yourself, to deflect unwanted attention away from the older one. Having said that, don't interfere when the older dog tells the puppy off. He must be allowed to put the pup in his place, or the youngster could make the older dog's life a misery.

Very often, you find that bringing a young puppy into the household can revitalise the older dog, so don't worry too much, just be sensible.

Whilst on the subject of having second and subsequent dogs, please don't be tempted to get two puppies together, as this can have disastrous consequences. I have a friend who says that "puppy plus puppy equals puppy squared" and it will certainly feel like that at times – two puppies together can wreak the havoc of four!

Firstly, the puppies will always relate to one another, before you, especially if they are litter brothers or sisters, as they will have been together since birth. Two puppies living together will form an attachment that is far more important to them than any human attachment. They will gang-up, as together they are a pack. Because they are a pack, they may become aggressive to other, single dogs.

If one is a chewer, he will influence the non-chewer, not the other way around. They will compete with one another at every opportunity. Walking on the lead will turn into a race, as will getting out of the front door, getting to their food, etc. If one is a barker, he will encourage the other to bark. Having two together will lead you to lump them together, rather than letting their individual characters emerge. When it comes to house training, the slower of the two to become clean will influence the other into being dirty again.

I could cite many more examples of why having two puppies together could be a dreadful combination. If you feel that I am coming strong on this subject, it is because many years ago, I did exactly what I'm trying to deter you from doing. I obtained two dear little cross-bred puppies – I just couldn't separate them – and the ensuing round of catastrophies led me to joining a dog training club and getting hooked on dog training! I would add that both dogs lived to a grand age, but not before they had made a good job of trying to wreck each other, my home and my nerves! Since then, I have met many people who have made the same mistake and were pulling their hair out over the antics of their puppies. So, if it is your intention to go and get two puppies, please think again. Get one first, let him reach maturity, then go and get the second.

Full Circle

So, you've just bought your second dog home. Turn back to the beginning of the book . . .

INDEX